LETHBRIDGE-STEWART

THE LAUGHING GNOME: CODA
ON HIS MAJESTY'S NATIONAL SERVICE

John Peel

CANDY JAR BOOKS · CARDIFF
2019

On His Majesty's National Service © John Peel, 2019
Additional material by Andy Frankham-Allen and Alyson Leeds

Characters from The Web of Fear
© *Hannah Haisman & Henry Lincoln 1967, 2019*
Lethbridge-Stewart: The Series
© *Andy Frankham-Allen & Shaun Russell 2014, 2019*

Doctor Who is © *British Broadcasting Corporation, 1963, 2019*

Range Editor: Andy Frankham-Allen
Editor: Shaun Russell
Editorial: Keren Williams & Alyson Leeds
Licensed by Hannah Haisman
Cover by Steve Beckett & Will Brooks

ISBN: 978-1-912535-45-3

Printed and bound in the UK by
Severn, Bristol Road, Gloucester, GL2 5EU

Published by
Candy Jar Books
Mackintosh House
136 Newport Road, Cardiff, CF24 1DJ
www.candyjarbooks.co.uk

For my friends Ly Cao and Nathan Skreslet

With thanks to David McIntee,
Nick Walters and Alyson Leeds

THE OBSERVER I

IT WAS the night of Monday 9th January 2012, and their first day back home after the funeral of Brigadier Sir Alistair Lethbridge-Stewart. Bill Bishop, and his wife, Anne, sat in the living room of their Scottish home, enjoying a moment of silence. She was reading a book, while he sat in his chair looking at the ugly gnome that rested in his lap.

Anne peered up from her book. 'I don't know why he left you that. It's an ugly thing, and quite frankly caused us no end of trouble.'

She was referring to events from a couple of months earlier. Alistair had discovered the Gnome in the graveyard after a funeral. He said he'd felt drawn to it, and with good reason as it turned out. It had been left by an old friend as a parting gift. Being a time traveller, this friend knew Alistair's time was almost up. The Gnome allowed Alistair to reflect on his life before his death. It was, really, a lovely idea. Alistair was astral projected throughout his life, reliving events, meeting people he hadn't seen in years, learning and understanding parts of his life that had always been a mystery to him. A chance to come to terms with regrets, with mistakes. Of course, as ever with alien artefacts, things didn't go that smoothly and both Bill and Anne had found themselves caught up in Alistair's temporal wake, their essences cast through time. Although in real time they were away for barely any time at all, from their point of view they had been lost in time for months. Caught up in the lives of strangers and, occasionally, people connected to Alistair's life.

Bill smiled ruefully. In one especially memorable trip, he'd even been the doctor who had delivered baby Alistair into the world.

'I think you do,' Bill said to his wife. They'd talked about it on the long drive back to Scotland from Cornwall.

'I know you *think* you know why.' Anne smiled sweetly. 'That's not the same thing, darling. Are you sure you want to do this?'

'I am. We both know where Alistair came from, his childhood, and we certainly know the story of what happened to him after Sandhurst. But there's always been one mystery...'

Anne sat back in her favourite chair. 'I know. What made him change his mind?'

'Exactly. He grew up hating the military, intent on becoming a maths teacher...'

'Which he did. Eventually.'

'Yes.' Bill looked down at the Gnome. 'This might not even work, but...' He shrugged. 'I have to know, Anne. The Brig didn't leave me this for the fun of it.'

Anne placed her glasses on the edge of her nose and peered over at the Gnome. 'It could just be a remembrance.'

'Could be. But our last conversation was about his past, about his service. I asked him, "What did happen during your National Service? It's probably the only thing you've never told me." And do you know what he said? "One day, Bill, perhaps you will find out." And then I get this.'

Anne let out a sigh. 'We're too old for adventures, Bill.'

'I don't want adventures; I just want to know.'

'But what if you get lost, what if—'

Anne continued speaking, but her words faded. For a moment longer Bill sat there, watching her mouth move but hearing nothing. And then he felt it. That familiar pull.

Bill smiled.

One last time, he thought, and seconds later he heard the laughter and was off. Falling into the black...

It was a sensation Bill was very familiar with, after so many astral jumps through time. Suddenly seeing through the eyes of a stranger, sharing their mind. The thoughts of the host body hidden behind a wall, barely a sense of the person whose body he was...

No. This was different. He could feel emotion coming from his host, could hear the thoughts as clearly as if they were his own. He *was* Alistair Lethbridge-Stewart.

And he was a prisoner.

PRISONER 1

HOW LONG?

That was all he could think. *How long?*

How long had he been here? Days? Weeks? Or was it just hours? Alistair's mind was too fuzzy to be sure. It *seemed* like a long time, but was it really? Or was his exhaustion, lack of sleep, hunger and thirst simply playing tricks with his mind? Tricks with time?

How long would he be here? Was there any end to this? He couldn't remember when it began, didn't know what was happening, and couldn't picture an end to it. Would he be out of there in a few minutes, or would this captivity encompass the remainder of whatever life he had left?

And, of course, the most important *how long?* of them all: How long could he hold out? How much more of this torture could he stand up to? How long before he broke? Before he simply went insane?

Or – had he already gone insane? Been broken? Was this all simply some kind of a hallucination? No, it couldn't be – if he were imagining all of this, he'd surely invent something more pleasant than being stuck in a cage in a jungle in North Korea. Something with pretty girls, not brutal Chinese guards… This had to be real, and he still had to be sane.

Shame, really. He'd really enjoy insanity if it had pretty girls in it, and not these—

There was a sharp cry, and a blow to his chest. Alistair's eyes cracked open, and he stared dizzily, dumbly, at one of his captors. The enemy soldier withdrew the butt of his rifle that had been slammed into his ribs and said something unintelligible in Chinese.

He wasn't to be allowed to sleep, he knew that. He hadn't slept since he'd been captured and dragged here, thrown into this cage. It was six inches shorter than he was, and only a few inches wider, so he could neither stand up nor sit down. He was confined to a muscle-straining, agonising cramped position. His body burned in pain, his muscles spasmed. His eyes were aflame, and he couldn't think straight. The cage swayed slightly in the wind. It was suspended about a foot from the ground on a thick rope from a framework. There were two other cages beside his, both occupied. And there were further rows of cages, some with other unfortunates in them, some empty, awaiting more captives.

It was night, he realised. He didn't remember it being night a few minutes ago. His mind was playing tricks on him again. Or maybe he was simply imagining it was night because his eyes were failing. They were weak and crusted, so that had to be a possibility. He might be going blind following all of this abuse. Not even twenty-two and going blind. He'd never get out of here if he couldn't see, would he?

Or was he being naïve to even imagine he might get out of here? The Chinese wouldn't simply let him go, would they? No, they wanted to break him. And once they'd done that, they'd just discard him, the rind of some fruit that had been drained of all its goodness, fit only to be left to the flies and vermin.

How long would it be before that happened?

There was someone else vaguely in view now. It was an old man, a native. He was shuffling along, being pushed from time to time by one of the soldiers. With a startling unreality, Alistair saw that the old man was carrying a silver tea tray, the kind you might find in a genteel drawing room back in England. It needed a good polish, but it was clearly valuable, and yet without value to the man who carried it. On the tray were small wooden bowls. They contained a cupful of dirty rice, and the old man was pausing beside each of the slowly swinging cages. The guard would pick up one of the bowls, stare at the prisoner inside the cage, carefully spit into the rice and then hand the bowl over.

It was his turn now. The old man didn't look at him; he kept his gaze down-turned, not wanting to see the man he was serving. The soldier looked, though, and smiled before spitting in the rice. Then thrust it out.

Alistair gagged at the thought of eating the contaminated food. His stomach reminded him that he was starving, hadn't eaten in God knows how long. But the thought of what had been done revolted him. The guard shouted something, and hit him with his free fist, and held out the bowl again. Alistair took it, not wanting another blow, and the old man and the guard moved on.

He stared at the disgusting mess. He'd sooner starve than touch it.

'Eat it.'

What? He looked around, and then realised it was the man in the adjacent cage.

'Eat it,' the man repeated. *Clipped accent. Maybe a decade older than Alistair. Forthright. Officer.*

'He spat in it,' Alistair protested.

'Just be glad he didn't piss in it. They do that sometimes. Eat it. You'll need your strength.' His companion tried – and failed – to straighten up. 'That's an order.'

Damned Army, always expecting you to follow orders. And look where he had ended up as a result of that! Beaten, starved, tortured and hanging in a cage in the Korean jungle. And now he was being ordered to eat filth.

He reached into the bowl with a shaking hand and pulled out a small, sticky globule. It took him two attempts to get it even close to his mouth. He finally forced some between his lips, trying not to think about it or taste it.

How long?

THE OBSERVER II

BILL WAS an observer. Up until now, each time he had been in the driving seat of his host-bodies. But not, so it seemed, with Alistair Lethbridge-Stewart. All Bill could do was observe, see life through Alistair's eyes, feel Alistair's emotions, hear Alistair's thoughts…

After they had all returned from their astral journey through time, Alistair, Anne and he had shared stories, compared notes. They'd each travelled to the same point in time; wherever Alistair had ended up, Bill and Anne had followed. When Alistair jumped, after finishing whatever purpose had brought him there, Anne and Bill jumped too. Except for one time. Bill and Anne had returned to the present first, while Alistair was sent on one more adventure, one that involved his granddaughter, Lucy, in 2018, and his brother, James, in 1937. Alistair had explained that when he had arrived in 1937 he had found himself in the body of his child-self, and unlike all the other jumps, he had been unable to affect anything. He was just a presence in the mind of his younger-self; an observer.

And now it was Bill's turn to play observer.

Well, he said he'd wanted to know what had happened to Alistair during the Korean War. And now it looked like he would find out. Not by living it, but through observation…

Once again Bill felt himself pulled away. His mind temporarily cast into the black until, once again, he found himself sharing Alistair's mind. And in his hand – Alistair's hand – Bill could see an envelope marked 'On His Majesty's National Service'…

YOU'RE IN THE ARMY NOW

'**OH, DAMNATION**, Jumbo!'

The other student, draped lazily across the chair, went as far as to open one eye and blink before pronouncing: 'Whatever it is, I didn't do it. I probably wasn't even in the country when it happened.'

'No,' growled Alistair. 'This isn't something you've done for once.'

'Told you.'

'It's HM Government.'

'Oh, well, *everything* is their fault.' Jumbo's nose twitched, so he scratched it. 'What have they gone and done now?'

'They've called me up, Jumbo. National Service!' Alistair waved the letter he'd just opened. A second slip of paper wafted to the floor and he snatched it up. It was a railway warrant, made out to Salisbury. At least he wasn't expected to pay his own fare to purgatory.

'Called you up or sent you up? There is a difference, you know.'

'Damn it, this isn't a joking matter. This is serious.'

Jumbo shook his head. 'Comedy is when *you* slip on a banana peel,' he uttered. 'Tragedy is when *I* slip on a banana peel.'

Alistair glared at his roommate. 'Why they didn't call you up?'

'Because even HM Government knows I am thoroughly useless.' Jumbo put on a very fake posh accent. 'James Chalmers? God, no – we don't want *him*. He'll crash every wretched plane we have.'

Alistair was walking up and down their room, filled with

anger and nervous energy. He sometimes forgot Jumbo's real name; he'd got so used to the nickname over the last few years at the University College of North Staffordshire. For some reason Alistair always thought there was an irony in rooming with a young man called James, but for the life of him he couldn't see why he felt it ironic.

'It's not for the RAF,' Alistair growled. 'It's the blessed Army.' Which was something, he decided. The RAF had taken his father from him; he had no intention of serving with them. He didn't wish to do military service at all, despite the family traditions. Or, more precisely, *because* of them.

'Maybe it's for the cavalry?' Jumbo asked archly.

Alistair ignored the remark and let out a frustrated sigh. 'And so close to graduation and my first teaching position...'

Jumbo shrugged carelessly. 'Ah, don't worry, Al. With your luck, you'll get posted to some sunny spot where the sultry, dusky maidens frolic in the cool night breezes. And I'm sure there's nothing that would please you more than a nice moonlight frolic.'

Alistair raised an eyebrow. He'd never spoken about his family history to Jumbo. His friend had no idea why the idea of National Service was so repellent to Alistair.

'I think I need a pint, Jumbo. Maybe several, in fact.'

Jumbo jumped to his feet. 'Ah! I knew if I let you ramble on long enough you'd say something sensible. Let's go.'

Nothing more of any significance was said until they were both grasping pints of bitter and seated in a smoky corner of the lounge bar in the nearby village. Being the closest watering hole to the college, it was mostly occupied by fellow students and the odd navvy or two taking a drinker's lunch.

'It's dashed bad luck,' Jumbo said. 'Fancy them waiting for a chap to graduate and be all set to make his mark on the world – and then *that*.' He sighed deeply and then drank deeply. 'I know it's not what you want, is it?'

'It's the last thing I want,' Alistair replied, bitterly. 'I want to do something *useful*. I had the future all mapped out. But teachers, it seems, aren't considered *essential*, unless it's teaching recruits how to kill a man seventeen different ways with a shoelace...' He took a draught. 'I mean, Jumbo – can you see me as a mindless drone, taking orders from some twit who's only an officer because his daddy had no other idea what to do with him?' He put on an exaggerated cut-glass accent. 'I say, chaps, that foreign-looking Johnny over there. Five rounds rapid, what?' Reverting to his normal tone, he went on: 'It's enough to make a man weep, Jumbo. Lieutenant Alistair Lethbridge-Stewart? Bah.'

His friend nodded sagely. 'It's not *you*, Al, is it?'

'Following pointless orders,' Alistair complained. 'I won't be able to do it. I want to *use* my brain. And here I am, destined to waste two whole bloody years in this farce. National Service. Service – I ask you!'

'You don't happen to have flat feet, do you?' Jumbo asked. 'My brother Tom, he had flat feet. Did his National Service in the typing pool because they said he couldn't fight with flat feet. They should have asked *me*; I'd have told them that he could fight far too well, even with flat feet. We fought throughout our childhoods. Probably still be fighting now, if I ever saw the blighter.'

'No such luck.'

Jumbo scratched his nose. 'I thought the military was something of a tradition in your family, though?'

Alistair raised an eyebrow. 'And how did you know that?'

Jumbo grinned. 'People talk, Al. Including you when you've had one too many.'

Alistair took that in his stride, and had to admit he appreciated that Jumbo had never mentioned it before.

'Oh, it is,' Alistair agreed. He smiled ruefully. 'My father, my great uncle, and my grandfather; all career officers. Even my Uncle Matthew, for a time. Lethbridge-Stewarts and military service go back hundreds of years, as my grandfather has endlessly told me. He's been trying to convince me most of my life to join up and follow in his glorious footsteps.'

'Well, can't he pull a few strings for you? Get you a cushy posting in a nice fancy regiment or something? One with bearskins and brass bands?'

'I'm sure he'd like nothing better,' Alistair said bitterly. 'But I'm not playing dice. They may be able to press-gang me legally, but I'm going to fight the whole thing all of the way, and that means sod a commission. They'll never make a willing warrior out of me, you mark my words.'

And with that, Alistair fetched them two more pints of bitter, and they focused on their drinks for a few minutes.

'Look on the bright side,' Jumbo finally recommended.

'There's a bright side?' Alistair shook his head. 'Two wasted years of my life? Two years of *yes, sir, no, sir, three bags bloody full, sir*? How is there a bright side to that?'

'You'll get to go to some glorious exotic country like Malaya at full government expense.'

'And spend the entire time knee-deep in muck in some godforsaken jungle,' Alistair complained. 'Miles away from a decent pint.'

'I hear that those overseas girls are… well, *willing*, if you know what I mean. You could learn a lot from them, you know, old man.'

'According to what I've heard, mostly to do with unpleasant personal diseases.' Alistair shook his head. 'No, Jumbo; it's going to be two solid years of hell.'

'Maybe you *should* try and get your grandfather to intercede for you?' Jumbo suggested. 'I mean, if you *have* to be in it anyway, why not take the high road instead of the low one?'

Alistair shook his head. 'Your dad's a CEO, isn't he? You probably got to see more of him growing up in a month than I saw my father in my entire life. Wing Commander Gordon Lethbridge Stewart…'

'MIA, right?' Jumbo patted his friend's arm. 'Sorry about that, old man. Damned tough.'

'It only meant that his absence became permanent,' Alistair replied. 'Before that, he was posted all over the place. I can't recall a single one of my birthdays he was present at.' He took another pull of his beer. 'I couldn't condemn a family of mine to that sort of life, Jumbo.'

'Steady on, old chap, you don't even have a girlfriend yet…'

'Not if Vera had anything to say about it.'

'Ah, still sending you those letters?'

'She never lets up. Besides, it's the principle of the thing.' Alistair sighed. 'I want a life that's strictly nine-to-five, then home to hearth and family. I want *my* family to see me and know me. And I don't want them to get a note one day from

HM Government saying *We regret to inform you...* No, Jumbo, the military is no life for me. I'll do my duty and then I'll make a belated start on real life.' He snorted. 'I've not even started yet, and I already can't wait to get out of it...'

PRISONER II

IT WAS almost impossible for him to think coherently. His entire world was now a pain-filled box, swaying above the filthy ground of Korea. Prisoners weren't let out for any reason, and the stench of urine and worse was inescapable.

Why was he being held here, a prisoner and mistreated? What had he done to deserve this? He didn't know why he was thinking of Jumbo and good English ale, except that it was a hell of a lot better than thinking about his current situation...

There had to be something about this land that made it desirable, but he couldn't imagine what. The Japanese had invaded it back in the '30s, and now the Reds were after it twenty years later. And for what? Alistair didn't really understand it completely, even when his head was clear. Now it made no sense at all to him.

One of the guards was making the rounds again. If he found any of the prisoners had fallen asleep through exhaustion, there would be blows and punishments. Then there were often blows and punishments for absolutely no reason at all. Their captors were sadists, and enjoyed inflicting pain and terror. Not just to the prisoners, either – they did it to the locals too. That poor old man who brought the meagre rice ration once a day was cuffed and kicked, and then punished if he so much as cried out.

The guard had reached the officer in the cage next to Alistair. There was a blow, and spitting, and then the guard moved on to glare through at him.

Alistair blinked through burning eyes at the evil creature outside the cage. The man raised his fists, and Alistair cringed, trying to prepare for the inevitable blow.

It didn't come. The guard unfastened the cage door, and shook it. Caught off-balance by this unexpected action, Alistair scrambled and then fell from the cage to the ground. As he lay there, shaking, the guard kicked him, hard, in the ribs. The fresh pain was agonizing. The soldier was shouting in – what, Mandarin? Cantonese? Alistair didn't know, couldn't understand a word of it. Another kick, and he rolled over, trying to get away. He was too weak and shaky to move properly.

More Chinese commands, and Alistair prepared for more kicks, but they didn't come. Instead, the old man was there, bowing to the soldier, and then bending over Alistair. He said something equally unintelligible, and reached down and tried to help Alistair to his feet. It was all pointless, really, as he simply had neither the strength nor the co-ordination to be able to rise.

The old man said something deferentially to the guard. The soldier glared down at Alistair, and then yelled a command. Two other soldiers came into view. The first man barked an order, and the two new arrivals grabbed Alistair roughly by his arms and pulled him upright.

Get up, man! You can do this!

Alistair tried to stand, but his legs refused to listen to his brain's commands and stayed stubbornly useless.

As the two soldiers dragged him along, following behind the first guard, Alistair had the strangest thought. The voice in his head – it didn't sound like him at all. It was older, had an accent...

He really was losing his marbles.

The old man disappeared somewhere, probably glad to be away from all this. Alistair couldn't blame the poor old chap – he'd have loved to be away from there, too.

It was daytime, he realised suddenly. Hadn't it just been night? When had the sun risen? He couldn't remember. He only knew it was day because he could now see his surroundings.

'Stay strong, man.' That officer in the next cage again, calling orders. Or was it meant to be encouragement? The first guard struck him with the butt of his rifle, causing him to groan in pain.

Stay strong? How was Alistair supposed to do that? There was no strength left in him at all. He couldn't even stand up.

He idly wondered where he was being dragged and why, but couldn't really understand much more at that moment than he was out of that cage, and could stretch out at last. The muscles in his arms and legs hurt like hell, but at least they were no longer cramped. Oh, yes, there was pain in his side, too, from where he'd been kicked, but that was almost incidental.

He was hauled into a tent, and the two soldiers let him go. He dropped immediately to the ground and lay there. Perhaps they were going to allow him to sleep, now? That would be nice.

A pair of highly polished boots came into focus in front of his face. Alistair stared at the boots. Somebody had done a lovely job on them. Sergeant Mullins would *love* those boots. He'd always been after the recruits to get a proper shine on the LPCs (Leather Personnel Carriers) they'd been issued in training. Some could never quite get the hang of it. Whoever owned these boots, though – he knew how to do it properly. Alistair couldn't help admiring them.

'Get up,' a voice ordered in heavily accented English, gently, politely. A moment later: 'That is an order, soldier!'

'I'm trying,' Alistair mumbled. He struggled to force his legs to co-operate, but they were being as stubborn as ever. They were one blaze of pain. 'Can't do it,' he said, finally. 'Too much… too much…'

'Oh, dear,' the voice said. 'And I *did* so much hope we would become friends. But there isn't much chance of that, is there, if you can't even manage to get up.'

Alistair tried afresh, but the pain was too much. He couldn't think, he couldn't move, except to roll over onto his back. At least that enabled him to look up at the person speaking.

He was a Chinese soldier in a very smart uniform – not like the guards, who always looked like they'd been dragged through a hedge backwards. He was tall and thin, and didn't look to be much out of his teens. An officer, obviously. His face was impassive, but he held a cigarette like a pen in his right hand which he took an occasional draw on.

He stared down at Alistair as he stared up at him. Then he shook his head slightly.

'I won't get any sense out of you, will I? Dear me.' The officer turned to the first guard and barked a rapid string of Chinese. The guard saluted, and the other two soldiers dragged Alistair upright again.

The officer smiled tightly and without much humour at Alistair. 'Perhaps next time…' he murmured, and then Alistair was dragged out of the tent like a sack of rotten potatoes.

COMMUNICATIONS

BASIC TRAINING lived down to Alistair's every expectation of it. Jumbo drove him to the station, and gave him a stiffly awkward emotional send-off. 'Try to not get yourself killed, you idiot.'

'I'll do my level best,' Alistair promised.

'Though I'm sure you'd make an excellent target. Might be safer if they aimed at you, in fact.'

'Thanks, Jumbo. I'll bear it in mind.'

They shook hands, and Jumbo drove off, waving carelessly as he did so.

Next came the train journey down to Salisbury, where he was met at the station and taken to camp. There were other lads on the train, all with a standard small suitcase they'd been advised to pack, all looking equally at sea and nobody looking forward to the end of the trip. At the station, there were a couple of beaten-up Bedford lorries waiting, with a couple of bored-looking soldiers. All the new arrivals ambled over and gave their names to a corporal with a clipboard, who ticked them off and snapped out which truck they were to go onto.

They were dismal vehicles, stinking of petrol fumes, waxed canvas and cigarette smoke. *Not the best combination*, Alistair thought. He took a place on the long plank that served as a seat and waited until the lorry filled up. Then the canvas flap at the back was closed, and somebody slapped on the side of the vehicle. With a throaty roar, the lorry lumbered off.

'Not even a bleedin' window to look out of,' somebody complained.

'What do you want to look at, then?' somebody else shot back.

'The last pretty lasses we'll see for a while,' the first replied. 'It'll just be your bleedin' ugly face from here on in.'

There was other banter, but Alistair had no enthusiasm to join in. He wasn't the only one to remain silent; obviously a lot of the other lads felt much the same way as he did about this.

They were all putting their real lives on hold to play soldiers, and had absolutely no say in the matter.

When they reached camp, the lorry coughed and spluttered to a halt, and they were ordered out and to form up. Everybody shuffled vaguely into place.

'God, what a shower.' This came from a sergeant; a stocky chap of middling age. 'I swear, they're really sending us the dregs out here. Well, we'll see if there's the makings of a real man anywhere among you. I'm Sergeant Stokes, and you lucky lads will be in my charge for the next six weeks. And do you know why you're lucky?' He glared at them all.

Alistair knew better than to try and reply, but there was always one, of course.

'No, sir,' a youngster answered.

Stokes marched over and glared up a few inches at the taller recruit. 'I am not a *sir*!' he yelled. 'Officers are *sir*. I am not an officer. I am a sergeant, and that is what you will all call me. Do you understand, you 'orrible little man?'

'Yes, sir – er, Sergeant.' The youngster looked cowed.

'Good. And the reason you're all lucky is because you're in my squad, and I'm the kindest, most humane sergeant in the modern Army. Now, the first thing we're going to do is to show you all how to march.' Stokes was walking along the line, and stopped to glare around. 'And do you know why that is?' This time around nobody was stupid enough to volunteer a reply. A slight smile touched Stokes' face. 'Because we here in the Army are terribly concerned that you keep your legs healthy and strong, that's why. 'Cause you're going to be using them a lot, I can tell you! So we're going to test your strong, healthy, limber legs by Corporal Potter here marching you over to the Quartermaster's to be issued with all your lovely new kit. And having a lot of lads whose legs aren't up to snuff would make me very unhappy – and you don't want to make your sergeant unhappy, do you?' Silence. Stokes halted, and turned to the nearest recruit – who happened to be Alistair, unfortunately. 'I asked you a question!' he barked. 'And when I ask questions, I expect answers! You don't want to make me unhappy, do you?'

'Not me, Sergeant,' Alistair replied.

'I'm very glad to hear it. Right, listen to my orders and do exactly what I say. First of all, is there anybody here who doesn't remember their left from their right? There had better not be. Squad, 'shun! Left - *wait for it* - face!'

Naturally, three of the others turned the wrong way.

And so it went. They had been assigned their barrack room in a drafty pre-fab left over from the war, the whip-thin corporal in charge of their platoon had somehow managed to march them all over to the stores to be issued with a mountain of kit. All of which, he had informed them, was to be correctly labelled in time for morning parade. Soldiers behind a long desk in a fresh hut gave the men a quick once-over and then produced clothing for them. It looked rough and itchy, and Alistair realised it was highly unlikely to fit accurately and that absolutely nobody cared.

This stage of the proceedings almost passed without further incident. Almost. Unfortunately, on being issued with his brand new, dull ammo boots, the lad in front of Alistair in the queue had been naïve enough to ask where they got their shiny boots from. Behind him, Alistair inwardly groaned as Potter's eyes sparkled with delight at the God-given opportunity.

'You'll find out before tomorrow morning, lad,' he said with an evil relish.

Wonderful.

Then they were marched back to barracks, told to change and what time the cookhouse and NAAFI opened. Potter bid them an ominous adieu, ready for the 'real work' to begin tomorrow.

That evening, Alistair sat on the edge of the rickety bed, carefully writing his name and Army number on the strip of tape he had just sewn into the collar of his horrible denims. All things considered, though, his first few hours as a soldier hadn't been all that bad; at least he had known what to expect.

Following the subdued journey earlier that day, bounced around in the back of an Army lorry with nineteen other young men he had met only half an hour beforehand at the railway station, Alistair had learned the names of some of his fellow inmates. There was the requisite Smith who had immediately become 'Smudge', a 'Dusty' Miller and 'Sticky' Glewe. There wasn't much shortening of any of his own names, the only real option being 'Stewpot', and nobody seemed that eager to try for the obvious 'Lofty' or 'Titch'. Alistair was grateful; nicknames never seemed to stick to him – unlike poor Rogers and Nightingale, who were now irrevocably 'Ginger' and 'Florence'.

He also had observed with some dismay that he was easily the tallest. They always picked the tallest in the squad for right hand marker when it came to drill. As such his plan to keep his head down, physically as well as figuratively, was compromised from the start.

The bed next to Alistair was occupied by the lad who had been unfortunate enough to fall victim to the tender mercies of Potter. He had introduced himself as Frank Campbell. He was a little younger than Alistair, about medium height, somewhat skinny in build, with short brown hair that stuck up awkwardly at the back.

Watching Campbell now, though, Alistair was not entirely convinced that Potter would be proved right in regard to his footwear. Campbell was doing his best, but he clearly had no idea how to go about bulling boots. Another hissed expletive indicated that, yet again, the young man had succeeded in removing just as much polish as he had applied.

'Should've kept your mouth shut,' Smudge chirped from the other side of the room.

Campbell shot him a frustrated glare. 'I wasn't to know, was I?' he bit out.

Smudge just smiled, taking a drag from his cigarette. 'That sort of question'll get you in trouble no matter where you go,' he said, shaking his head as if he were imparting sage advice. 'Common sense, really.'

Campbell screwed up his filthy duster and lobbed it at Smudge. He missed and hit Ginger over in the next bed, who stabbed himself with his sewing needle and let fly an exclamation more suited to a vicarage tea party than an Army barracks.

Amid the chorus of high-pitched gasps and faux-swoons, Alistair at last allowed himself a small smile. They would all get on fine, he had little doubt about that, but so far they had failed to grasp the most important issue surrounding Campbell's boots – nor did it look as if they were going to any time soon. He had been wondering whether he ought to say anything, but having watched Campbell's previously-yellow duster turn black over the past half hour, Alistair finally decided enough was enough.

'You do know that Campbell's not the only one in the soup, don't you?' he remarked to the room in general.

This had the unfortunate effect of bringing all other conversation to a standstill, and as nineteen pairs of eyes turned on him, Alistair found himself having to resist the urge to cringe.

'I'm not?' Campbell asked, puzzled.

'It's a test,' Alistair said carefully. There was no going back now. 'As far as Potter's concerned, we're supposed to work together, so if one man's at fault, it's everyone's responsibility. If Campbell's the only one who turns up with shiny boots tomorrow, Potter will label us all as idle buggers and have us on jankers quick as lightning. Campbell included.'

'But that's not fair,' Nightingale piped up from the back.

Alistair shook his head. 'No, it's not fair,' he said. 'But that's the point. It's us versus Potter, and the only way we win is if we watch each other's backs.'

'So, if we all turn up with shiny boots tomorrow...?' Sticky said, cottoning on.

Alistair nodded. 'Right. He'd never expect it from new boys like us.'

'And how do you know?' Smudge demanded. His expression was one of genuine curiosity.

Alistair hesitated a few seconds before answering. 'Army family,' he said simply. 'There's things you can't help but pick up.'

'You staying in, then?' someone else asked.

Alistair fixed his face into an attitude of determination.

'No,' he said firmly. 'I'm going to be a Maths teacher.'

The room went quiet again, and Alistair turned to Campbell.

'Give it here,' he said, holding out his hand for the boot. 'And someone see if they can find me a candle.'

Taking up the polish and finding a miraculously still-virgin corner of the duster, Alistair set to work on Campbell's boot. In quiet fascination Smudge, Ginger, Sticky and the rest drew around to watch.

And that was simply the start of it. Their early wrong-footing of Potter was a brief, small victory which quickly gave way to drilling, then obstacle courses and hikes, and then more drilling. Eventually, they were issued rifles and target practice commenced. Alistair found this more to his liking, as he had an eye for it, and turned out to be the best shot in his platoon. Unfortunately, there was too much of everything else, and too little shooting.

Then there were classes in various different matters, from map-reading to radio transmitter operation. He realised that the Army was using these classes to determine each recruit's final destination. Naturally, the recruits in training weren't informed of the results of any of this testing.

He found he was right, and the other members of his squad were pleasant enough for the most part. He didn't feel particularly close to any of them besides Campbell, but they were decent, reliable chaps – with the exception of Hannigan, who had a lazy streak and a tendency to skive off. The only aptitude he seemed to display was for peeling spuds, something he was condemned to do on a very regular basis.

Instruction and training lasted six weeks, and then it would be the turn of the next bunch of conscripts. By the end of the sixth week, the Army had made up its mind as to what it would do with each of them. Alistair was surprised to discover he'd been assigned to the Royal Corps of Signals. That meant another railway journey for him, this time to Catterick Garrison in Yorkshire. He didn't know about seeing the world, but he *was* seeing plenty of Army grounds…

Two others from his squad, one of which Campbell, were also assigned to the Signals, so they travelled north together (after a traditional thank-God-we're-out-of-here in the NAAFI the night before), with a slight headache.

And instead of the rank of private, they were now signalmen.

Alistair discovered that he was starting to enjoy his trade training with the Signals. He'd done a little ham radio operating in his school days, and he found it easy and fun. This was cranking it up a gear, and he liked the extra power and range of the equipment he was training with. Not only that, but he soon learned that the vast majority of the Signals trainees went from Catterick to the British Army of the Rhine. They'd be close to the Ruskies, but there was no active outbreak of hostilities, so it was a pretty safe posting.

And German beer was legendary. And as for those blonde Rhine maidens... Yes, he was fairly certain he could spend the remainder of his National Service happily settled on the Rhine. And picking up a smattering of German could prove to be useful in the future, too – there were lots of German mathematicians, so it couldn't hurt to be able to read them in their native language.

Naturally, the Army proved it couldn't be as obliging as all that. In his cadre, only two others of the recruits weren't assigned to the Rhine. One man was sent to Malaya – jungle warfare.

And Alistair and Campbell were assigned to the 1st Commonwealth Division... Korea. Aiding in the 'military intervention'.

Wonderful. Abso-bloody-lutely wonderful.

PRISONER III

ALISTAIR HAD been taken back to a different cage, slightly larger. He still couldn't rest, but he had a little more room for his legs, so they didn't cramp up as much. He was a couple of rows back from his previous position, and away from that bloody officer. There was nobody in the cage next to his, but – judging from the stench and drying blood – it hadn't been empty long. He didn't even have the strength to wonder what had happened to the previous inhabitant.

He was given a little filthy water and more of the spat-in rice before he was taken back again to the immaculately neat officer. This time he was able to shamble along slowly, and to stand, shaking, in front of the man.

Taking a slow, deliberate drag on his cigarette, the Chinese man said: 'I am an officer. You will show me the proper respect.'

'Sorry,' Alistair mumbled. 'Don't get enough water to be able to spit in your face, old man.'

Impassively, the man gave a slight nod to the two guards. One of them picked up a club and swung it against the back of Alistair's legs. With a cry of pain, Alistair collapsed forward.

'That's better,' his tormentor said, gently. 'Kneeling before me is respectful.'

Alistair attempted to rise, but the guard with the club gestured with it, and he decided to stay where he was.

The officer gave a slight inclination of his head. The second guard hurried to fetch a chair and positioned it beside the officer. He sat down gingerly in it, and then looked down at Alistair.

'Good. Now we can have a little chat, eh? You are no doubt

wondering how I speak such good English?'

'No,' Alistair said, honestly. He didn't care in the slightest.

'I shall tell you anyway. I was born and raised in Anshan, where there was a Christian mission before the war.' He waved his hand airily. 'Not *this* war, of course – the one with Japan. The elderly Englishman who was in charge of the mission took a liking to me, and he was a great believer in education, so he took me in hand. He taught me a large number of subjects, primarily English. I was a good pupil and learned quickly and well, wouldn't you say?' Alistair said nothing. 'No? Well, I'm sure you'll prove to be chattier once you get to know me.' He pretended shock. 'Dear me, how remiss of me! I am forgetting my manners – we haven't yet been introduced. Permit me to correct this breach in etiquette. My name is Peng. The old missionary thought that was a heathen name, so he always called me Peter. Even when I killed him, he still called me Peter, and not Peng. I am certain that you will not make that mistake, will you...? Ah, but now *you* are being impolite. You have not told me your name. Please, correct this oversight.'

A lot of this nonsense had simply flown over Alistair's mind, and it was difficult for him to focus. This foreign chappie wanted his name, did he? Well, he was allowed under Army regulations to give his name, rank and serial number, but he didn't really feel like co-operating with this person in any way. He'd been thinking about Catterick, hadn't he? And that lovely, lovely cinema they had. Maybe he could take a name from the last film he'd seen? Nobody too obvious, though... But it had to be a name he'd be able to remember...

'Clitheroe,' he said, as firmly as he could. 'James, Signalman. Serial number 6... 4...' He shook his head slightly. 'Can't remember the rest of it.'

Peng raised his eyebrows in mock surprise. 'Don't let that worry you, Signalman Clitheroe,' he said, in a sarcastic tone. 'I'm sure you'll remember a lot of things before we're done talking.' He took another puff of his cigarette. 'Yes, a lot of things.'

SNAFU

THE FIRST thing you learned in the Army was that it was even more strictly segregated than civilian life, and that you had better know and stick to your place. Privates (or signalmen in Alistair's case), of course, were the lowest of the low, and had to take orders from everybody. At least that made things simple. Complications only set in if you managed to get yourself promoted. He'd managed to dodge the bullet of a commission via the War Office Selection Board (or 'Wosby', as it was commonly known) in Basic Training, by simply refusing to attend when his name was put forward. Stokes had howled at him for a good ten minutes, which Alistair had endured steadfastly. They couldn't *make* him attend, after all. After this promotions could only happen if you forgot the second rule: never volunteer for anything. Keep your head down, follow orders and let other people make the decisions. That's how you (mostly) survived. At least, that was the theory. It didn't always work.

You also learned that the Army loves acronyms and had nicknames for everything and everyone. You didn't use the proper name for anything. And, naturally, there were plenty of unapproved acronyms that made the rounds. One obvious one was RHIP – 'Rank Hath Its Privileges'. That was clear-cut, too. Officers didn't bunk with their men; they had separate quarters, separate messes (with better food and even table service!). Even sergeants had their own hang outs, where they didn't have to fraternise with the troops they'd spent their days terrorising. Privates, of course, got the minimum of everything.

And then there was the inevitable SNAFU... 'Situation

Normal All Fouled Up' (though 'fouled' was only used in mixed company). It was the one inevitable fact of Army life: foul-ups happen. There was nothing that you could do about it beyond wait for it to happen and hope it wouldn't prove lethal.

Being assigned to Korea was, as far as Alistair went, a real SNAFU. Korea wasn't even classified as a war – it was a 'military intervention' (a war in everything but name). It was a fallout from the war. Japan had invaded Korea before the war, and had finally been driven out when they had surrendered after Hiroshima and Nagasaki. That had left a power vacuum, and *they* never lasted long. 'Nature abhors a vacuum' he'd learned in school, and that applied to human nature as well. The Russians – just a hop, skip and a jump away in Kamchatka – had seen this as a chance to annex more territory and to win converts to their political philosophy. The newly formed United Nations (the foundation of future peace, as far as many were concerned) had been persuaded by the Yanks that this would be a terrible thing to allow to happen, and so they (under the prodding of the self-same Yanks) had decided to 'help' out. Korea split into two opposing factions, the Ruskies piled in, and then so did the Yanks.

As if *that* wasn't bad enough, the Chinese – freshly inspired by their own brand of Communism – saw an opportunity as well, and decided that they wanted a hand in all of it. How the resulting mess didn't get to be called a war was beyond most… *participants*. But it didn't matter what you called it, it was hell.

It would be a long trip to Korea, but the NCOs tried to fill most of it with activity. The one good thing about being aboard ship was that they couldn't order ten-mile loaded marches. They could, however, have the troops do daily PT. Which Alistair didn't mind – he'd shot up during his mid-teens (after having always being too short) and found himself quite adept in the gym. And another good thing was that he at least had Campbell's friendship for company.

There were classes to explain the situation in Korea, and weapons, ships and aircraft to keep an eye open for. Plus, they and a few others had extra training on the RT (the only part of all of it that Alistair actively enjoyed). There he found himself thrown together with another signalman in particular

– a happy-go-lucky northerner.

'Stan Hodgeon,' the young man had introduced himself in his thick Mancunian accent. 'From Wigan. Shouldn't really be here, you know, but, well – SNAFU.' He grinned. 'I actually wanted to be a cook, see?'

'Good grief! Why?'

'It's me background,' Stan said. 'Me family are butchers – me dad, uncles, great-uncles, the lot of 'em. I'm to be one when I get out. So, I thought I'd like doing kitchen duty – keep me hand in with meat, like. Then they discovered I were good with radio, and here I am. That's the Army for you, eh? What about you?'

'Oh. Alistair Lethbridge-Stewart.' He shook Stan's hand. 'My friends call me Al.'

'With a name like that, Al, you should be an officer, not a lowly peasant like me.'

'Not interested,' Alistair said, flatly. 'I just want to do my stint and get back to being a teacher. I was just about to graduate when I got the… call.'

'What was you going to teach, then?'

'Mathematics.'

Stan snorted. 'You could practice on me, then. I'm no good at sums.'

'Maybe I will, in all of our copious free time.'

Stan laughed, and they were somehow then friends.

Alistair knew that a lot of people made good friends in National Service, but he'd pretty much avoided trying, apart from Campbell. He didn't want ties to the Army – he just wanted to do his duty and get back to real life. Despite himself, though, he somehow discovered that he got along with the skinny northerner.

They had absolutely nothing in common, really, outside of their daily life on the ship. Stan was from one of those families where everybody had seven or ten kids, and they married second cousins and had a dozen kids of their own. It all sounded horribly chaotic to Alistair, whose closest relatives were a couple of cousins he barely saw. He'd never even had a brother, while Stan had a regular troop of them. And pictures of the lot, which he showed his new friend.

'Me sister, Mary Anne,' he said of a stiff but fairly attractive young lady. 'If you're ever up Wigan way after this is over, you'd like her.'

Alistair didn't want to be set up with anybody right now, let alone a girl with a thick accent and a bunch of brothers. And his mother's Christian name. He just nodded non-committedly.

They were leaning against the guardrail of the transport ship in one of their rare off-duty moments. Campbell was below deck. He and Stan got on fine, but the training rotation meant that Alistair and Stan spent more time together than Alistair and Campbell did. There was nothing visible but sea and sky, which were both pleasant enough. Alistair didn't suffer from sea sickness, thankfully, though a number of the men did. Luckily, they weren't currently around heaving their guts up into the sea. Nothing bothered Stan, of course. He went through life oblivious to a lot, and uncaring about most of the rest. He didn't even resent being called up – it was just another lark to him. There were times when Alistair envied him his calm acceptance, because it was something he could not bring himself to feel. He resented every minute of this imposed life.

Stan pulled out a pack of Players and offered Alistair one. Alistair hesitated – he'd never really enjoyed smoking, but he'd discovered that in the Army it was sort of a bonding experience. You shared ciggies with your mates, smoked them and grumbled about military life. He accepted the offered cigarette and they stood, looking out to sea and contemplated the horizon in silence for a while.

'What do you think Korea is going to be like?' Stan mused.

'Blackpool on a rainy Monday?' Alistair guessed, and they both laughed at the thought.

Alistair had taken geography in school, of course, but Korea certainly hadn't been on the curriculum. It had been mainly the British Empire, naturally, the produce of Australia, the length of the Irriwady, New Zealand lamb... Some European stuff, of course, and a bit about the United States. But Korea was too small to bother with. And Stan had left school at sixteen – he was only seventeen now – with the bare minimum of a British education.

'Well, you don't need to know too much to be a butcher,' he said, cheerfully.

Again, Alistair envied his friend's simple acceptance of the way things were.

'What will you do when this is over?' Alistair asked him.

Stan grinned. 'I'll join me dad in the shop,' he said. 'And I've got me eye on me cousin Gladys. And she's given me a nod, you know.' Inevitably, he had a picture of her – a skinny girl in a floral frock and a rather ridiculous hat. They'd be a good match, no doubt. 'And you?'

'Back to university and graduate.'

'You'll be good teacher,' Stan said. 'I'm learning a lot just listening to you natter.'

'I want to be able to make a difference in people's lives,' Alistair said. 'I had a couple of really fine teachers in my time, and I'd like to pass it on to other youngsters.'

They smoked quietly, and then they both flicked their butts into the sea below before going inside.

And so it went: exercise (almost like being back in Salisbury again), training (he could strip and reassemble his Enfield in the dark), education (what's a MiG and what's a B-29 Superfortress?), food (even Stan couldn't say anything good about it beyond 'At least it's dead') and smoking. Day after long day.

But, eventually, Korea was at hand. They were only a day or so out when the relative calm broke. Alistair and Stan were, inevitably, smoking at the rail when Stan gestured.

'Bit black over Bill's mother's,' he commented.

'I beg your pardon?'

'Sorry, northern slang, mate.' He pointed to the horizon ahead of them. 'There's rain in store.'

Alistair could see that he was quite correct: huge, dark clouds were gathering in the distance, curling and advancing with considerable speed. 'Maybe it *is* Blackpool on a rainy Monday,' he muttered, tossing his half-smoked ciggie away. 'We'd better get inside before that strikes, or we'll get soaked.'

'Sergeant won't like us getting our uniforms wet,' Stan agreed. There was a jagged flash of lightning that reflected off the sea, followed by the bellow and crash of thunder. They hurried below, and then heard the sound of rain slamming against the deck and bulkheads. 'Ee, this is gonna be a rough one.'

That was a severe understatement. The ship started to lurch and toss as the sea shook. Rain hammered away, and a couple of men came below, soaked to their skins. The dipping and rising was even starting to make Alistair a bit queasy. The men who'd had trouble with the relatively calm seas could be heard heaving away in the ship's latrines. That didn't help matters much. Alistair struggled to keep his stomach where it belonged.

The storm howled and pelted and flashed all around them. The transport slowed, unable to make much headway in these rough seas. The bulkheads shivered and shook, and the decks absolutely refused to stay horizontal. And it went on for hours.

They retreated to their hammocks, but there was no relief in sleep. The hammocks swung wildly, almost tossing them out, and there was no way they'd be able to get any rest like that. They couldn't even enjoy a good smoke, as that would make them sicker than they already were. Everybody just sat around, moaning and complaining. A couple of men tried to play cards, but their hands kept flying off their makeshift table as the ship rocked and rolled.

It was a very hard night, and it seemed endless. This was a huge storm – perhaps even a typhoon, Alistair realised – and they were stuck, helpless, in the midst of it.

'Think we might drown?' Stan asked.

'It might be preferable,' Alistair answered.

'I wonder if Gladys would miss me.' Stan shrugged. 'Well, I'm sure she'd find another fella.'

That' a cheerful thought, Alistair mused.

The ship bucked and rocked like a drunken thoroughbred, and shook them all up. Finally, long after what should have been dawn, it began to peter out. The ship started to shake less, and the sound of the rain that had been constant for hours now started to lessen in its drumbeat. Eventually, it died down altogether.

The good news was that PT on deck was cancelled, as it was far too wet, but that just meant doubling up on other training. News began to filter back that their arrival would be delayed, that not only had they made no progress during the storm, but had been blown further out to sea and had to retrace their course. Alistair didn't know how accurate the gossip was, but it soon proved to be true.

They didn't even sight land that day, nor could any lights be seen by night. Well, he wasn't disappointed by the delay – one less day of problems to face.

Around lunchtime the next day there was a cry from the observer aloft. About ten minutes later, a slash of coast was visible on the horizon.

'Land at last,' Stan commented. 'I hope I can remember how to walk when the ground stays steady beneath our feet.'

Alistair grinned at the comment. He could empathise with that feeling. They'd been on swaying decks and in swaying hammocks for well over a month now, with only a couple of short port stops in between. It would be wonderful to stand on something that didn't try and slip away from you.

Their sergeant ordered them to start their packing, ready to go ashore. It would be hours before that was possible, but it was at least something to do. It took them all of ten minutes to layer everything they owned in their kit bags, and then they were back to the inevitable waiting. They had their orders in their pockets; everyone in the squad would scatter, but he and Stan were the only two with the same posting, and they'd be leaving their comrades as soon as they were ashore. 'Ashore' in this case would be Seoul, the Korean capital.

They could hear the bustle of the city even down below (they weren't allowed on deck in case they got in the sailors' way), mixed with the cries of seabirds and blares of ships' horn. Eventually, they felt the engines slow to a crawl, and then the grinding sound of the mooring chains singing out. Bumps, grinds, calls and, finally, all motion stopped except the slight rise and fall associated with being afloat. It was another fifteen minutes before they were ordered topside. They grabbed their kit backs and ascended to the deck for their first look at Seoul.

It didn't look that different to an English port at this point – mostly warehouses and cargo storage. The main difference was in the colour of the workers' skins and the style of their clothing. Voices were raised and people cried out in English and what was presumably the Korean tongue. There was plenty of motion ashore, not so much on the ship. Then the landing plank was run out, fastened into place, and the troops began to shuffle off.

Alistair and Stan were among the last to disembark, naturally, and sadly Campbell was one of the first, so by the time they reached land the other signalman was gone. At the end of the dock they looked around for some sort of guidance. The main body of troops were plunging on ahead, through a corridor consisting of natives offering trinkets, fruits and even brightly coloured birds in wicker cages for sale. There were men and women, all crying out in a sort of pidgin English, seemingly not realising that nobody was stopping to buy anything. There were a couple of RMPs at the dockside, keeping a loose eye on the natives. Desperate, Alistair crossed to them.

'Sorry, Sergeant, we're looking for Dispatch.'

The man eyed him sceptically for a moment, then pointed. 'That way, third building. And don't stop to buy anything on your way.'

'Absolutely not, Sergeant,' Stan promised. Hefting their kit bags, they headed off in the indicated direction. 'And I thought training barracks were a madhouse,' he muttered, as they pushed past wildly gesticulating and yelling locals. 'Mind, there's a pretty face or two here.'

'I think the order *don't buy anything* applies especially to the local girls,' Alistair warned him.

'I know. But a lad can dream, can't he?'

They finally managed to get through the would-be vendors and made it to Dispatch – there was a sign on the door – and inside. With the door closed, it was a lot quieter. There were a couple of desks in the room, at which a pair of clerks sat. Alistair picked the closest, and marched over.

'Sigs Lethbridge-Stewart and Hodgeon reporting for transport,' he said, noting the man was a signalman himself.

'Papers?'

They handed them across and waited as the young man skimmed them. Then he scowled, checked a clipboard and then stared back at the papers in his hand.

'You were supposed to be here yesterday,' he complained.

'Not our fault,' Alistair replied. 'We had a run-in with a storm.'

'Well, your transport's gone.'

Stan rolled his eyes. 'Does that mean we can head back to Blighty, then?' he asked hopefully.

'You must be bleedin' joking.'

'Yes, I thought I must.'

'What *do* we do?' Alistair asked, pointedly.

That stumped the lad, as did Alistair's accent, apparently. 'You'd better wait here,' he finally decided.

Obviously, this was a problem above a clerk's powers of decision. He waved them vaguely in the direction of a few empty chairs and then shot off through a door in the rear of the room.

'SNAFU,' Stan decided, emphatically. 'That's the Army for you – travel half-way round the world, and they expect you to keep to a bloomin' timetable.'

'Maybe someone should have ordered that storm to step aside?' Alistair suggested. 'Some officer's not doing his duty, if you ask me.'

'I wonder how long it'll take them to sort this out?' Stan settled down on one of the uncomfortable chairs. 'What's the chances that they'll decide it's best just to forget we're even here?'

'We're in the Army,' Alistair pointed out. 'They have to account for everything – and everyone.' He took another chair.

The second clerk was typing away, paying them no mind. He was probably breathing a thankful prayer that this problem had gone to his companion and he didn't have to sort anything out.

After a wait of about five minutes, the inner door opened again, and a captain strode out, carrying their papers and frowning. Alistair and Stan shot to their feet.

'Stand easy,' the captain said, distractedly.

The clerk slipped quietly back into the room behind him and into his seat. He focused on shuffling some papers about.

'This is dashed difficult,' the captain observed. 'Your transport's gone. And there won't be another run out to Imjin until the next transport arrives in a week.' There didn't seem to be much they could say to that, either. He glanced at the two clerks, who were desperately attempting to look busy. 'I don't suppose either of you has any ideas?'

Alistair sighed inwardly. Definitely SNAFU. Bloody typical of the Army, really. Neither clerk seemed to want to contribute any ideas (assuming that they had any). The captain looked at the papers again, as if this might magically conjure up an answer from the heavens.

'Oh, dash it all! We can't just have you hanging around and making the place look untidy for a week or more.'

Alistair could see that Stan was itching to suggest they be sent home again, but, thankfully, he knew better than to open his mouth at this juncture. This was an excellent time to remain dumb.

'I'm sure the Americans don't have problems like this,' the captain muttered to himself. Then his face lit up. 'The Yanks! Of course.' He moved to put the papers in his hand down on the nearest desk, but had second thoughts. 'Wait here, chaps.' And he shot out of the door.

There was a momentary increase in the sound of offers to sell anything and everything before the door swung shut behind him.

Stan sighed. 'I don't suppose there's anywhere to get a cuppa?' he asked hopefully. 'Or, better yet, a pint?'

The clerk they'd been talking to laughed bitterly. 'If there was, mate, d'ye think we'd be sitting here?'

'I'm starting to dislike Korea already,' Stan said to Alistair.

'Look on the bright side; it has to get better, because it could hardly get worse.'

Alistair and Stan sat in silence, waiting. The two other privates carried on with whatever paperwork they had before them.

About ten minutes later, the door opened again, and the captain hurried back in, beaming.

'Right, men,' he announced. 'It's arranged. The Americans will give you a ride with them out to the Imjin River. Once you're there, you'll be directed to the British lines. Safe travels, lads.' He looked down at them. 'Come on, get the lead out; the Yanks are leaving very shortly.'

'Ah, where do we go, sir?' Alistair asked.

'Oh, yes, right. Danvers, take these two over to the American post. Compound Three. Off you go.'

Danvers turned out to be the clerk they'd been dealing with. 'Sir,' he said, and glared at Alistair and Stan. 'Come on, you two – shift it!'

There was no use pointing out that the muck-up wasn't their fault. Alistair grabbed his kit bag, and followed Danvers out of the door. Stan hurried to stay with them. They passed through the crowd of offers again, Danvers expertly fending the natives off with the ease of familiarity. Not that there was any time to take in the view – there wasn't much to see, anyway.

It turned out the Americans were stationed almost next door, so their trip was brief. Danvers led them to the motor pool in the compound, and gestured them to where there was a single jeep idling. There was a pile of boxes in the back, but nobody visible.

'That must be it. Bon voyage,' Danvers said, then he turned and hurried away.

'Friendly fellow, eh?' Stan muttered. 'Speaking of which, where are the Yanks?'

'Over here, Limeys.' A lean shape unwound from the back seat of the vehicle and managed to unfold somehow into a human form. 'Izzy Rivkin. Stu's the driver; he's just picking up a few last-minute items. Stow your bags, and settle in.' He grinned and held out his hand. Alistair shook it and introduced himself and Stan. 'Your boss just caught us in time,' Izzy added. 'Lucky for you, we're a little slow off the mark today. We were supposed to be on the road an hour ago. Well, maybe it's lucky – kinda depends on your point of view, don't it?'

'The Imjin River a trouble spot?' asked Alistair.

'You could say that. The KPA are causing a spot of bother.'

'KPA?'

'Korean People's Army.' Izzy grinned. 'Say, you're a bit short on the intel, aren't you, guys?' He sat up a little taller. 'Here's Stu now.'

Alistair raised an eyebrow as he saw the other GI running to the jeep. His arms were overflowing with packs of nylons. 'You boys dress a little oddly,' Alistair said.

'It's for the gals,' Izzy explained.

'Girls?' Stan looked puzzled.

'Locals,' Izzy explained. 'They go nuts for the nylons. Do anything for them. And I do mean *anything*.' He winked, and Alistair tried not to feel too embarrassed.

Stu reached the jeep, and tossed the packs into the back seat. 'Hey,' he said, cheerily. 'Stu Reiss.' He shook their hands. Izzy stayed in the back, so Alistair took the spare front seat and Stan clambered in the back. 'Mind the pantyhose, friend,' Stu called. 'I want them all in good shape when we reach the river, hear?' Then he laughed and sent the vehicle dashing across the deserted lot. 'So, who's got the map?'

Alistair didn't quite know what to make of their new acquaintances. They seemed friendly – but more than a trifle undisciplined.

'How far is it to the Imjin?'

'Don't rightly know,' Stu admitted cheerfully. 'Couple a' hundred miles, most likely. Got plenty of gas, so don't worry. Izzy, you found the goddamn map yet?'

'Me? I thought you had it.'

Alistair sincerely hoped that they weren't all going to have it.

THE OBSERVER III

INSIDE ALISTAIR'S mind, Bill smiled. Observing the twenty-something Alistair Lethbridge-Stewart was quite an experience. His antipathy towards military service was very real, and so far removed from the officer who had first taken Bill under his wing back in 1969. Clearly a lot had happened in between 1951 and then. Bill knew some of it, but the circumstances of Alistair's conscription was new.

He still wondered, though, what was making him jump from the prison to Alistair's first days in the military and back again. Certainly, the slightly older Alistair was thinking back on those earlier days, but surely that wasn't enough?

And as Stu drove off, Bill felt his mind being dragged forward in time back to the prison.

Hello, old friend, he thought as he returned.

PRISONER IV

ALISTAIR WISHED his mind would clear; everything was hazy and surreal. And he was sure he could still hear that strange voice in his head. Clearly a side effect of what Peng's men were doing to him. Of course, that's what his captors wanted – they were trying to break him, and the foggier everything was, the harder it was for him to think, the easier it would be for them. It was therefore vitally important that he tell them absolutely nothing that could be of any use to them.

If only he could *think* about what that might be.

He might let something vital slip without even realising it. Not that he knew anything vital, of course; he was only a lowly signalman, after all, and not in a posting to encounter anything truly sensitive. The thought struck him as funny for some reason, and he found himself giggling.

'This situation amuses you?' Peng asked. He held his cigarette to his mouth, sucked, and then breathed smoke in Alistair's face. This made Alistair cough, and stopped his fit of giggles. 'Are you laughing at me?' There was genuine emotion in Peng's eyes now, and it was anger. 'It is very dangerous to laugh at me.'

'I was laughing at myself,' Alistair tried to explain, but that made as little sense to Peng as it did to himself.

Peng abruptly back-handed him, sending him sprawling. His jaw ached from the blow, but he could see the Chinese rubbing his hand; it must have hurt him as well. Maybe there was some sort of a moral in that? Hurt others and you hurt yourself? That was sort of funny, too, wasn't it? Alistair had to fight another attack of laughter.

He was vaguely aware that he was getting hysterical. This

was not a good thing – if he could only remember *why* it was not a good thing…

Peng turned back again, his face impassive once more. 'So, let us begin again, Clitheroe. I am an officer, and you are trained to obey the commands of an officer. And I order you to tell me everything that you know.'

'Not my officer,' Alistair informed him. 'Order your own men. Can't order me.'

Peng glared down at him, then gestured to the two guards. They hauled Alistair back into a kneeling position, and then backed away. Peng smoked for a moment, and then looked down at Alistair.

'Do you know why you are here?'

Well, *that* was an easy one to answer. But *should* he answer? After all, his captors knew perfectly well why he was here already, didn't they? So, he wouldn't be telling them anything useful. On the other hand, telling them anything at all – even useless material – might be considered aiding and abetting the enemy. Maybe the best thing would be just to keep his mouth shut.

Rule number two: never volunteer for anything! Or was it *never volunteer anything?* Oh well, it was something like that.

After waiting for some response, Peng became impatient, and nodded slightly. One of the guards slammed the butt of his rifle into Alistair's shoulder, wrenching a cry from him, and knocking him back to the ground again. The guard then grabbed Alistair by the injured shoulder and jerked him painfully back to his knees.

'Do not be impolite,' Peng advised him. 'When I ask a question, you will answer, or you will be punished. Do you understand?'

Well, *that* much made sense to Alistair: Peng was annoyed. Peng was the enemy, and Peng was annoyed. Therefore… therefore… Oh, yes! Therefore Alistair was doing his duty, and fighting the enemy. Best thing to do, then, was to stay silent, since it didn't give the enemy anything. That was it. That was the way. Stay silent.

He screamed again as the guard slammed his rifle into the other shoulder. Then, mercifully, he lost consciousness.

KOREA

ALISTAIR LOOKED around as the jeep sped along the roadway through downtown Seoul. His first impression of the city was that it was an overcrowded tip. The roads were none too good, with rain-filled potholes all over the place. It was lucky they were in a jeep, which could ignore these conditions. Mostly. He didn't like to picture what it must be like riding the streets in a Bedford, lurching and bumping constantly. The buildings were alternately flimsy shacks and sturdier but battered houses. The air was thick and humid, and filled with the odour of cooking. There were people everywhere, some active, others huddled about cooking fires even in the streets.

Stu was sounding his horn constantly, warning people out of his way. There were even people driving a few straggly cows along, and chickens and other birds in wicker cages all over.

Izzy grinned at him. 'First time in Korea?'

'First time out of England,' Stan said before Alistair could answer.

'Culture shock, eh?' Izzy grinned. 'You should see Brooklyn some time.'

'It's a bit… mucky,' Alistair commented.

'It's a war zone,' Stu offered. 'Can't expect it to be spick and span. It's the maid's day off, boys.'

He was making fun of them, and Alistair could hardly blame him. 'Sorry. We were hoping it would look a bit more…'

'Exotic?' Izzy asked. He grinned again. 'Oh, there's lots of places that are real pretty.' He gestured vaguely. 'Plenty a' temples and palaces and such. Just not in the best of shapes right now. The locals are nice folks – but pushy, tend to forget to share the road, but basically decent enough folks. And some of the gals are real pretty and friendly.' Then he scowled. 'They may not call this a war, fellas, but make no mistake about it – that's what it is. And these folks know it, and they're just trying to survive.'

'They've had a real tough time,' Stu added. 'An awful lot of 'em have never known what peace is like. The Japs invaded them in the '30s, so anybody younger than twenty has never really known freedom. And, not too long ago, this city was in Commie hands. We freed 'em, but I'm not entirely certain that's the way everybody here sees it.'

'That's bloody awful,' Stan said.

'Dead right.' Izzy grinned. 'But Uncle Sam's here now – along with you Limeys. We'll sort this lot out in no time. Show them what freedom can mean, once the fighting's over.'

Alistair realised that these Americans were rather brash, and more than slightly mercenary, but their hearts were in roughly the right place. If they were a representative sample of the troops here, things might not be so bad after all.

'Have you two been here long?'

Stu laughed. 'We were among the first,' he answered. 'That's why we know our way around. Stick with us, you'll be okay.'

It was always good to have somebody who could show you the ropes. 'Thank you. How long will our route take us?'

Izzy shook his head. 'Eager to be in the thick of things, eh? You Brits! Don't be so quick to get yourselves killed.' Then, answering the question: 'Three, four days, depending.'

'Depending on what?'

'The weather, for starters. This is not yet the monsoon season, but storms can still get pretty intense. We may have to sit out a few downpours. Then there's this little thing called *war*. The North pushes south, we push north, lots of fighting and the like. It's not a tidy affair.'

'Imjin's the big river out west,' Stu added. 'Runs sorta north-south. Both sides want it, so it's hot ground for fighting. That spills over, so we'd kinda like to avoid as much as possible.'

'Then there's the air show,' Izzy continued. 'The Ruskies have handed the north a bunch of MiGs, loaned them some pilots to teach them the ropes, and set 'em loose. They like to shoot up the roads from time to time, so keep your eyes peeled.'

'It sounds like rather a mess,' Stan said.

Izzy laughed. '*Rather a mess* – yeah, I'll say it is. Especially for the poor locals. Hey, there's a temple now.'

Alistair caught a glimpse of a tall wall, with an ornate gateway, a path leading through trees to a quaint-looking building, and then they were past it before he could make out any details. Except for the gaps that had been blown in the wall.

Seeing the expression on Alistair's face, Izzy shrugged. 'Your first war, eh? Well, Stu and I were in the Big One – 1st Infantry Division; Sicily, then the Ardennes. Only the scenery changes.'

'And the girls,' Stu added.

Stan looked puzzled. 'How long have you been in the Army, then?'

'Twelve years,' Izzy answered.

'And you're still privates?'

'Not *still*,' Izzy laughed. '"Again". We keep getting promotions, but it don't sit well with us.'

'So we get busted down again,' Stu added. 'If we're caught with those nylons – well, we can't get busted any lower, at least.'

'Maybe we could claim they belong to these Brits?' Izzy mused. 'Everybody knows the Limeys dress funny.'

'Not *that* funny!' Stu spluttered, while Alistair felt himself go red.

'Take a bit of advice from us, guys,' Izzy confided. 'Never let yourselves get promoted. That way lies madness.'

The buildings and people started to thin out, finally, as they reached the outskirts of Seoul itself. Alistair could see that the town was ringed by mountains, though it lay on a flattish floodplain. It would have been a lovely place to hike, had it not been for the war. There were small farm holdings scattered around now, and natives working the fields. Rice, he imagined, and other crops. Not a lot of livestock. Nobody paid them any attention; the locals were clearly used to military traffic.

They drove on. The roads improved somewhat as they moved further from strategic targets and into the countryside.

They weren't paved, but they had been levelled, at least, and cleared. At one point, Stu cursed, and pulled off the road, heading a short distance into the undergrowth.

'Planes,' he explained, pointing at a bunch of small dots in the sky.

'Theirs or ours?' asked Alistair.

'Too early to tell. But not too early to take precautions.'

They watched as the planes grew as they flew southwards. They could belong to either side…

'F-86s,' Alistair announced, recognising their silhouettes. 'Sabres. Your chaps.'

'He's right,' Izzy agreed, shading his eyes. 'They're our boys all right. Hoorah for the flyboys, eh?'

'Aren't you going out?' Stan asked.

'Nah,' Stu answered. '*We* can tell who *they* are, but all they can see at the rate they're going is a vehicle on the road. They might strafe us just to be on the safe side. Even with recognition patches.'

'Charming.'

'Didn't they ever tell you guys that war is hell?'

The roar increased, and then the aircraft were overhead, and then flashing off south. Izzy yelled and waved his hat to encourage them. Then he sat down.

'Show-offs,' he muttered.

They continued on their way. After another hour, Stu announced: 'I'm beat – time for a break.' He pulled off the road beside a small stream, and they clambered out and stretched their aching limbs.

'I'll mash us a brew,' Stan volunteered. He started to rummage in his kit bag for his supply and a billy can.

'Tea?' Stu laughed. 'Don't you guys drink *real* stuff? Or at least coffee?' He reached into one of the boxes in the back of the jeep and pulled out a bottle. 'The only good *mash*,' he explained. 'Kentucky straight.'

'Ah… it's a bit early in the day for me,' Alistair said. He wondered, without saying it, whether their driver should be taking a nip or two… Still, it wasn't as if there was any other traffic, at least. Nor, thankfully, any pedestrians for him to run into.

'Well, alert me when it's late enough, and I'll bring it out again.' Stu laughed, took a good-sized drink, and then handed the bottle over to Izzy, who repeated the performance. The two Yanks watched in considerable amusement as Stan made tea for himself and Alistair, and then chuckled as it was drunk. 'I thought you guys always drank tea with a stiff pinkie?'

'Only in drawing rooms,' Alistair assured him with a straight face.

'Gotcha.'

Alistair was certain Stu would repeat that as the gospel truth later.

Alistair looked around as he sipped. They were on the verge of a small wood, the trees getting thicker up a small hill. Everything seemed to be so pleasant and peaceful; it was hard to believe that there was a war anywhere near here. This could be a very beautiful country, given half a chance. It was such a waste for people to be killing one another instead of living quiet, gentle lives. Not unlike his own situation.

Somehow, Izzy caught onto his mood. 'Yeah,' he said softly. 'Wonder what the locals will do with this place once the fighting's done?'

'They probably won't know what to do,' Alistair said, sadly. 'You say most of them have never known peace. War… where does it ever get you?'

Stu laughed, breaking the mood. 'Well, it got *you* here. Lucky you.'

'Yes,' said Stan, glumly. 'Lucky us.'

They moved on, bumping along the roadway. After a while, Alistair could make out fields, and then farms, and finally a huddle of houses. These were mostly built of wood, and didn't look any too secure. There were locals out, wearing tunics, pants, sandals and straw hats to protect them from the sun. Most of them were working in the fields, and some paused as they saw the strangers approaching. There were children of varying ages, too, a bunch of whom started yelling and running towards the jeep as Stu slowed down.

'Hey, Joe! Hey Joe!'

'*Yeoboseyo*,' Izzy called. He reached into another of the boxes and pulled out a handful of foil-wrapped packets.

'*Chingu! Chingu!*' He started handing them around to the kids running alongside. 'Not you, you got two already. Here ya go, doll...' Then he was waving behind them as they drove on, and he settled back down. 'Kids,' he said. 'Who can resist 'em?'

'Does that happen a lot?' Alistair asked.

'Every chance they get,' Stu said. 'They know Izzy's a soft touch.'

'Kids should have *some* fun in life,' Izzy replied, defensively.

'Did I say otherwise?' Stu glanced at Alistair. 'Good education for ya, though – learn a bit of the local lingo. *Yeoboseyo* – that means *hi*. And *chingu* is *friend*. Never know, might come in handy sometime. Works on kids and dames alike. The gum don't hurt none, either.'

'Works better than offerin' 'em cups of tea,' Izzy added helpfully.

'I'll bear that in mind,' Alistair said drily.

They drove on, back up to about thirty now that the road was clear again. An hour or so later, Stu pulled off again.

'Far enough for one day,' he decided. 'Gotta give the old gal time to cool down and get replenished.' He patted the bonnet. 'Want her to get us where we're goin'.'

'I gotta get replenished myself,' Izzy said. 'Just rations, guys, sorry.'

Stan looked thoughtful. 'Are you in any hurry to eat?'

Izzy looked at him. 'You got an idea?'

Stan wiggled his fingers. 'I'm a butcher back home in Wigan,' he explained. 'And a cook. And I know a thing or three about catching animals and birds. Is there anything eatable on the hoof here?'

'Depends how hungry you are.' Izzy considered the matter. 'There's wild boar, if you can find 'em.'

Stan shook his head. 'Too big. I don't mind eating pork, but I hate to waste good meat, and we could never eat a whole boar.'

'They're not so simple to catch,' Stu informed him. 'And they might have a fifty-fifty chance of eatin' *you.*'

'Didn't I hear that the Brits like fair play?' Izzy asked.

'Something smaller,' Stan said firmly. 'Rabbits, mebbe?'

'Yeah, plenty of them. And pheasants. You Brits like your

pheasants, right?'

Alistair's head filled with memories of trips to the family estate in Glen Cladach, and the many over-the-top meals there. It was no wonder his parents had preferred the simple life of Cornwall. Especially his mother. Alistair smiled slightly; he was more his mother's son than his father's.

'They'd be perfect. A brace of them, eh?' Stan rubbed his hands together. He rummaged around in the boxes in the jeep and found some wire. 'See you soon, lads.' He hurried into the bush.

Alistair watched him go, and laughed slightly.

Izzy grinned. 'You Limeys might turn out to have your uses after all. Think he can really do it?'

'I've no idea,' Alistair confessed. 'But *he* seems to think he can do it. And if he doesn't, we could always eat rations.' He glanced around. 'I'll get some wood and build a fire – just in case.'

'Smart thinking,' Stu agreed. He had the bonnet of the jeep up and was looking inside. 'Sing out if you find a pond or a stream, will ya? Our ride is a bit thirsty.' He went to the back of the jeep and unslung one of the extra petrol cans. 'Meanwhile, I'll gas her up.'

Alistair scouted around, and began collecting kindling and larger branches. It took him half an hour or so, but he had no real trouble in scrounging up the fuel he needed. He came across the path of a stream, and pointed it out to Stu. The American went off with a water bottle.

The sun was starting to go down when Stan strode back out of the woods. He had a pair of pheasants, and held one by the feet, plucking it as he walked.

Izzy glanced up and grinned widely. 'Attaboy!'

'Well done, Stan,' added Alistair. He had the fire going well by now, and was using extra wood to make a spit. 'I'm sure this will be the best meal we've had in months.'

Stan blushed slightly, and went on dressing the two birds with deft hands and his bayonet. He gutted them and disposed of the entrails at a distance while the birds began to cook. 'Shame we don't have some stuffing, but I dunno if the local nuts are safe to eat.'

'I think we'll be eating darned good,' Stu commented. He'd finished checking over the jeep and seemed satisfied it was in good shape for the morning. 'You already got my taste-buds all fired up.'

Stan proved to be as good as his word. He roasted up the pheasants beautifully, and they all ate with gusto. They may not have been as good as the pheasants Alistair's grandmother tended to cook – no time to leave them to hang – but they were, however, superb. It might just have been because Army food strayed into the bland side a lot, but he doubted it. Stan was obviously just what he claimed – a good butcher and a fine cook. He might even teach Granny McDougal a thing or two.

Stu pulled out the Kentucky bourbon again. 'Is it still a little early for you fellas?'

'No,' Alistair said. 'On the contrary, I think now might be the perfect time for a glass.'

Stu made an exaggerated face. 'Oh, he expects a *glass*? These Limeys!' He shook his head. 'Sorry, milord, but you'll have to drink from the bottle, like the rest of us slobs.' Then he grinned and handed it across.

Alistair held the bottle a moment, and then drank. He shuddered as the burning liquid slipped down his throat, but he managed to avoid choking. He wiped off the bottle and handed it back, giving himself time to ensure that he would be able to actually speak again.

'Interesting taste,' he managed to say. 'But it will never beat tea.'

Stu laughed and handed the bottle across to Stan, who took a healthy swig of his own. His eyebrows shot up, and he shook his head.

'I could pickle pigs' knuckles in that.'

Izzy grinned. 'I don't know if that's a compliment or an insult,' he admitted. 'But it's probably true.'

'I'll let you know once I figure it out,' Stan promised. 'Hoo, I think I'll stick to beer from now on.'

'*Warm* beer,' Stu jeered.

'Can you get anything else in this country?' Alistair asked.

And so the night went, until they settled down to sleep.

PRISONER V

'YOU DO not seem to enjoy these conversations of ours, Mr Clitheroe,' Peng said. He was in his chair again, and Alistair was on his knees before him. 'Really, you will find them more productive if you respond to me.'

'I have nothing to say to the enemy.'

Peng pretended that he was offended. 'But I am not your enemy, Mr Clitheroe! I am your friend.'

'Friends don't torture friends.' Alistair was pretty certain he was right in saying that.

'This is not done to you as *torture*. It is done to you to free your mind. You have been lied to all of your life – kept in thrall to those over you. They fear your enlightenment, so they must keep you down, away from your rightful place. I am doing this to you to help you.'

'Don't do me any favours.'

Peng laughed. 'But it is my *duty*,' he explained. 'I must free you from your bondage, from the lies that tie you down. Do you believe in God, Mr Clitheroe?' When Alistair remained silent, he shook his head in mock sorrow. 'Come now. Even if you think I am your enemy, how can it harm you to answer such a simple question? Do you believe in God?'

There probably wasn't any harm in replying, but there was still a part of Alistair's mind that was certain that this was all a trick, and that no matter what he answered, he'd be playing into Peng's nasty little plan. So, he remained silent.

'You're an Englishman,' Peng finally said. 'No doubt you were raised Church of England, eh? Did you sing along with the Christmas carols and all of the hymns? I used to enjoy some of the hymns myself – even though I was never stupid enough to believe in them. But they have nice tunes, don't they?' He lit a fresh cigarette, and blew smoke again into his prisoner's face. 'Do you like hymns? What's your favourite?' Again, Alistair refused to answer, so Peng shook his head again. '*Jerusalem*, no doubt; it's *so* patriotic, after all. Or perhaps *Onward Christian Soldiers*? That would be appropriate, wouldn't it? You know what mine is? No? Not even a guess?' He shrugged. 'Well, I'll tell you. It's *All Things Bright and Beautiful.* I always loved that one. I used to sing it quite well. Even the Reverend Father liked to hear me sing it.' Peng smoked again, and then looked heavenward. 'I sang it when we buried him.' He leaned forwards. 'Now, *there* was a man who believed – I mean, *really* believed. He trusted in his god, and I killed him. I mean – seriously – if his god *really* existed, would a benign deity just stand back and let me murder somebody who believed so fervently in him? Of course not, right? And if there was a god, would he allow me to do all of this to you?'

'You're trying to help me, aren't you?' Alistair asked, and then wished he'd just kept his mouth shut. *Anything* could encourage the enemy.

'Yes, Mr Clitheroe, I am.' And then Peng gave a sharp, barking laugh. 'Oh, you're attempting to be funny! Why, how impressive of you. None of the others have the strength to make little jokes like that.'

So, he was torturing others, too? Ha! *He* was getting information from Peng, and not vice versa! He giggled again, unable to stop himself.

Who else was here? He'd been with other men, but he couldn't quite remember their names, or faces… One of them was an officer, he remembered, but he couldn't recall his face or name. If he could just sleep – long, relaxing, blessed sleep… If he could…

Stay with me, Alistair. Don't let your mind be distracted.

What? What was that?

'I have to confess, you worry me a little, Mr Clitheroe,' Peng informed him. 'If you can still keep that vaunted British stiff upper lip, then you'll never be freed from your shackles. And you *do* want to be free, don't you? Of course you do. But the only way you will become free is to throw away all of those lies you've been taught. You have to unlearn it all, and then we can start putting you back together again, whole and hale and hearty. You do want that, don't you?'

'I want...' Alistair's voice dribbled out. 'I want...'

'Yes, Mr Clitheroe? What is it that you want?'

'Want to... spit in your eye.' He started giggling again.

'Fool!' Peng snarled, his mask of indifference broken. He picked up a swagger stick and started to beat Alistair about the shoulders. 'Why do you insist on provoking me? Why do you make me punish you when all I wish is to help you? Why? Why? Why?' He struck him again and again.

The pain was crippling, but it served to focus Alistair's mind. He concentrated on the agony, and refused to listen to his torturer. Eventually Peng stopped thrashing him, and stood there, panting, until he managed to regain his composure.

'It really is too bad, Mr Clitheroe,' he said. 'Now you will have to go back into your box and be punished further until you co-operate. And then we will speak again.'

He nodded to the guards, who jerked Alistair to his feet. He almost passed out from the pain in his arms, but they dragged him from the room and back to his cage again.

THE OBSERVER IV

HE HADN'T imagined it. That time Alistair had definitely heard him.

Inside Alistair's mind, Bill smiled. Perhaps he wasn't just an observer, after all? He may not have been able to control Alistair's body, participate in events – not that he'd want to, in this instance, mind – but he could, it appeared, communicate with Alistair. At least on some level.

Perhaps this is why the Gnome brought him to this point in time? To help Alistair keep his mind through the torture.

Bill locked on to that idea.

Yes. One last favour returned to the man who had done so much for him.

But before Bill could test that further, he found his mind cast back to April 1951 again...

IMJIM

EACH OF the party took turns to stand sentry during the night. Alistair had taken the first watch, and then got to sleep the rest of the night. Nothing had happened, except for the passage of animals from time to time. He wasn't at all sure what the nocturnal passers-by were, but none came near the fire. He did see glints of eyes from time to time, but nothing more. He wasn't awakened until after sunrise, so clearly the same situation had prevailed during the remainder of the night. They had cold pheasant for breakfast. Stan brewed up some tea, but the Yanks had coffee – probably spiked with the bourbon.

Then they were on their way again, still moving northward.

'The Imjin is on our left,' Stu informed them. 'But travel's better here. We don't need to head west until we're nearer our lines.'

'When will that be?' Alistair asked.

Izzy chuckled. 'Don't worry, you'll have no doubts. There are plenty of troops – on both sides of the river. You Limeys are there in force. We're pushing the Chinese and KPA back, but they don't have the sense to know when they're beaten.'

'What about your lot?' Stan asked.

'We're on your guys' left,' Izzy said. 'We'll drop you off before we finish our run.'

'Right-o,' Alistair agreed.

They had to hide from aircraft twice. The first time, it was from Yak-9Ps, four of them. They were North Korean, but old-fashioned prop jobs – no match for any of the American fighters. They didn't hang about, but circled around and headed back north again. The second flight were B-29 bombers, most likely supporting the combined forces at the river.

There were still few locals to be seen – they were, after all, approaching the front – but there were now signs of the various armed forces ahead. In several places, there were deep shell holes, some with bits of vehicles remaining in them. They even passed a couple of burned-out lorries, hauled to the side of the road, beyond being salvaged.

Up until now, there had been the cries of birds and other sounds of the forest – only heard when they paused for breaks and shut down the jeep's engine – but now there was only silence. Even the wildlife seemed to have deserted the area.

'Must be getting close,' Stan muttered.

'Nah. *Close* is when you start hearin' the shooting,' Stu called back.

'I thought you said it would take three or four days to reach the river,' Alistair pointed out. 'It's not even been a full day yet.'

'I may have misjudged it a bit,' Stu answered, unapologetically. 'I always overestimate travel times so's to impress folks when we get there so early.'

'So, how long will it *actually* take?'

'Couple a hours, most likely.'

Alistair barely managed to restrain a laugh. 'And how accurate is *that* estimate?'

Stu guffawed. 'I think these Brits are getting wise to us,' he told Izzy.

There was movement on the road ahead. Stu pulled off the road, and they all brought their rifles to the ready position. Izzy made a chopping motion.

'It's our guys,' he announced, with some relief.

'Guess that means we're still holding our line,' Stu commented.

It was a supply truck from the American lines, which pulled over as they approached the travellers.

'Any news?' Izzy asked the driver.

'Yeah,' he responded. 'You're headin' into the thick of things. Big build-up ahead.' He grinned. 'Where'd you find the Limeys? Out for a con-sti-tutional?'

'Nah. They got left behind in Seoul, so it was Brooklyn to

the rescue – as usual.'

The driver shook his head. 'They may not thank you when you see what's ahead. There's gonna be plenty of trouble. And soon, too.' He waved, and then drove off.

'I've heard better news,' Stu muttered.

Izzy shrugged. 'And worse. Shift it, kid.'

They drove on.

A couple of miles later, they heard more engines ahead. Alistair exchanged a worried look with Izzy.

'Got to be our guys,' Izzy reassured him. 'That driver woulda told us if the enemy were this close.'

In a few minutes they had reached a temporary camp that had been hastily thrown up close to the road. It was no more than a cluster of about two dozen tents of varying sizes. There were a couple of lorries there, and stretchers were being unloaded.

Stu pulled over, watching a moment, and then a driver came over. He saw that they had no further casualties, and was about to leave when Izzy asked what was going on.

'Patrol got shot up,' the driver said. 'North of the river. It looks like the North is moving decidedly south. Where you headed?'

'Directly for trouble, by the sound of things,' Izzy answered. 'Anything we can do here?'

'Not unless you know how to patch up the wounded or resurrect the dead.'

They drove on. Alistair looked back, watching the turmoil as the wounded were processed into one of the larger tents.

'Mobile Army Surgical Hospital,' Stu explained. 'They can pack up and be on the road in an hour. Move 'em in when needed, move 'em out when the fighting changes place. They're good guys, and badly overworked.'

This was the first time Alistair had actually seen directly one of the results of conflict. He'd heard plenty of stories during the last war, of course. Not only from his father, but many of the men in Bledoe had been called up. Alistair and his friends had heard plenty. But, of course, hearing and seeing were very different things. And it didn't sit well with him, knowing that those were human beings back there, bleeding and maybe dying. War... Bloody, stupid, pointless war.

'Don't go all broody on us, lad,' Izzy said, serious for once. 'You're thinking any of those could be you, aintcha?' He shrugged. 'Well, yeah – it could be. But be thankful it ain't.'

'Yet.'

'Well, yeah, there's always the *yet*. But the end result of thinking like that is desertion, and the brass takes a dim view of that. It gets you shot by your friends instead of your enemies.'

'Izzy,' Alistair said at great length, aware he was possibly going to show his true colours. But seeing those people, and thinking about his family... 'You've been a soldier for more than a decade. Is there *really* any point to it? Does it do any good?'

'Probably not to you. But – to other people? Yeah. Remember those kids in that village yesterday, all *Hey, Joe* and grabbing for gum? It makes a difference to *them*. When this is over, they'll have a real shot at a decent life, which they wouldn't get under the Commies. And it made a huge difference in the Big One. I'm just a simple Brooklyn Jew, kid, but we saw what the Nazis were doing to our cousins in Europe. You didn't see the concentration camps, the women and children murdered just for being what they were born. The gas chambers, the medical experiments... It was real bad, but we did real good, saving folk from that.'

Stu nodded. 'And there's the gals,' he added. 'Don't forget the sex appeal we get from wearin' this uniform.'

That broke Alistair's brooding mood. 'Is that all you think about?' he asked, with mock severity. 'Women?'

'Nope. There's also booze.'

At that, Stan laughed. Alistair had almost forgot his friend was there.

'Stu's got a point,' Stan said.

Alistair just nodded, unable to simply let his mood go entirely.

Traffic was picking up on the road now. Troops were moving about, and there were other jeeps rattling around. As they approached the front lines, there were tanks and field guns scattered around, and lots of activity. And troops – hundreds and hundreds of troops.

'Here's your guys ahead,' Stu announced. 'This is your

stop. Next stop, Fifth Avenue, Bryant Park.' The jeep skidded to a halt. 'All ashore that's goin' ashore.'

Alistair and Stan grabbed their kit bags and stepped down. They turned to Stu and Izzy.

'Thank you for the ride, gentlemen.'

Stu laughed. 'Youse guys are welcome,' he said in a mock accent. 'Get on with ya. See ya when the war's over.' And the jeep roared away.

Alistair took a deep breath. He was going to miss that crazy pair. Izzy had certainly given him something to think about. But, right now, they had to find out where they were supposed to report. He stopped a soldier hurrying past.

'We've just arrived,' he explained. 'Where should we report?'

'Fresh meat?' The main pointed to a tent. 'Captain Carter is over there. I'm sure he'll tell you where to go.' He hurried off.

Alistair and Stan exchanged glances, shouldered their bags and walked over to the tent. There was a soldier on duty outside and he challenged them as they approached.

'Sigs Lethbridge-Stewart and Hodgeon reporting for duty,' Alistair announced.

'Hang on.' The man popped into the tent, and then emerged. 'Captain Carter will see you.'

They marched into the tent and saluted smartly. The worried-looking captain nodded back.

'At ease, men. You have your papers?' He took them and scanned them. 'Ah, you're the Signals boys. You're a bit late, aren't you?'

'The weather wasn't too co-operative, sir,' Stan explained.

'Yes, well.' Carter explored the table he was using for a desk, and then stumbled across the paper he was seeking. 'You're both assigned to the Glosters, so I'm sure their OC will fill you in.'

'Sorry, sir, but where *are* the Glosters?' Alistair asked.

'Oh, right. Yes.' Carter raised his voice. 'Corporal!'

The guard came in and saluted. 'Sir?'

'Find someone to point these men to the Glosters, will you?' He nodded to Alistair and Stan. 'Dismissed.'

They saluted and followed the guard out of the tent, while

Carter went back to examining his paperwork.

'The Glosters, eh?' the guard said. 'Well, they'll keep you busy, right enough.' He glanced around. 'Mac, escort these lads to the Glosters, will you?'

The soldier he'd picked on came trotting over. 'New, eh? Come on, follow me.'

They did so, hurrying out of the area and directly northwards.

'Expecting trouble?' Stan asked.

'There's a build-up,' Mac answered. 'Bound to be an attack soon. You boys'll be handy. Scalies are a bit thin out here.' Mac led them along a rudimentary pathway. 'River's this way; we'll find your post along here.'

The woodlands thinned out a bit as they came over a rise and they had their first look at the Imjin. It didn't look too impressive at first. There were steep cliffs on either side of it, something like seventeen hundred feet apart. Alistair had read the river itself was only about a hundred and fifty feet wide and very deep, but there were a couple of pontoon bridges across it, about half a mile apart.

'Not much to look at,' Stan commented. 'Now, the Douglas back home in Wigan – *there's* a river.'

'It may not be impressive,' Mac said. 'But we're on this side, mostly, and the Northern troops is on the other.' He pointed down towards the pontoons. 'Your lot is down there. Couple of miles upstream, there's the Northumberland Fusiliers.' He picked out the road leading to the bridges. 'That's Route Eleven, the main supply line. And over the river, see that hill? That's 194. Nobody can pronounce the local names, so we numbers them all. And there's a Belgian Battalion on it, keeping an eye on things. The rest of the circus to the rear and west of here. Yanks, mostly, but good in a scrap. And, beyond the river, are the Chinese and the Koreans.'

'Quite a spot.' Alistair studied the far bank carefully.

Mac held out his hand. 'I think you can manage without getting lost now. I'd better get back. Lots to keep me busy, you know.' And then he was gone, leaving them on their own.

'On the whole, I really wish that we were by the Douglas right now,' Stan admitted. 'The calm before the storm, eh?'

'Afraid so,' Alistair agreed. 'Come on, let's go.'

They started down the slope, following the footpath. It was a bit further than it looked, and it was almost ten minutes before they were challenged by a couple of sentries, after which they were escorted down to the encampment by the river.

There were no tents here – not even trenches or more than strands of barbed wire. There were just soldiers, waiting and watching. Many were smoking, some were brewing tea. Alistair and Stan were taken to a spot on the escarpment where they saw a lieutenant and a sergeant. Again, they had to produce their papers.

'Signals, eh? Good show.' The officer nodded. 'Sergeant Brady, get these men a couple of radios and the manuals.' He glanced at them. 'Hodgeon, you stay here with me. Lethbridge-Stewart, when you've got your radio, head over to the second bridge and report for duty.'

'Sir!' The sergeant hurried off and was back in a few minutes.

Two soldiers carrying radio packs followed him, and they handed the devices across. Alistair checked his out quickly. The battery was fully charged, and the signal seemed to be moderately strong. He slipped the codes book into a flap, shouldered the radio, and then hurried down towards the pontoon bridge.

There was plenty of activity now. Some of it was clearly of a military nature, and some simply men at ease. The troops looked tired, but alert. He wondered how long they'd been here, and then how long they (and he) would remain here. Everything seemed to be temporary; no real defences, nobody dug in. Maybe they were expecting to fall back if there was any trouble?

He reached the bridge, and saw that there were simply a couple of squads there, guarding their end. There was a lieutenant there in charge, and he reported in.

'Good man,' the officer said. 'Find yourself a place to flop.' He gave a brief smile. 'At the moment, it's all sit and wait.'

Alistair glanced around and saw a mid-sized rock to one side of the bridge that would provide a little cover in case firing commenced. There were a couple of squaddies there, smoking, but plenty of room for a third man. He moved over, and they shifted to make room for him.

'Can't get the Light Programme of that thing, chum?' one of them said. 'Bit of dance music would go over well right now.'

Alistair smiled as if this was the first time he'd heard that joke.

'I don't think they take requests,' he said, expertly ignoring the man's double-take at his accent.

'Yeah, well. We're in the Army, lad. We take anything that's offered, you should know that.'

The other man held out a battered tin mug. 'Fancy a brew? It's not good, but it's strong. Bit like my old woman.'

Alistair accepted, grateful, and discovered that the description of it had been spot on. Still, it was hot and wet – and, as the other fellow had said, you accepted what you got in the Army.

'Is there much action here?'

'Not at the moment,' the first soldier replied. 'But it's coming. You can always tell.' He nodded. 'I'm Canning; he's Brewster.'

'Lethbridge-Stewart.' He sipped some more. 'Do we have any cover?'

'Couple of twenty-five pounders back there, and some four point twos.' Mortars, Alistair realised. 'Some Centurians back up the road. Apart from that...' Canning slapped his rifle butt.

Which reminded Alistair. He'd checked out his radio but forgotten about his Enfield. He quickly checked it over to ensure it would be operational if needed. It could be fatal if he forgot that simple check again in the future.

And then it was simply that old situation in the Army – hurry up and wait. Either the enemy would attack, or they'd be ordered to advance. Until one or the other happened, there wasn't much to do.

PRISONER VI

IT WAS still very difficult for Alistair to think. The only 'rest' he'd managed to get was when he'd passed out from pain as he was being beaten. His entire body was one huge ache, except where it was simply burning from agony. His mind was slipping away, he knew, and there was nothing he could do to fight this. He knew that the official orders on coping with interrogation were to try and concentrate on friends and home and family, but his brain was so foggy that he couldn't recall any such things. It was as if his entire life to date had been nothing more than pain and captivity. He was hungry, thirsty and weak. He didn't object to eating the filthy rice any longer. The guard had stopped spitting in it, now that Alistair no longer cared, which was a very slight victory.

How long could he hold out?

Longer than you realise.

That strange voice in his head again. It had vanished for a while. Alistair assumed that now it was back, it was a sign that his sanity was continuing to slip.

Although, considering the voice kept urging him on...

You're made of much stronger stuff, Alistair. You're a Lethbridge-Stewart, which means you continue to fight. Never give up.

He tried to place the voice. Perhaps he was imagining his grandfather's voice? It was an old man's voice, certainly. But there was no Scottish lilt there. Something London, maybe...

Focus, man!

Alistair swallowed. A painful thing to do.

He didn't want to be a weakling, to fail himself and his companions. The one consolation he had was that he'd been of absolutely no use to the enemy, since he couldn't possibly recall anything that might be of use to them. If he broke now, they'd get nothing more from him than gibberish. Ha! That would teach them!

That's the spirit. That's the Alistair Lethbridge-Stewart I know.

Alistair frowned. *Who are you?*

Ah. For the first time there seemed to be hesitation in the other voice. *I'm your inner core, the strength you didn't know you had.*

Alistair wanted to laugh. The voice was as convincing a liar as Jumbo was.

And then guards came for him again.

He didn't know how long it had been since the last time, but, really, what did it matter? He was taken into the tent, where Peng sat, waiting. Alistair knew that his tormenter was waiting for him to kneel, but he'd be damned if he did that. He might break, but he would show no willing obedience to this man.

Peng grew tired of waiting, and motioned to the guards. One kicked the back of his leg, and Alistair stumbled forwards and down. The guard then pushed him to his knees.

'Why do you persist in torturing yourself?' Peng asked him. 'Why will you not simply obey?'

'Why don't you… stop talking?'

Peng shook his head in mock sorrow. 'You English – so proud, so perverse, so difficult to enlighten. You think it is your task to enlighten us, that we are savages. But this is our country, and you are the invader.'

'Not your country,' Alistair said. He managed to nod at the old Korean, who was standing silently to one side. 'His country.'

'We are here to free his people,' Peng explained.

'Doesn't look very free to me,' Alistair muttered.

'He is merely a foolish old man, who – like you – doesn't see how simple it would be for him to be free. All any of you have to do is to allow me to enlighten you.'

Alistair remembered something from a previous conversation. He was surprised that he could remember anything, but this one fact remained. 'You like to sing.'

'I have a good voice,' Peng said, with a certain pride. 'The missionary father told me so. Do you wish to sing?'

'Do you know *Rule Brittania*?' Alistair asked, and then couldn't stop the giggles. 'Rule Brit—'

One of the guards hit him across the shoulders.

'You are being even more foolish than usual. Is it that you somehow don't think that I am quite serious? I am here to save you, even if I must kill you to do it.'

'Bloody silly thing to say,' Alistair managed to utter. The guard raised his rifle to strike, but Peng made a chopping gesture.

'No, I think we need to be a trifle more graphic with Mr Clitheroe. We have to show him how serious we are.' He rose to his feet. 'Come along, Mr Clitheroe – let us walk together. Ah – you walk two steps behind me. I am your superior officer, and you must show the clearest respect for me.'

'Piss on your respect,' Alistair growled, and then broke into giggles again. He'd never imagined he could ever be so crude out loud.

The two guards grabbed his arms and dragged him outside the tent and into the bright, harsh sunlight.

Peng led the way to where the other cages hung. Alistair could see that there were other soldiers in them, all looking as battered and tired as he felt.

'Are any of these men friends of yours, Mr Clitheroe?'

'Don't have any friends. Nobody in the whole world. Don't know anyone. Don't know anything.'

'Stay strong, man!' It was that damned noisy officer again.

'Do you know him?' Peng asked.

Alistair tried to shake his head, but it refused to move. 'No,' he said, instead. 'Don't wanna know him, either. Won't shut up. Always giving me orders.'

'Well, you don't have to obey his orders anymore. You only need to obey *mine*.' Peng moved on to the next cage, and rapped on it with his swagger stick. 'How about this man?'

Alistair's vision was fading in and out, but he could make out the man's face. 'Not him,' he said. 'Not been properly introduced.'

'Such a shame.' Peng decided. 'Well, this is only a demonstration, so I'm sure he will be adequate.'

He gestured to the old Korean, who stumbled quickly

forward and unfastened the cage. The soldier inside it fell out, and was unable to get to his feet. Peng glowered down at him.

'I am your superior officer! Stand to attention!'

The prisoner was shaking all over. 'Can't,' he mumbled. 'Too sick.'

'Sick? Then you have only one use left to me.' Peng stepped up to the man and unbuttoned his holster. Pulling out his pistol, he stooped slightly and shot the soldier through the back of his head.

The man fell forward. Alistair caught a quick glimpse of the gaping hole in his forehead as he fell, and then there was simply a stench of blood and a spreading, dark pool.

'You filth!' the caged officer cried. 'Murderer!'

'You be silent or be next!' Peng snapped back. He turned to Alistair. 'Look at that man,' he ordered. 'You can see that I am very serious about my task. If you will not allow me to educate you, then you will be my next demonstration.' He held up his gun, and wagged it under Alistair's nose. 'I will save you even if I have to kill you.'

FIREFIGHT

DINNER WAS rations before sunset. Canning chewed glumly. 'Bet you didn't eat like this on the road,' he complained to Alistair.

'No,' Alistair agreed, straight-faced. 'We had pheasant last night.'

Brewster stared at him suspiciously. 'You're kidding.'

'No.' Alistair smiled. 'It helps when you travel with a butcher and part-time poacher.'

'Sod it, Canning, I'm travelling with this bugger from now on.'

There wasn't much for Alistair to do. Once in a while, a call would come through to check up on the situation. Since nothing had happened, he was able to simply give an all clear. Lieutenant Pereira nodded at each request for information.

'Must be seeing some movement,' he mused. 'Better be ready, lads.' He sent a runner to the men of the Ulster Rifles down the road, and he, too, reported back that nothing was happening.

Darkness fell. There were no lights allowed, so there was not much to see. Alistair could just about make out the dark shape of the bridge, and nothing else. Time ticked slowly on.

Canning checked his wristwatch from time to time. 'It's past my bedtime,' he complained.

'You want a bedtime story?' Brewster asked.

'There are other things I'd prefer in my bed. Preferably blonde.'

There was a sudden burst of gunfire from the other side of the river. The flashes illuminated the darkness slightly, and Alistair could make out several man-sized shapes. Some of the

Ulstermen trotted forward and returned fire.

'PVA patrol,' Pereira muttered, and then looked to Alistair. 'Get on the radio and report this to HQ.'

'Yes, sir.' Alistair sent the call signal, and he heard Stan's voice on the other end. 'Enemy incursion,' he reported. 'Small patrol, by the looks of things. Over.'

Stan acknowledged, and then replied: 'You're to hold position. Over.'

'Roger. Over.'

There was another short burst of firing from the enemy, a little closer to the bridge now. The riflemen shot back, as they rushed forward onto the pontoon. It was almost impossible to see anything, except in the light from the gunfire. It looked like the Irishmen were advancing, hoping to drive back the attackers.

'Damnation,' Pereira complained. 'They've skirted around the Belgians. They must be intending to wreck the bridges and cut the poor chaps off.'

Alistair acknowledged, got on the net and gave the contact report.

'Hold present position,' Stan responded. 'The RUR will move forward to safeguard the other end. Repeat: Hold position. Over.'

More gunfire broke out at the far end of the bridge.

'They're bringing up more troops,' Lieutenant Pereira realised. 'I hope the Irish can hold them.'

'They're good fighters, sir,' Canning pointed out.

'Yes, but it depends how many enemy troopers they have to face. It looks like the North have slipped a fair number past Hill 194.' Pereira chewed on his upper lip. 'This isn't good.'

In the distance, further gunfire broke out, coming from the direction of the hill. More of the riflemen hurried past, on their way to defend the bridge. There was no supporting fire yet from either guns or mortar; there were no real targets for them to aim at. Just lots of gunfire now, from both sides of the river.

The radio sounded again, and Stan came on. 'The enemy are attacking Hill 194,' he reported. 'In full force. No word yet on how long they can hold out. Over.'

If they can, Alistair thought. They were the only allied force on the north of the river, and their only line of retreat was over these pontoon bridges. If the PVA held the far side – or even destroyed them – the Belgians would be completely cut off. The situation was getting serious.

And then there was more gunfire down the river, closer to the spot where the Fusiliers were stationed. The enemy must have made another attack down there.

'River's pretty shallow down there,' Brewster explained. 'They must be wading across.' He shook his head. 'Bloody hell, this is getting serious.'

'Two-pronged attack,' Pereira mused. 'They're throwing a lot of men into this.'

Down on the bridge, the Ulstermen were facing heavy fire. More PVA troops were arriving every minute now. The Belgians were clearly isolated, and unable to halt the flow of the enemy past Hill 194. They were converging on the far side of the river, at the far end of the bridge.

The wounded started to retreat from the bridge. Those who could walk, ran, crouched over, trying to staunch the flow of blood. Some of the worst hit were carried by their comrades. Many were down by the bridge, dead or incapacitated. Alistair didn't really have the time to consider all of this. He was relaying messages to and from Lieutenant Pereira and keeping his head down. The bullets hadn't reached this far yet, but the enemy were clearly established on the north side of the bridge. The RUR were doing their best, but they were hopelessly outnumbered and outgunned.

The order came down from HQ for them to pull back, which they did – forced to leave a number of their men dead.

The retreat was orderly, but the fighting Irishmen were exhausted and many even of the fighting men had wounds that had been hastily bound up. The battle hadn't lasted very long, and already it looked as if the enemy were winning.

Then the order came for the Gloucestershires to start falling back. Alistair could see the enemy starting to make their way across the bridge, firing constantly now. He wasn't really worried yet, though he was disturbed by the sight of the wounded and dead. He had often wondered during training how he would feel when the training became real, and people were actually intent on killing him. He had liked to believe that he would be cool and unflappable under fire. He knew that some people panicked, and he had really hoped that wouldn't be him. He'd heard so many war stories from his grandfather and great uncle, even a few from his father, and they had always sounded to be calm and concentrated. He had hoped that this was a Lethbridge-Stewart trait that he would somehow have inherited.

And now the reality was here? He was more irritated that he had to run away from his first fight. He could just imagine people back in Blighty asking: 'What was it like, your first battle?' And he'd be forced to say: 'Well, actually, we ran away.' What an excruciating thing to have to admit.

As they retreated, the men kept up firing back at the advancing enemy. Perhaps there were some among them in *their* first action. At least if they were asked, they could say: 'We made the yellow dogs run!'

Was any of this fighting doing any good? Young men were being injured and dying. These were men who had their whole lives before them, but who were now maimed or dying in a far-off country, away from their friends and families, sacrificing their futures, and for what? Fighting for the freedom of a country most people in England would never see, people they would never know… People who might not even *want* to be fought over. Did it *really* matter what sort of government they had? Most of these people had never even known freedom, anyway. They'd been invaded by the Japanese, and now by the Communists. They'd spent their entire lives being beaten down. Maybe they just wanted to be left alone?

Alistair knew that, as a soldier, he wasn't supposed to make any kind of moral judgments. Just to obey orders. He was supposed to trust the men above him on the chain of command, believe that they knew what they were doing, and were issuing orders for the best. But how could he be *sure* of that? There had been far too many cases of generals giving stupid or even fatal orders to their men, showing a callous willingness to sacrifice hundreds of young lives for no real purpose. How was he supposed to just accept this?

If he was injured or even dying – which he might well be soon – then what would it all be for? Would it be the slightest comfort to know that somebody whose name he probably didn't even know had decided that his sacrifice was required and worth it? He doubted his mother would think so. She'd lost her husband to the last war, losing her son to this one...? No wonder his Uncle Matthew had resisted so much in the last war. For the first time in his life, Alistair truly appreciated the reasons behind his uncle dropping out of military service.

Alistair was sweating now, but – thankfully! – not from fear. It was from the strain of carrying the radio pack, some sixty pounds in weight, as well as his normal gear. Canning and Brewster stuck with him, turning back to fire at the enemy from time to time.

'Does anyone know where we're going?' Brewster asked.

'Backwards,' Canning grumbled.

Lieutenant Pereira ordered a halt, and they moved to cover the road behind them. He crossed to Alistair.

'See if you can find out what's happening,' he ordered.

Alistair donned his earphones and listened in to the network. A few minutes later, he had some answers, but they weren't good ones.

'The enemy is on the advance, sir,' he reported.

'We noticed that,' Brewster grumbled.

'Not just here – all down the line. They've attacked the Fusiliers' positions in large numbers, and we've lost Hills 152 and 257. The Fusiliers have pulled back, and the Koreans are bringing more troops across the river. We're to join A Company on Castle Hill, which is probably the Koreans' next target.'

'Right, that's over to the east. Must be that slope over there. Let's go.'

They were on the move again, Alistair feeling the strain. Running uphill with a radio pack on your back while the enemy were shooting at you was not mild exercise. Maybe those horrible cross-country runs back in training hadn't been entirely useless after all.

Up they went, through the grasses and scrub brush, bullets zinging all around.

The Hill was just ahead of them now, and Alistair could see where the men of A Company had settled in. They were able to provide covering fire so that Alistair's squad could make it safely. It was a huge relief to be able to flop into the dirt and rest for a moment.

'Bracing, innit?' one wag called out. 'The gnats are a bit aggressive this year, though. Have to go to Margate next time.'

There was a short pause, and the enemy stayed downhill. Even in the poor light, though, it was obvious that their numbers were swelling by the minute. Well, they had to have control of the two bridges by now, so they were most likely pouring troops across the Imjin.

He glanced at his wristwatch and saw that it was just after oh-four-hundred hours. Grief! They'd been under fire now for almost six hours! It certainly hadn't felt that long. He wondered what time dawn would be. Maybe then they would be able to see what their situation was.

Maybe it would be better if they didn't.

With the time for a breather at last, Alistair was starting to come down from the adrenalin high. He could see that the wounded were still accumulating. There were field medics moving around, checking to see if anyone needed attention. They dressed the simple wounds, and then had stretcher bearers move in for the seriously injured. Alistair saw one man with blood over more than half his face. He was breathing with difficulty, and there was fresh blood bubbling around his mouth.

There were others, with wounds, some of them patched up, others waiting, their faces tight with pain, for the medics to reach them. Alistair felt for them all, knowing that any of them might have been him – and still might be. Radiomen were a preferred enemy target, hoping they could cause confusion if the squaddies couldn't get through for orders. He was wearing a sixty-pound bullseye on his back.

Sunlight started to tinge the horizon. Alistair watched the sun start to rise, and light flooded the plain and river below. As it brightened, he could see that hundreds of enemy combatants were hurrying over the two bridges and up the slope to reinforce the men at the base of Castle Hill. It wouldn't be long before the opposition commanders decided that they had more than enough men to take on the few hundred British troops awaiting them.

And then what?

Pereira slid across to him, staying low to the ground.

'Report to HQ that A Company is in position and ready to defend Castle Hill. Tell them there are large numbers of the enemy to our front.'

'Sir!' Alistair did as he was told. Stan was still on the other end, and reporting that thousands of Chinese had crossed the river and striking hard all down the line.

War wasn't hell, Alistair decided – it was chaos incarnate.

There was a barked command from somewhere down the hill. With a howl of anger, rage and pride, the Chinese started up Castle Hill, firing as they came.

'Steady, lads,' Pereira said, holding his pistol at the ready. 'Wait for the word.'

And then the command, from further up the hill. 'Fire!'

PRISONER VII

ALISTAIR WAS dragged into the interrogation tent once more. He couldn't remember how many times he'd been here by now, but it didn't really matter. Things never changed. He was still weak, and exhausted and determined to hold out, even if it killed him. Partly, that was due to loyalty – couldn't let the side down, old chap! – but, at this point, it was mostly because it was the only way he had left to fight back. They wanted him broken, and the only way he'd break would be completely. To be honest, he'd probably welcome death as an escape from this.

Never surrender, Alistair. You will *get out of this.*

He appreciated the certainty in the voice. Even if he didn't share it. Still, there was some satisfaction in seeing how annoyed Peng was becoming. The fake veneer of charm and friendliness had worn and cracked now, and he was starting to develop a tic near his left eye.

That's right. You *wear* him *down. Show him what Lethbridge-Stewarts are made of!*

'Clitheroe,' Peng growled, 'why do you persist in provoking me?'

Alistair thought about the question for a moment. 'It's a hobby.'

'You British!' Peng paced up and down, tapping his left hand with his swagger stick. 'You think you're so much better than everyone else. So arrogant of you!'

'Rich... from a torturer.'

'This is not torture!' Peng yelled. 'This is re-education.'

'Never been a good student,' Alistair slurred. It was getting harder for him to think of answers now. Was he close to breaking? Maybe so, but if he was, he would not give Peng the satisfaction of knowing it.

'I killed your friend,' Peng said. 'Doesn't that tell you anything?'

'You're a sadist?'

'Fool!' Peng struck out with his stick, across Alistair's arm. Alistair couldn't prevent his cry of pain. 'You refuse to learn! You will be the next to die, as an example to the other Englishmen.' Then he managed to calm himself down. 'But I do not wish this, Clitheroe. I wish for you to understand and to accept. Why is it so hard for you to see this? I am your friend.'

'Funny sort of friend.' Why didn't this idiot just give and leave him in peace? Or shoot him; honestly Alistair was beyond caring which he did.

I care, said the voice in his head.

Good for you, old chap, Alistair thought back.

'You must be freed from the lies of your past,' Peng insisted. 'Those in power in your country have fed you lies since you were born. They have told you to behave this way, dress that way, obey your orders, think as they tell you... Lies, all lies! You must free yourself of these lies, learn how to be free, like me.'

'By dying?'

'I am like a surgeon,' Peng said. He clearly liked the thought, and nodded. 'Yes, think of me as a doctor. You have been infected, as have all of the English. It is my task to cut away the diseased portions of you, so that the healthy portions may live. Sadly, there are times when there is too little healthy flesh, when a person is so corrupted they cannot be saved. In such cases, they must be killed to prevent the spread of infection.' He lowered his voice, confidentially. 'I think that you are healthy enough to be saved, Clitheroe. Do not prove me wrong, and force me to slay you to prevent further infection. Allow me to cut away the rot, and to preserve the living.'

Alistair was unable to think straight through the fog enveloping his brain. He wished he could have thought of something intelligent or witty, but the best he could manage was, 'Piss off.'

Peng gave a cry of frustration. 'It would appear that I was wrong about you, Clitheroe. It would seem that the disease has taken too firm a hold in you. If you continue to live, you will harm your friends and prevent me from saving them. I can see that drastic measures must be taken in your case. Very drastic…' He shook his head. 'Do you still hope for rescue? Do you think that your Army will come rushing in to save you in the nick of time, like in those ridiculous *Boy's Own* stories you British love so much? Let me assure you that this won't happen. The England that you imagine loves you has abandoned you. This camp is your life now, and you can leave in only two ways. Either you surrender and allow me to show you the true state of things – or you will die. There is no other hope, no impending rescue, no *Gunga Din* rushing to your aid. It is just this small circle, Clitheroe – you and I, and this camp. This is your world now. Come to terms with it.'

He turned his back on Alistair, and made a sharp gesture with his swagger stick. The two guards grabbed Alistair's arms and hauled him out of the tent and back to the even smaller world of his cage. They fastened the door, and left him in the sun.

Alistair didn't even have the strength to despair. He couldn't bring any clarity into his mind. There was only fogginess and that eternal pain. He was in Dante's Inferno, being punished endlessly, and he couldn't even remember why. Why should he suffer so much?

And then, on the edge of his consciousness, he was aware of the old Korean man limping along the row of cages, offering a small cup of filthy water to the men inside.

Drink it, Alistair. Filthy it may be, but it will keep you alive a little longer.

And then? He waited for an answer. *Do you know, I'm starting to think you're not me at all.*

Why do you say that?

You're far too sure of things.

For a moment the voice was silent. Then, *Perhaps I'm from the future?*

The old man reached him and, seeing the uncontrollable shaking in his hands, held the cup with its pitifully small ration to his lips. Alistair drank, almost reflexively. As he withdrew the empty cup, the old man whispered a single word. Just one word, but it was enough to manage to make Alistair think again.

'*Chingu.*'

Friend…

And, it seemed to Alistair, the voice in his head smiled.

DISASTER

NOW THERE was fear, of course. Alistair would have been mad not to feel it. The enemy troops had started their rush up Castle Hill, firing – often wildly – and yelling. They didn't seem to be bothered by how good a target they made themselves. They ploughed upwards. The defenders fired back, picking off targets as best they could. The noise was deafening.

Alistair was glued to the radio, listening to and relaying reports. The problem was that information wasn't too accurate in the midst of a battle, and having to have Stan repeat things over and over because of the noise didn't help.

Their big guns had opened up, now that they had targets that were visible, and their deep-throated howling also didn't help matters. The four-point-twos poured mortar fire into the enemy ranks, but without making any noticeable difference. Explosions downslope threw rocks, dirt and mangled bodies into the air, leaving devastation in their wake.

'Fall back!' Pereira yelled. 'Fall back!'

Alistair lifted the radio onto his aching back again, and ran doubled over behind the officer. Canning and Brewster ran on either side of him to provide cover, shooting as they went. The whole of A Company appeared to be on the move, retreating from the horde of advancing enemy. Castle Hill was too open and exposed, with too little cover for them to be able to regroup. There was wire strung around the base, but they managed to clamber through it. It wasn't until they reached the bottom of the far side of the hill that the order to hunker down came through. The Company flopped down, grabbing any cover that they could. Alistair dropped with his back against a tree.

The PVA had reached the summit of the hill, and stopped, advancing no further. They found their own positions, firing down at the troops below. There was movement up there as they brought in a machine gun and crew, getting it into an abandoned bunker. There was a short burst of test fire, and then the crew were settled in. It was impossible for the British troops to break cover now without becoming sitting ducks.

They were in desperate trouble. Alistair fought to quell the fear in the pit of his stomach. There wasn't a chance for any of them as long as that machine gun nest was there. It seemed somehow more absurd than terrifying that it looked quite likely that he would die here, at the bottom of a foreign hill, shot to pieces in his very first battle. Was *this* to be the climax of his life story, being killed in Korea?

'We'll be cut to ribbons if we move,' Lieutenant Pereira muttered. 'And if we *don't* move, the enemy will simply swamp us...' He wasn't issuing orders or asking a question, so Alistair remained silent. What could he say, in fact? The officer was quite correct.

Then, from further along the line, he saw another lieutenant and a handful of men starting forward, back up the hill again. Were they crazy? The enemy was bound to spot them... And, indeed, they did, opening fire at the small squad. The other lieutenant went down. Despite the intense fire, three of the men moved determinedly up to him and managed to drag the badly wounded man down, through the wire and back to relative safety. Alistair let out a sigh of relief, as it looked like the brave man had survived. Still, it had demonstrated the impossibility of a direct assault.

Except – the lieutenant was on his feet again, and, amazingly, heading back up the hill on a limping run. This time, though, he was alone. He had a string of grenades, and lobbed one after another towards the bunker. That merely made him a better target, as he had to pause each time to throw. None of the grenades reached the bunker. The officer pulled the pin on his final grenade and threw it, hard and accurately. As he did, a stream of bullets from the machine gun nest sliced through his body, and he fell.

There was a huge explosion, and then silence from the bunker. The last grenade had fallen well inside it. The nest was destroyed, at the cost of the life of a brave man. Three of his men jumped up and headed up the hill. They managed to retrieve the body and carry it back down. Several of the troops there saluted as the dead man was carried past them.

It had been an amazing act of bravery, and had given the embattled men a fresh chance. There was a surge of men, but rifle fire from the summit sent them steadily back – save for those whose bodies littered the side of the hill. Despite everything, there was no way that the hill could be retaken, and the order was given for a slow, steady retreat.

Alistair resumed contact with Stan, passing along the news as he heard it to Pereira.

'The Americans have managed to get some reinforcements to the Belgians,' he reported. 'They've been under heavy fire, but they're managing a strategic retreat. We're to try and cover their movement.'

'Understood.'

The officer started to issue orders, moving men in position to cover the reported path that the Belgians would be taking. From being ahead of the Glosters, the troops would take up defensive lines to the south of them now.

And so it went.

Alistair couldn't keep a clear picture in his mind of what was happening. Lots of shooting, lots of movement. The large guns booming, mortars exploding – and, all the time, the Koreans advancing, slowly but inexorably. The allied forces were being pushed back, away from the river.

They had no other option but to withdraw. Lieutenant Pereira gave the order for a slow, steady pull-back, but they were facing a terrible fire from enemy lines. There was no chance to get anywhere near where the Belgians would be, and Alistair reported this to HQ.

'We're to pull back to Hill 235,' was the message he relayed to Pereira.

'Let's hope there's some cover there,' the officer muttered. 'Right, chaps, let's move.' He stood up, and then abruptly spun about and collapsed. Blood was pouring from a deep wound in his right shoulder.

'Medic needed!' Brewster called, as he and Alistair moved to check on the fallen man.

'We've got to stop the blood,' Alistair growled.

'Well that's flamin' obvious!' Brewster snapped. 'Where's the damned medic?'

Alistair called on the radio and was simply told to stand by.

'We've got to retreat,' Brewster said, urgently. 'We'll have to carry him.'

'No point, if we can't staunch that wound,' Alistair observed.

He tore at Pereira's sleeve, then used his bayonet to rip it free. Wadding it up, he crammed it into the site of the wound. Canning used the bayonet to tear a strip from his own shirt to tie the pad into place. But there was a lot of blood seeping around the edges of the cloth. They couldn't get enough pressure to halt the flow.

Bullets were still flying all around them as the enemy kept advancing. It had been a lucky – or unlucky, depending on your point of view – shot that had actually hit the lieutenant, but the enemy were certainly finding the range.

'Get the men moving,' Canning snapped to Brewster. 'If they don't get out of here, they'll be sitting ducks. We've got to move.'

Brewster nodded, taking temporary command, and urging the rest of the squad to retreat in some kind of orderly fashion. Alistair helped Canning to half-drag, half-carry Pereira, moving as swiftly as they could while keeping their heads down.

It wasn't quite a rout, as the men kept their heads for the most part. Brewster led the way towards Hill 235. The remainder of A Company were making their way there, too. And there were pitifully few of them. Alistair couldn't even see an officer, but there was limited visibility, which might have accounted for it.

They were being slaughtered, that much was clear. The PVA must have made this a major assault, pouring their troops into the area in almost reckless numbers. They'd forced the Belgians to retreat, taken both bridges, driven back the Royal Ulster Rifles, and laid down continuing fire at the Northumberlands. The allies were retreating on all fronts, falling back under the tremendous power of this attack.

Thankfully, they had laid down no minefields, and only limited amounts of barbed wire, so they didn't have to worry about getting caught in their own traps.

Where were the tanks? There were supposed to be Centurians, but there was no sign of them. Fire from the twenty-five pounder guns had fallen silent, too – probably the gunners were afraid of hitting their own men. Alistair guessed that their men had to be getting low on ammunition, and that no further supplies were likely to move into the area while there was the chance that the enemy might get their hands on the munitions.

It was looking more and more likely that his first battle would also be his last.

'Hold on,' Canning gasped out. He sounded exhausted, and he wasn't even carrying a radio pack, as Alistair was. 'Let him down a minute.' They lowered Pereira gently to the ground, and Canning pointed. 'The bleeding's stopped.'

Alistair did a quick check, and found no pulse. 'That's because he's dead,' he said, grimly. 'No point in dragging him any further.'

'We can't just leave him,' Canning protested, uncertainly.

'If we don't, we'll be caught or killed ourselves,' Alistair pointed out. 'We don't have a choice.'

He plunged on, following in Canning's wake. Broken plants and shrubs indicated that they were not the first to pass this way, which was a good sign.

The light was starting to fade again. The day was almost over. That was insane; how could it have passed so quickly? It was as if time sped up during periods of stress. He hadn't eaten all day, but he wasn't hungry. He *was* thirsty, but he'd wait until they reached some measure of safety before sipping from his canteen.

There! Up ahead! They were on the lower slopes of a hill, and he could see other soldiers clambering ahead of them now. Without the burden of Lieutenant Pereira to slow them down, they had caught up with the main body of A Company again. They climbed the hill behind the others, hoping that they'd reached 235, where they were supposed to be.

The men were falling, utterly drained, wherever they

could when they reached what they hoped was a safe height. There were pitifully few of them. By the time it was completely dark, they huddled close together, watching and waiting. Alistair got onto the radio again, to listen for further news of orders.

It was worse than he had even imagined: HQ was withdrawing to Hill 235 as well, falling back as the enemy advanced. D Company had been forced to retreat, and were making for Hill 235. B Company, so far, had not been attacked, but their position was not good. With D Company gone, their left flank was exposed, and then the Fusiliers were targeted and forced to pull back. B Company was now stranded on Hill 316. There was no way for any troops to reach them, reinforce them or to cover their retreat.

Really, it was as bad as Alistair had ever imagined. Had no one in the Allied Command seen this coming? How had so many PVA troops managed to reach this area without anyone giving warning? Just how stupid and incompetent was the military mind, anyway?

The night was dreadful. There was a little firing around Hill 235, but it wasn't very accurate or effective. However, the sound of warfare continued in the distance. It was concentrated on B Company and Hill 316.

There was movement close by, and Alistair managed to pull his rifle into position. Then, with considerable relief, he saw that it was Stan. The two of them greeted each other enthusiastically.

'What's happening?' he asked his friend.

'HQ's moved here,' Stan said. 'I've been told to get some rest. As if anyone can sleep through all this racket. B Company's taking some beating, I'm afraid, poor lads. How about you?'

'There's not a lot of A Company left,' Alistair said, regretfully. 'We took a thrashing ourselves.' He shook his head. 'This is being badly handled. That's the military mind for you.'

'Intel wasn't good,' Stan agreed. 'As for the rest – well, I'm sure they're doing their best.'

'Their best,' Alistair said, bitterly, 'is hopelessly

inadequate. This is a damned fiasco, and it's cost a lot of good lads their lives. And there will be more to pay when it gets light again.'

'Aye.' Stan shook his head, sorrowfully. 'Well, let's try and get some rest, eh?'

Alistair's mind was in such turmoil that he didn't think he'd be able to sleep. But sometime in the night, he managed to get a few hours of fear-tossed rest. When he awoke, he felt as if he hadn't slept at all.

Hill 235 turned out to be fairly packed with survivors from the previous day, including a bunch from Supplies, so there were rations and tea to be had, as well as small amounts of extra ammunition parcelled out among the men. Canning was still with Alistair, but Brewster had vanished during the night, most likely on the far side of the hill. Morale was not good.

There had been roars from the twenty-five pounders in the night, but Alistair had been so tired that he'd barely registered it. He got onto the radio, and started to gather some information.

B Company had passed through hell in the night. The Chinese hadn't let up at all, and thousands of them had surrounded Hill 316, determined to take it at any cost. There had been six assaults on the Hill, B Company outnumbered almost twenty to one. The last assault had been so intense that the commander in charge had called on the guns to blast the hill to break it up, risking being killed by their own twenty-five pounders. A seventh assault had started with the coming of light, and the tiny remnant of B Company was retreating in as orderly a fashion as it could to join them on Hill 235.

Which meant that at any time, the enemy would be free to turn all of their attention onto 235…

The survivors of B Company began to trickle in – less than two dozen in all. The rest had been annihilated. Worse, the PVA had driven their assault deep south, cutting the party on 235 completely off from the Royal Northumberland Fusiliers. The 29th Brigade was now all concentrated on Hill 235, and in very grave danger of being completely cut off. If the Chinese managed to swing around behind the hill, it would be impossible to retreat.

Alistair and Stan were kept busy, as HQ sent out requests for status reports and attempted to determine what their options were. The Americans had managed to bring some of their own forces across, and they ordered the Philippine 10th Battalion forward to help out the Brigade. This would involve armoured support, thankfully – the Americans sending a batch of M24 tanks along the road to Hill 235, backed, finally, by some of the long-missing Centurians.

The men cheered when they saw the tanks approaching from the south. This would be of great help, providing them with extra firepower, and, with luck, enabling them a dignified and reasonably safe relief.

They received no such luck, of course. The Chinese had already brought in some of their own guns, and opened fire on the approaching column. Booming shots exploded all around the head of the column, and then the lead M24 erupted in flames. The crew scrambled out – those who survived, but the vehicle was immovable, and blocking the advance of the other tanks. As the enemy guns pounded away, the relief column was stopped dead – easy targets for the PVA artillery.

The Americans had little choice. The tanks started in motion again – but in reverse. The road rocked with fire as they disappeared from view again. Morale plunged again as everyone realised that there was going to be no relief, at least for the time being. Meanwhile, the enemy pressed forwards.

Alistair closed his eyes briefly, anger and frustration bubbling inside.

Two days of battle, and the situation kept deteriorating.

PRISONER VIII

SNAP OUT *of it, man!*

It was somehow night again, as Alistair's awareness came back to him. He kept fading in and out, his mind too tired to keep concentrating. He hadn't slept; it was as if his mind had simply shut down for a while.

And all the while the voice continued to urge him on.

He'd eaten his meagre daily ration of rice, and the guards had taken their turns around the cages, banging on those of anyone who looked as if they might have fallen asleep. One of them passed by him, sneered as he saw Alistair was blearily looking back at him, and moved on. Alistair was a little surprised the man hadn't punched him anyway, just out of pure malice. Ah, well, maybe the soldier was in a relatively good mood tonight.

So, you're from the future, are you? Alistair asked the voice.

I said perhaps.

I see. So, perhaps, I have a voice in my head from the future?

Alistair would have laughed had the idea not been so absurd. But why not? He was very clearly becoming delirious. Why not invent a voice from the future?

In that case, future voice, why are you here?

Well, that's the thing. I'm not entirely sure. I wanted to see how you fared in the Korean War, what changed you from a man with such a belligerent attitude to service, to become the officer I knew.

Knew? Past tense. So, according to this voice he'd created in his own head, in the future he was dead. No doubt died in this camp. But then the voice had said officer.

No chance of that, Alistair thought. *If I escape, once I've done my two years, I'm going back to teaching.*

For a moment the other voice was silent, as if considering. *Don't be so sure of that, Alistair. You have quite a future ahead of you.*

If you say so.

Nothing more happened for a little while, and then there was movement again. The guards had left the area, probably playing games of chance in their tents.

The shape moved closer, and he saw it was the old man. He held a finger to his lips in the universal sign for silence. Then he slipped closer, smiled a mostly toothless smile, and softly unfastened the cage. Then he made a beckoning motion. Alistair's mind was so confused that it was a moment before it all sank in.

He was free! He pushed open the door to his cage and got out (mostly a barely controlled flop-and-fall). The old man fastened the cage door again, grinning happily to himself. The old man – right! He'd said he was a friend earlier, and now he was proving it. Alistair realised that he wasn't the only one the old man had let out of the cages. There were two more people on the ground, stretching their muscles and trying – like him – to rise. Alistair finally made it to his feet and shuffled over to the closest of the other freed captives.

It was the officer who'd called either orders or encouragement to him earlier. Alistair didn't know the man, but they were comrades in adversity. He stooped and helped the officer to stumble to his feet. Together, they went to the third man and helped him to silently rise. This man looked somehow familiar, but Alistair couldn't place the face. Oh, well, it would come to him.

Clear your head, man, the voice said. *You do know him. Very well.*

They glanced around, and the old man was making urgent gestures for them to follow him. The officer managed to shake his head, and he moved over to the next occupied cage, and fumbled with the rope that held it closed. The old man made a soft grunt and shook his head, gesturing for the officer to stop and follow him.

'We're not leaving anyone behind to be tortured by those fiends,' the officer growled. 'It's all or nothing.' He helped the prisoner within to climb down.

The old man was panicking now, gesturing around, and then pointing for them to come with him.

The other man seemed to understand. 'He's worried about the guards coming,' he hissed. 'We *have* to get out of here. We can't chance being caught – who knows what they'll do to us?'

This made sense to Alistair. 'We can send help to rescue them later,' he said.

The officer seemed unconvinced, but he hesitated and then finally nodded. He helped the fourth man to his feet, and supported him as they followed the old man carefully to the edge of the encampment. The Korean pointed out a pathway, and urged them to take it.

The officer frowned. 'Come with us.'

The old man clearly didn't understand English. The officer thought for a moment, then he moved his hand in a circle to include the four captives. Then he pointed at the old man, and gestured that he should come into the circle. The Korean shook his head firmly, and pointed at the ground. He clearly intended to stay there.

'But why not, man?'

The prisoner Alistair vaguely recognised said, 'I think he wants to stay and help the others to escape later.'

'But the Chinese will kill him; they're bound to know it was he who let us out.'

'They don't think he'd dare. Peng will probably assume that one of the guards didn't lock the cages properly.'

'Maybe,' the officer agreed, dubiously.

'We can't force him to go with us,' Alistair pointed out.

'That's true.' The officer nodded. 'All right, let's go, then.'

He led the way down the path. The fourth man seemed to be strong enough to walk on his own now.

Alistair fell in beside the man he vaguely recognised. 'Do I know you?' he asked softly.

'Of course you do,' the other replied. 'I'm Stan. Surely, you remember? Stan?'

Stan. Your best friend, Alistair. Remember?

Oh, right, yes, his best friend, Stan! How could he have not known that immediately? He grabbed Stan's arm and gripped it enthusiastically.

'Stan! Stan! Of course!'

'Ssshh!'

'Oh, right.'

Stupid!

They moved through the night forest, leaving the light of the camp behind them. The moon hung low and gibbous in the sky, shedding a morbid sort of glow over things. It was good to have light to walk by, though. They came to a fork in the path, and the officer paused, confused.

'Which way?'

'Left,' Stan suggested.

'Why?'

Stan shrugged. 'It's as good as any.'

'True.' The officer started down that path, and they followed.

They saw no signs of animal life, heard nothing but the chatter of insects. It was like walking through some alien landscape, but Alistair was excited. They were *free*, and that was all that mattered.

And then, a few paces further, they were suddenly blinded as lights shone in their eyes. Unable to see, Alistair stumbled, and felt the pain of several blows that knocked him down. From the ground, he looked up and saw Peng, smiling down at him.

'Surely, Mr Clitheroe, you did not think that escape would be as simple as that?'

THE LAST NIGHT

'**NOT A** pretty picture, eh?' Stan commented.

That was an understatement. The pitifully few survivors of the Glosters were isolated on Hill 235, digging in as best they could. Hardly any of them had any trenching tools, so the hard earth had to be broken by bayonet or by hand. In some places the earth had been cratered by artillery fire, which helped. But the hill provided far too little cover. On the other hand, there weren't more than a few hundred soldiers left.

Down below, in the valleys between the numerous hills, the PVA was assembling, ready for an all-out assault. It wasn't easy to make out, but there had to be thousands of them. How badly were the Glosters outnumbered? It was impossible to tell, but it may have been as much as a hundred to one.

This is very likely it, Alistair concluded.

With the best will in the world and the best of British luck, they were facing an overwhelming foe. And here he was, only twenty-two. And young Stan with him was barely eighteen.

Abruptly, he remembered his English Lit classes back at Liskeard Grammar, and studying the so-called War Poets – more like anti-war poets, of course – like Wilfred Owen and… well, the names didn't matter. How did that one go? Oh, yes…

> *If I should die, think only this of me:*
> *That there's some corner of a foreign field*
> *That is for ever England.*

A bit sentimental, but looking more and more likely. And then there was that bitter *Dulce et decorum est…* That was more like his mood, to be honest – regret and anger. Here he was, facing death, and for what purpose? Had any of the dead soldiers here perished for a single good reason? Was any of this helping the Koreans at all? Tearing up their country, dropping bombs, waging war – what was it *really* all about?

Whatever way you looked at it, this whole affair was a bloody mess – in every meaning of the term. And what about those soldiers down there? No doubt they were all young men, too, who were convinced that they, too, were defending their homeland. And they were dying by the hundreds as well. He just couldn't see the point of it all, that any of the fighting would solve anything.

He snorted; there didn't seem to be very much chance that he'd ever know. Unless there was some truth to all the stories about Heaven and a reward in the life to come. Alistair wasn't sure he either believed or disbelieved any of that religious stuff. Well, he'd soon discover the truth of it, one way or the other… But, supposing it *was* true? Were there people or angels sitting up there in Heaven looking down at them even now? And, if so, what were they thinking? *Bloody idiots*, most likely. It was certainly what *he* was thinking. He might have been safe and useful, teaching mathematics to snotty-nosed schoolkids, instead of dying pointlessly here in a land he didn't know and couldn't really care about. What a turn-up for the books, eh?

The radio crackled with new messages, and he returned to the here and now, listening to fresh information and orders for the few officers the 29th still had left. Needless to say, the news was far from good.

He reported to the captain that there had been another attempt to push the tanks through to relieve them, but that it hadn't been able to make it. They would try again. The captain nodded, and hurried off to report to Lieutenant Colonel Carne, the senior officer on the Hill.

Alistair settled back down again, watching as the Chinese below kept up their movement. It was impossible to tell if there were more troops coming, or if they were simply repositioning the ones that they had.

A short while later, Alistair received the report that a second attempt by the tanks to break through had failed. Their situation was getting worse by the minute. There would not be another attempt to push the tanks through – and, in fact, they were retreating back, since the PVA was still moving forward.

There was a sudden burst of gunfire, and the Chinese started up the Hill. Alistair lodged his radio firmly, and grabbed his rifle. If he was going to die, then he'd at least go down fighting. His stomach was churning, and the palms of his hands were sweating. He tried to dry them on his uniform sleeve, but that, too, was soaked with sweat. Fear, anger, and sheer annoyance at the stupidity of it all mixed together in his mind, but he tried to concentrate on picking out targets, and awaited the command to open fire. He knew there wasn't much ammunition, and he couldn't afford to waste shots.

'Steady, chaps,' the captain called. 'Wait for the order...'

They *were* waiting for the order – couldn't he see that?

The enemy came on, through the shrubs and tall grass, like lions hunting their prey.

'Fire!'

Rifles cracked all around him. Alistair shot, but he couldn't tell if he'd hit anyone. Some of the enemy went down, but many of them returned fire.

The radio demanded his attention, and he squirmed around in the small depression he'd dug to answer it.

'They're going to airlift in supplies, sir!' he reported to the captain.

'Jolly good show; we can certainly use them.'

As the men fought, firing at the advancing enemy, Alistair kept glancing at the sky. It seemed like hours (and it might have been), but he heard the drone of engines, and then saw the outlines of the planes. He felt elation rising. Fresh supplies! The first good news of the day.

The Chinese started up with their big guns, and he saw bursts in the air all around the Hill. They were trying to stop the planes from getting to Hill 235...

The planes circled, and then – *no!* – they pulled back and disappeared into the distance. The attempted resupply had failed. Alistair's hopes sank. No relief by road, no supplies by air. Could the situation get any worse?

Somehow, though, the enemy were forced back, and there was a brief respite. Alistair took a short drink from his almost empty canteen, and realised that there was another problem now. With no fresh supplies, they had no reserve water. What they did have would barely last the day. Rations had to be getting low, and he didn't even want to think how badly they were off for ammunition.

Another message – one that he had been more than half-expecting and dreading. He reported to the captain, who now had his left arm in a makeshift sling. There were very few medical supplies left, it seemed, as well.

'Sir, orders from HQ for Colonel Carne. He is to use his discretion to decide whether to surrender the Hill or not. There… there won't be another attempt to resupply us.'

'Right.' The captain disappeared, taking the message along.

'What do you think's gonna happen?' Stan asked, clearly as worried as Alistair.

'What *can* happen? We've been abandoned, and we can hardly hold out forever. I shouldn't imagine that the colonel has much choice, really.'

The captain was back. Seeing their expressions, he said: 'Orders are to hold our positions for now.' He refused to say any more. Alistair wondered what the captain thought of that order, but he couldn't read the officer's expression.

They ate a few scraps of their meagre supplies and waited. The enemy attacked, and were somehow beaten back again. Ammunition was getting dangerously low, and then, suddenly it seemed, night was falling, and both sides settled down to await the dawn and better conditions.

'What do you think they're doing down there?' Stan asked.

'The Chinese?' Alistair shrugged. '*They* can bring in more supplies, so they're probably getting into position to strike in the morning.'

'What are our chances?'

'Who can say? If Carne doesn't order a retreat, then I imagine we're doomed. To be perfectly honest, I'm surprised we've lasted this long.'

Stan licked his lips, no doubt as thirsty as Alistair felt. 'If… if I don't make it and you do, Al, will you do me a favour?'

'Don't talk like that.'

Stan shook his head. 'I've *got* to talk like this. It's a real possibility, ain't it? But – if you do make it, will you go to Wigan and tell me Gladys that I were thinking of her at the end? Because

I am. I just wish—' He broke off and shook his head. 'Will you do that for me?'

Alistair swallowed. 'Of course I will,' he promised. Somehow, he managed a smile. 'I may even take Mary Ann on a date.'

That made Stan chuckle. 'It'd be nice to have you in the family,' he said. 'If… if it's the other way round, is there anyone you want me to speak to?'

Alistair considered this. He couldn't think of anybody who would really miss him.

'There's just my mother,' he said. 'And she'll get one of those telegrams… *We regret to inform you…*' He laughed, grimly. 'Maybe you could tell your Mary Ann what a great opportunity she missed out on, never meeting me.'

'Aye, I'll do that.'

The night was long and tense. Alistair managed a little sleep, but woke, sweating, from a dream that the attack had begun again. He held up his hands, palm down, and watched to see if they were shaking. Would it turn out that he was a coward, after all? So far he had met his fear and managed to keep it on a leash. It was there, constantly, in the background. Hell, he'd have to have nerves of steel not to be afraid right now. But the question was – who was in charge? Him or the fear? Right now, *he* was – but how long would that last?

And what would happen in the morning? No food, no water, no medical supplies, very few bullets… And they had a lot of wounded men, most of whom wouldn't be able to fight, and many of whom wouldn't have the strength to move if they even were ordered to evacuate. What a terrible, terrible state they were in.

And suppose the colonel did decide to call for a retreat – what then? The enemy were all around them – where could they go? HQ wasn't supporting them – hell, the tanks had pulled back. All they had now were the twenty-five pounders down the road and a few mortars left working.

What a damned mess they were in! Alistair knew that the Glosters were brave men, and would do whatever they were told. He couldn't help but admire their ferocious courage. They'd taken a pounding already that most men would never know in their lives. But how much longer could even they endure this?

One thing was perfectly clear, though: the rising sun might

well be the last any of them would ever see…

What a waste. What a stinking, horrible waste.

When the dawn came, the blood-red sun rose slowly over the horizon, looking far too much like an omen even to the unsuperstitious Alistair. He looked down the Hill as the morning mists dissipated in the sunlight.

There were thousands of Chinese soldiers down there; there couldn't be more than a few hundred English troops up here on the Hill. There was an uncanny silence, not even the chorus of the dawn from the local birds. It was as if all of Nature was waiting to see what would happen.

The radio came to life, and he started taking messages for the captain.

'The Americans have implemented Plan Golden A,' he reported.

'Golden A?' The captain's face paled. 'Bloody hell – they're pulling back.' He scurried off to inform the colonel.

'That doesn't sound good,' Stan muttered, in a worried tone. 'If the Yanks are giving up…'

'It's known as a *strategic withdrawal*,' Alistair replied. 'But you're right – it *isn't* good.' He gestured. 'Listen to our twenty-five pounders.'

'I can't hear anything.'

'Precisely. They're probably following Golden A, too.'

They were even more isolated now, but he didn't need to point out the obvious.

There was no help for them now. None at all.

It was just them alone, virtually out of all supplies, against a large section of the PVA. There was absolutely no light on the horizon for them now. They had exactly two options: stay where they were and get cut to pieces, or retreat – and, most likely, get cut to pieces anyway. They had been abandoned, left to die. That was the Army for you.

Alistair sighed. So, this was it, then. Twenty-two, never to be twenty-three. So much potential in his life – and it would be over very shortly, all of the fine promises unfulfilled. He had not made a mark on the world, and now he never would. The British Army had called him up, trained him up – and now strung him up. Damn them all to hell.

He should have been afraid. He should have been angry. But

all he could manage to feel right now was horribly weary.

The captain moved back to join them. 'The order is being given to retreat,' he informed them. 'Every man is to make his way back to our lines by any means possible.'

Stan snorted, and pointed down the Hill, where the Chinese were waiting. 'Are there any means possible?'

'God knows,' the officer admitted, frankly. 'You've both done splendid jobs, though. There's one more task for you to do before you go. You've got to destroy your code books; can't let the enemy get their hands on those.' He fished in his pocket and pulled out a silver Ronson lighter, handing it to Alistair. 'Keep it; I'm trying to quit smoking anyway.' He smiled mirthlessly, and moved on to pass along the orders.

One last duty – quite possibly the literal truth. Alistair fished out his code book, and Stan found his own. The lighter caught on the first attempt, and they set the books alight. They had to wait to ensure that both were completely consumed, so that there would be no possible information for the enemy.

'We'd better destroy the radios, too, mate,' Stan said. 'Just in case.'

'Right.' Alistair watched as the last few pages burned to ashes. 'Just in case.'

There was howling from below, and then the Chinese surged up the Hill. This time, though, there was no returning fire. The Glosters all around were dropping everything and trying to make it down the Hill. Alistair and Stan used their Enfields to shoot out the radios, so that nothing useful to the enemy was left behind.

The enemy surged up the Hill, firing from time to time, or clubbing if the Glosters didn't fire back. The British, faced with no choices now, held up their hands to surrender.

Alistair had heard plenty of horror stories about how the Chinese treated their foes – especially those that they thought knew something useful. He was determined that he wouldn't be taken alive. His had only three bullets left in his rifle, but maybe he could make them count. Two for the enemy, one for himself.

What a way to go.

And then the enemy were all around, screaming, yelling and shooting or striking. Alistair raised his rifle. At this range, he could hardly miss.

And the Enfield clicked uselessly. The bloody thing had

jammed!

He struck out with the butt. Snarling faces surrounded him, and something struck him. There was a sharp pain in his shoulder, and then a second blow which—

When Alistair struggled back to consciousness, he could see nothing at first. He was a mass of pain from his left shoulder to the back of his head. Had he somehow been blinded? Or killed, and this was what the afterlife was actually like? He tried to move, to straighten up or fall down – he didn't really care which way he went – but he couldn't.

What had happened to him?

Gradually, though the pain didn't recede, he started to be able to make things out. He wasn't in total darkness after all, and he wasn't blind. It was night, that was why it was dark. He must have been unconscious for a whole day. He'd been struck down by the Chinese, and clearly was now their captive. He realised that he was in some sort of a cage, but one that seemed to be rather unsteady. Was it on the back of a transport, maybe? And it seemed to be so cramped – maybe it had been intended for a native, somebody a lot smaller than him?

He felt the bars, made of sturdy wood, clearly cut from whatever trees were available, because the bars were only vaguely straight. As his vision cleared at last, he could make things out.

His cage was suspended from a framework, and it was swaying gently, a short distance above the ground.

He was a prisoner.

A PRISONER

PENG CALMLY lit a cigarette and smiled – or, rather, smirked – at them. The two guards stood on either side of him, their rifles held ready, bayonets pointing at the four men.

'So, gentlemen, you now see that there is absolutely no hope for you. Even when we allow you your freedom, you come directly to us.'

'Yes,' the officer said, slowly. 'And how is that, I wonder?' He glanced at the rest of them.

'It is very simple,' Peng said. 'One of your own has betrayed you.' His smirk grew wider, as he revelled in the situation. 'And you will never again know whom you can trust – except for me. You can only trust me.'

'You told them!' Stan screamed. 'You promised me you wouldn't, but you *told* them!'

Alistair was stunned. All the time they'd spent together… Even the voice in his head was silenced by the revelation.

'Stan? What did you do?'

'I'm sorry,' Stan said, openly weeping. 'I couldn't take no more. I didn't mean to do it. I just couldn't take no more.' He glared at Peng in hatred. 'You promised me you'd never tell them!'

'And I didn't, you idiot,' Peng said in contempt. 'You told them yourself.'

Alistair was still having trouble processing this news: Stan had betrayed them? The whole 'escape' was no more than a plan of Peng's, an attempt to break them by showing them that there *was* no escape… So that old Korean man had only been pretending to be their friend. And he'd rushed them out of the camp because he was only supposed to free the three of them, and he'd panicked when the officer had started rescuing others. And Stan was with them to ensure that the 'escapees' took the right path – straight to Peng.

A trick. It was all nothing but a trick. And now they would go back to their cages and more torture.

Alistair, now is not the time, the voice in his head said. *There will be—*

The hell with that!

'You traitor!' he screamed, as loudly as he could, and took a very uncertain swing at Stan.

Stan back-peddled, and Alistair overbalanced – exactly as he had hoped. The two guards laughed as he stumbled, apparently too weak and ineffectual to even hit the man he had targeted. Except, he hadn't really wanted to hit Stan; as he flailed wildly, he got closer to one of the guards. He dived for his rifle, trying to wrest it from the man's hand.

Everything moved quickly after that. The guard yelled and jerked back on his rifle, but he hadn't been expecting this attack, and he fumbled and dropped it. The bayonet hadn't been attached properly, and it fell free. He backhanded Alistair, who stumbled and fell, right over the bayonet. He grabbed it, and managed to stagger to his feet.

The second guard had raised his rifle to shoot, but the officer jumped at the man while the guard was targeting Alistair.

Oh, I've just realised who he is, the voice said.

Alistair ignored it.

The officer and the guard staggered about drunkenly. The first guard snatched at his rifle again, but Stan, screaming incoherently, attacked him.

Peng was momentarily taken aback. He'd gone from the smirking certainty that his plan had succeeded to seeing it crumbling apart. He fumbled with his holster, to free his pistol. Alistair clambered to his feet, and raised the bayonet. He gripped Peng around the neck, and then brought the bayonet down in a vicious slice, burying it deep inside the Chinese torturer's collarbone. Blood spurted, as the point penetrated to whatever shrivelled remnant there was of his heart. The light went dull in Peng's eyes, and he was suddenly a dead weight showering blood everywhere. Alistair let go, and the body collapsed, dragging the embodied bayonet with it.

Alistair knelt, almost fell, beside him and jerked the pistol free of the holster. He looked around as there was the crash of rifle fire. The guard Stan had been struggling with had managed to pull the trigger. Stan let go, and staggered back, and then collapsed to the ground, bleeding. As the guard swung to bring the rifle to bear on Alistair, he raised the pistol and fired twice. Both bullets struck home, and the guard collapsed.

The officer had managed to beat down the guard he had been fighting, and the last of the prisoners had leaped on him from behind and was throttling him.

Able to ignore that threat, Alistair turned to Stan, who lay broken on the ground.

There was blood all over his friend's chest, and it was bubbling. The shot must have punctured a lung...

Stan blinked. 'I'm sorry, Al,' he said, his voice cracking and filled with pain. 'I didn't mean to do it, but I just wasn't strong enough. I couldn't take any more. I'm sorry.'

Alistair knew that, according to the Army code, he was supposed to feel nothing but contempt for anyone who helped the enemy. But this was his friend, and Alistair knew only too well what hell the poor lad had been through. He couldn't feel any anger, or contempt, only sorrow.

'It's all right, Stan,' he assured his friend. 'You did what you could.'

Stan coughed and tried to smile. 'You'll not tell Gladys?' he begged.

'I'll tell her, Stan,' Alistair said. 'I'll tell her you were the bravest man I ever knew. I promise you that. I'll tell her.'

'Thank... thank you.' Stan shifted slightly. 'Ee, it ain't half black over Bill's mother's...'

'I know,' Alistair said, helplessly.

And Stan was gone. Alistair felt tears on his cheeks.

Men weren't supposed to cry, he knew, but *dammit*! In a situation like this, what else could he be expected to do?

There was a gentle hand on his shoulder. Alistair wiped his eyes on the back of his hand and looked up. It was the officer, now holding a rifle.

'We'd better go now. They'll have heard the shots back at

the camp. With a bit of luck, they'll think it's just Peng shooting us, but they're bound to get worried when he doesn't come back.' It was just words, meaningless to Alistair. The officer shook him. 'Come on, Clitheroe.'

That made Alistair start to giggle. He couldn't help it.

'What's the matter with you, man?' the officer asked. 'Pull yourself together!'

'Not Clitheroe.'

'What?'

'Name's not Clitheroe,' Alistair explained, as best he could. 'I just told *him* that.' He gestured at the fallen Peng. 'Told him I was Jimmy Clitheroe.'

'Bloody hell.' Then the officer laughed, too. 'Well, you seem to have grown up a bit then, lad. Now, leave him. We have to go.'

'He's my friend,' Alistair protested. 'Can't leave him.'

'We have no choice, whatever your name is. We have to get out of here. Now – *come on*! That's an order, man!'

Alistair shook his head, but this was in an attempt to clear it, not to argue. He got to his feet and looked down at Stan, somehow peaceful in death. He saluted his friend, and then fell in behind the officer and the other escapee.

Together they hurried off as quickly as they could into the trees. He had no idea where they were going – no idea where they even were, come to think of it. But they were out of the cages, and that was all that mattered. He was free again, and had a gun in his hand. The other two men had the rifles they had taken from the guards. They quickly lost sight of the four bodies.

The vague moon helped them to see roughly where they were going, but all three of them were exhausted to begin with. Alistair knew that he wouldn't be able to travel very far, and he doubted that the other two men were any better off than he was.

'Have to rest soon,' he said.

'We can't rest yet,' the officer snapped. 'Too close to the camp. We have to get as far away as we can.'

'Are we going in the right direction?' the third man asked. Even under the dirt and grime, his blue eyes shone through.

'Any direction away from the camp is the right direction,' the officer said. 'We'll try and get our bearings when the sun comes up.'

They stumbled on in the night, all of them on the verge of collapse. Finally, the third man staggered and fell.

'Can't go on,' he announced. 'Better leave me.'

'Nobody gets left behind,' the officer said, firmly. 'Mr Not-Clitheroe, can you take one arm?'

Alistair considered the thought. 'No,' he finally decided. 'Can barely move. We have to rest, sir.'

The officer looked glum. 'Yes, you're probably right at that.' He looked around. 'Well, we'd better get off the path, at least. With luck, we can hide until first light.' He gestured off to the right, and they moved carefully about a hundred yards before the other man fell again.

'No more,' he begged.

'This will have to do, then,' the officer decided. 'You two rest, and I'll keep watch.'

Alistair didn't have the slightest will to argue. He simply crawled under a bush and closed his eyes. He was out in seconds, but it was a troubled sleep. He kept seeing images of Stan's face, bloody and dying, mixed in with that of Peng's, looking startled as Alistair stabbed him through the heart. All of his dreams were infected with death and blood.

It doesn't get any easier, the voice said.

When he finally awoke, it was late afternoon. He was completely disoriented for a moment, surprised he was horizontal and not vertical. He briefly wondered where his cage had gone, the horrible stench of urine… He could almost even think clearly.

Come on, Alistair, no time for that. Focus.

The voice was still there. Maybe his mind wasn't so clear as he'd thought.

It all came back to him in a rush, and he sat up quickly – too quickly. He had a face full of shrubbery. He batted it away and rolled painfully from under the bush. His legs and back ached, his head hurt, and he was both hungry and thirsty. But he was *alive* – and free, still. The Chinese hadn't found him again in the night.

Not just him, though – there had been two others. And Stan… Stan was dead, and abandoned somewhere back in the forest. There was nothing he could do for Stan now, but what about his companions? He looked around, and saw that both of them were still asleep. That officer must have tried to stay awake, but he had been in just as bad a shape as Alistair. All three of them had simply passed out.

They had been incredibly lucky not to have been found. The Chinese must have realised they had escaped by now and been searching for them. The brush where they were was pretty thick, though, so it was always possible that a search party had passed them by; if one had even been in the area.

Unless this was another of Peng's sly tricks? Maybe he *had* found them in the night. Alistair realised he was still clutching his pistol. Peng would hardly have left them armed, would he? Ah, but what if he'd unloaded the pistol and left it, so that Alistair would *think* he was armed when he really wasn't? He'd better check… He cracked the gun and saw that there were still three bullets in it.

And then he remembered – Peng was dead. He had killed the torturer. His first confirmed kill, and it couldn't have been to a more deserving victim. He could recall the blade slipping down behind the collar bone and into Peng's malicious little heart. He would never be able to hurt anyone again. Like poor old Stan… Alistair sniffed again.

Does it ever get easier?

No, the voice answered. *You remember every kill, every man who dies under your command.*

Command? Alistair hadn't been in command. If anything, it was the complete opposite. Desperation.

You'll learn, Alistair. Best to keep a distance from the rest of the men.

Good advice. But Alistair wasn't sure it was advice he could follow.

He looked over at the two sleeping men. Should he wake his new companions? It was quite likely that there was a search underway for them, and it might be best if they were on the move again before it reached them… But both men had suffered a great deal, and they might need all the rest they could get. They'd be more likely to be able to get away if they had the extra sleep. What to do? Why should he be faced with the decision? He wasn't an officer – just a lowly signalman.

For now.

Alistair almost laughed at the voice. *No,* he thought. *Not for now. Not ever. This is not the life for me.*

They had weapons and rounds between them. But they had neither water nor food. Just thinking that made Alistair realise just how hungry and thirsty – especially thirsty! – he was. Maybe he should scout around and see if there was a stream or pool anywhere. He wasn't even fussy about it being clean water, after what he'd had to drink in that cage. This seemed like a reasonable idea, so he moved off quietly through the shrubbery. Then he considered that he might have trouble finding his way back again, and reconsidered. He was agonising over what he should do when the officer twitched and gave a low moan.

Uh-oh... If there were Chinese out looking for them, they might hear the sounds.

He moved back, quickly and as silently as he could, and then shook the man. It looked like he was having a nightmare. The officer woke, and sat bolt upright. His mouth opened before his eyes, and Alistair clamped his hand over it swiftly, to prevent a cry. The man's eyes opened, and for a second he looked terrified, going rigid. Alistair held a finger to his lips, and the man relaxed and then nodded. Cautiously, Alistair removed his hand.

'Thank you, lad,' the man said, softly. 'Bad dreams...' He shivered, and then glanced up. 'Good Lord, how long have I slept?'

'No idea,' Alistair replied. 'I only woke a short while ago myself, sir. I've not seen or heard any enemy, but I can't be sure they're not nearby.'

'No, indeed.' The man rubbed his stubble – very nearly a beard, actually, just a little bit longer than Alistair's own. 'Well, perhaps we're better off moving by night, then.' He glanced around. 'Weren't there three of us?'

'He's over there.' Alistair indicated their companion. 'I didn't know whether to wake you or let you have more rest.'

'God, I'd love to sleep for a week. But we're going to have to get moving.'

'Where to, sir?'

The officer chuckled softly. 'Now that's a damned good question, actually. You don't happen to know where we are, do you?'

'No idea,' Alistair admitted. 'They knocked me out when I was captured, and when I came to, I was in that bloody cage. How about you, sir?'

'Something similar. I was close to the front line when they grabbed me and two other chaps. Marched us north-west, that's all I know, but then we were in the woods, and eventually reached that camp. Three or four days at least from the front – but in which direction does it lie?'

'South-east seems reasonable, sir.'

'Yes – *if* the enemy lines aren't also in that direction.'

There was movement from the other man, and he sat up. 'God, you two are making enough noise to wake the bloody dead. And I should know, because I'm pretty sure I *was* dead. And I'll be dead again if the Chinese hear us.'

'Yes,' the officer said. 'Well, now that we're all awake, it would probably be best if we started moving. Come on, lads.' He clambered to his feet, and started to lead the way.

Alistair wondered if he had any idea where he was going. After all, which way had they come from? But they had to go *somewhere*, so he fell in behind. The third man brought up the rear. He was limping slightly.

'You okay?' Alistair asked.

'Ankle's a bit rough,' he admitted. 'One of the guards cracked it with his rifle. I'll be okay, though. I'll keep up.'

Alistair nodded, uncertainly. Well, that was just abso-bloody-wonderful – *another* problem.

They walked for a while, and then the officer stopped.

'Game trail,' he said, softly, pointing to a faint pathway crossing the path they were on. 'They usually lead to water, so we'll follow it.' He bent and examined some tracks. 'Deer of some sort, heading this way. Maybe we'll be really lucky and find supper, too.'

The thought of water and food was overwhelming. It would be wonderful to slake his dust-dry mouth and put something more substantial than a small bowl of filthy rice into his shrunken stomach. It was all Alistair could imagine as they followed this fresh trail.

It ended at a trickling stream, oozing slowly over rocks. The three of them threw themselves down and scooped water into their mouths. It felt absolutely heavenly, and Alistair simply savoured it for several moments.

'That's better,' the officer said, sitting quietly for a moment. 'We've got nothing to carry water in, so we'd best follow the stream for now. Meanwhile, though, we should introduce ourselves.'

Brilliant, the voice said, clearly excited.

Alistair didn't share the excitement. *Oh yes, you think you know who he is, don't you? Who is he then?*

It occurred to Alistair that if the voice in his head got the name right… Well, he didn't quite know what it would mean. He had never met the officer before they'd been captured, but if the voice knew the man's name…

But before the voice could say, if it was even going to, the officer beat it to it.

'Second Lieutenant Spencer Pemberton, Parachute Regiment. And you two?' He grinned. 'I know you're not Jimmy Clitheroe,' he said to Alistair.

'No, sir. Sig Alistair Lethbridge-Stewart.'

'Sapper Brian Hooper.'

'The one who didn't make it,' Alistair said, thinking of his dead friend. 'He was Stan Hodgeon, also Signals. He was my friend.'

'Sorry, Stewart,' Pemberton said. He furrowed his brow. 'I wish there was some way we could go back and free the rest of our lads. But we'd just be captured again. They're bound to have reinforced the guards by now, and replaced that rat, Peng.' He reached over and placed a hand on Alistair's shoulder. 'Well done for offing him.'

Alistair didn't want to admit he'd had nightmares about that. 'Thank you, sir.'

'Well, best move on,' Pemberton said. He climbed to his feet, and the others followed as they moved alongside the tiny stream. 'If this widens up, we may even find some fish. In any event, it's bound to lead us to the sea, sooner or later. Once we're there, we may be able to steal a boat. Then it's just a matter of heading south.'

'Sounds like a piece of cake, sir,' Hooper said, laughing slightly.

'We're soldiers of the King, lads, we can do it.' Pemberton seemed determined.

Alistair admired his optimism, but couldn't help wondering how much depth there was to it. He was probably just trying to put a cheerful face on it. Right now, their chances were not very good. They were behind enemy lines – no telling just how far – with no allies, little ammunition, no food and their only water ran beside them.

On the other hand, given a choice between this and those cages...

They carried on through the forest. They could hear birds, and saw some flying overhead, but no signs of animal life. Well, given the noise they had to be making, that was hardly surprising, was it? Besides, most animals came to drink in the evening, or at night.

They had to stop and rest frequently; Hooper wasn't complaining, but it was clear that his ankle was playing him up. Pemberton was keeping an eye on it, and calling halt whenever he started looking unsteady on his feet.

Night was starting to close in about them when their little stream fed into a smallish river. This was about six or eight feet across, and a couple of feet deep. It ran much clearer, and was quite cool. Pemberton called another halt.

'Soak your ankle for a few minutes,' he ordered Hooper.

Gingerly, the engineer removed his boot, and what remained of his sock, and Pemberton looked at the ankle.

'I'm no medic, but it looks like a sprain. Soaking will help it. Go on.'

Hooper winced at the cold shock as he lowered his foot into the swift waters, and then sighed.

'How did they capture you both?' he asked, as they rested.

'I was with the Gloucestershires,' Alistair explained. 'We were stuck on Hill 235 when the enemy overran us.'

Hooper looked surprised. 'Me too,' he said. He chuckled. 'We must have just missed each other in the fighting.'

'And you, sir? Parachute problems?'

'Oddly enough, no.' Pemberton mused. 'I was aiding with a supply run to the Yanks. Lorry got caught in the shelling and it overturned. Knocked me out, and when I came to, the KPA had overrun it. Took me off with a bunch of other prisoners. I don't know where they ended up, but when the enemy realised I was an officer, they separated me and took me to that bloody camp.' He frowned. 'I recall seeing some more prisoners brought in – must have been you and others from 235. It must have been two or three days after me; I can't really remember properly. Hard to keep track of time there.' He looked at them. 'I don't suppose either of you has any idea how long we were there?'

Alistair shook his head. 'Could have been a week, might have been a month,' he admitted. 'Time was kind of hazy.'

'I don't think it was a month,' Hooper added. 'But definitely more than a week. I tried counting how often we were given rice, and I do remember thinking seven at one point.' He snorted. 'Of course, I could have been simply delirious. And I should stop thinking about food, even that swill.'

They waited a short while longer, and then Pemberton decided it was time to move on again. Hooper had to struggle to get his boot back on. He couldn't lace it up; the ankle was swollen too much, and it hurt too much to try. That wasn't good. Alistair didn't know how much longer the poor chap would be able to stay on his feet. But Hooper simply gritted his teeth, and pressed on. Alistair quietly fell to the rear so that he could keep an eye on his companion. Pemberton said nothing, but led the way downstream.

The moon was low again, a sliver thinner than the previous night. It cast a soft glow over the forest which – under other circumstances – might have seemed almost romantic or magical. Right now, it simply seemed oppressive. Hooper started to limp badly, but attempted to conceal the pain he was in. Pemberton spotted it, though, and called a halt again.

'We can't go on like this,' he decided. 'That dodgy ankle of yours will only get worse, and you'll not be able to walk at all.'

Hooper lowered himself to the ground, relief on his face

as he took his weight off the ankle. 'Maybe you'd best just leave me, then, sir,' he suggested.

'Don't be silly, man. We're not going to abandon anyone. You just need to rest up, that's all.'

'Go on without me,' Hooper urged. 'I'll only wreck your escape. I'm not much use to you, and I'm a definitely liability.' He grinned. 'Me mum always said I was a real liability, and it turns out she knew what she was talking about.'

'We're not leaving you, and that's final,' Pemberton said sharply.

Alistair agreed with this decision. Too many had been lost already. They had escaped together, and they should stick together.

POSSIBILITIES

They attempted to give Hooper's ankle support with some makeshift bandages, then moved on after a short rest. But Alistair saw that Hooper was trying to hide the pain he was feeling. Something clearly had to be done to get the poor chap off that ankle, but what? The trouble with that idea was that neither he nor Lieutenant Pemberton were very strong at that moment, so a stretcher was out of the question. They'd been fed starvation rations for – well, however long their captivity had been. Enough to keep them alive (barely), but not enough for them to build up any strength.

A travois, then, like those used by the tribes of America? Pulling one would be easier on them than carrying him, but it would leave an unmistakable trail behind them that even a blind badger could follow. That was out. So that left…

He looked at the stream – a raft? That had some potential, and it meant that the river would do most of the work. The downside to the idea, though, was that villages tended to be built alongside streams like this, and they might just float right back into the enemy's hands. He decided that he'd discuss ideas with Pemberton at their next rest stop.

That wasn't very long. They left Hooper bathing his foot in the stream, and moved far enough away so that he couldn't hear their conversation. Alistair outlined his thoughts, and Pemberton agreed.

'Yes, Grimnod, I was thinking much along the same lines.'

Alistair raised an eyebrow. 'Sir? Grimnod?'

Pemberton smiled slightly. 'You have a tendency to nod grimly a lot when you're thinking.'

Alistair almost grimly nodded in response, but forced

himself to resist the habit.

Well, I suppose I wanted a nickname, he decided.

Don't worry, it won't take, the voice told him.

Alistair chose to ignore the voice. He was out of the prison camp now. Time to get his mind back together.

'The raft is probably the best idea,' Pemberton was saying. 'We can scavenge around for wood when it gets light, and see if we can find creepers or something to tie logs together. We'll simply have to keep a very sharp lookout, that's all.'

Alistair glanced back at Hooper. 'I was just thinking about my school history, sir. Scott of the Antarctic. You don't think Hooper might do an Oates on us, do you?'

'Walk off for the sake of the party?' Pemberton shrugged. 'It's a possibility, I suppose, so we'd better not turn our backs on him. What we really need, Grimnod, is food.'

'There's probably fruit and mushrooms around,' Alistair said. 'But I don't know if any of the local stuff is poisonous or not.'

'That's the trouble, isn't it?' Pemberton glanced at the stream. 'The water looks likely for fish, so with a bit of luck and work, we might catch one or two. Can't risk a fire to cook it, though, but the Japanese positively relish eating their fish raw, and it doesn't seem to do them much harm.' He thought for a minute. 'Tell you what, Stewart, it'll be dawn in an hour or so. When it's light enough, you have a recce around for some wood for a raft. I'll stay with Hooper, and we'll try and catch some fish. Then we'll reverse roles. That way, neither of us will get too tired.'

'Right-o, sir.'

It sounded like a reasonable plan.

'I'm surprised you weren't put up for Wosby,' Pemberton said, abruptly. 'Fellow like you, languishing in the ranks. Criminal waste.'

Alistair snorted. 'My grandfather and great uncle would've liked nothing more, sir.'

'Grandfather was in the Forces, was he?' Pemberton mused for a moment. 'Oh, of course. Lethbridge-Stewart... I should have clicked. There was a Lethbridge-Stewart at Waterloo, as I recall.'

'Yes, sir.'

'Good to have a solid Army family behind you.' Pemberton raised his eyebrows at Alistair. 'You don't agree, though?'

'I want to be a teacher,' Alistair said, firmly. 'Mathematics. I don't aim to be a career soldier. I'm happy to stay a signalman for my National Service. Sir.'

'Good luck with that,' Pemberton said. 'I'm aiming to get you both Mentioned in Despatches when we get back.'

'I'd rather you didn't, sir.'

'Sorry, Grimnod, one of the jobs of an officer is to seek out and encourage potential in the men under his command. Whether they like it or not.'

Told you, the voice said. *Officer material, Alistair. I know Old Spence had something to do with it, but you never told me how.*

Alistair frowned. He refused to acknowledge the voice. He didn't care what a voice in his head said – maybe it was his ego? – he wasn't going to become an officer. Maybe the Brass wouldn't indulge Pemberton. He'd been through a lot of strain, after all, and there'd be plenty of other officers vying for a mention – for themselves or their protégés. With any luck, they might not trust his judgement.

Pemberton decided that they couldn't push Hooper any harder that night, and ordered a rest until first light. 'I'm probably the freshest here, so I'll stand watch. You two get whatever rest you can.'

Alistair settled down, his back against a tree, and fell asleep quickly.

Pemberton shook him gently awake. It was light now, and the dawn chorus was screeching, singing, howling and just generally carrying on in the background. Hooper was still sleeping.

'I'll leave him for now,' Pemberton said quietly. 'You have a shufti around, and keep your eyes peeled for any usable wood.'

'Sir.'

Alistair took a drink from the stream, and then moved off into the woods, heading further downstream. After only about a couple of hundred feet, he ran into potential trouble. There was a farm right ahead of them. They had almost walked into it in the night. The ground had been cleared, and what looked like a couple of dozen acres was now under cultivation. Rice paddies, fed by water from the river, and patches of vegetables. There were three rather crudely constructed buildings a few hundred feet from the river's edge. Alistair stood at the edge of the trees, taking all of this in.

This could be a disaster. There was absolutely no chance of building a raft now. If they sailed past the farm, they were bound to be spotted and reported to the local authorities. He, Pemberton and Hooper would have to head away from the river into the woods and go around the farm. The real problem, though, was that it was highly unlikely that there was only the one farm. They might be entering into what passed locally for a built-up area. How far would they have to detour to go around? He wasn't sure they would even have the strength and endurance to make it.

In the field of rice close by, a figure stood up, holding a hoe. It was an elderly woman, up to her knees in water. She'd obviously been weeding, and now she was staring directly at Alistair.

The obvious thing to do was to shoot her. But if he did, the shot would attract more people, and he had only three bullets. Aside from that consideration, though, he knew he would never be able to bring himself to shoot an old woman, even if she was technically the enemy.

If he turned and fled, there would be a hue and cry, and his companions would be discovered as well. Perhaps he could convince the woman that he was alone? It was obvious from his manner of dress that he was both a foreigner, a foe, and a fugitive, so there would be absolutely no chance of convincing her otherwise – assuming he could somehow make himself understood.

He was filled with terror. He would be taken back to that prison, and tortured again. It would be extremely unlikely he'd be able to withstand conversion this time. It had been a close call before...

The woman called something out, and the door to the closest building opened. A much younger man emerged, and then stopped as he saw Alistair. He looked puzzled, but then called out, '*Chingu!*'

Alistair had heard *that* before from native lips. There was no reason to believe that it was true this time, either. But if he pretended to believe it, then maybe Pemberton and Hooper would stand a chance of escaping. So instead of fleeing, he moved slowly forwards, towards the house.

The young man nodded enthusiastically, and beckoned to him to keep coming. '*Chingu*,' he repeated.

Alistair kept moving slowly down the pathway to the house. A small child – possibly a girl – looked out of the door, and then vanished back inside again.

The door to a second house opened, and another man exited cautiously. He was dressed, like the other man, in long pants, a tunic and straw hat, and wore sandals on his feet, and he slouched. When he saw Alistair, he exclaimed: 'Blimey!' and straightened up.

Alistair stood staring, mouth open in shock, for a moment believing he had finally lost the last of his senses.

'Frank?' he stammered.

And it was.

Frank Campbell.

Campbell's face split into a wide grin. 'Al! Dear God, am I glad to see you!' He rushed forward, and they met halfway, calf-deep in a Korean paddy field and neither cared in the slightest.

Alistair gave a bewildered laugh, still hardly able to believe it as Campbell gripped his arm and shook his hand vigorously.

Having got over the surprise, Campbell now took in the state of his clothes and his injuries, and frowned. 'Where the hell did you end up?'

'With the Glosters.' Alistair could hardly speak he was so happy. War, he supposed, made the world a small place. 'Got overrun and captured. Escaped. You?'

'Northumberland Fusiliers.'

'So, we were that close to each other all the time.' Alistair paused, gathering his wits and mentally telling himself to pull himself together. 'Okay, so I know how I got here, but what about you? What the devil are you doing here? And in that get-up.'

'Hiding out,' Campbell explained. 'I've been here a couple of weeks. Yung-Sun and his family have been hiding me.'

The Korean man came closer and bowed slightly. He tapped his chest. 'Yung-Sun,' he said. He pointed at the old woman – presumably his mother. 'Shin.'

'Nice to meet you,' Alistair said, rather inanely. He tapped his own chest. 'Al.' They'd never be able to pronounce his full name. He turned to Campbell. 'Can you speak the lingo, Oxtail?'

'Just a few words,' Campbell replied. 'Never been that good with languages, and theirs can be tongue-twisters at times. But we get along alright. Don't worry, Al, they can be trusted. They've been very good to me.'

Alistair was thankful for that. If they had been hiding Campbell all this time, he was fairly certain they could be trusted.

'There's two more with me. An officer and a sapper.'

Campbell raised an eyebrow. 'Crikey. We could start a branch of the Empire here, if we had a few women.' He turned to Yung-Sun, then pointed to himself. He then discretely held up two more fingers.

Somehow, the Korean seemed to understand. He nodded. '*Chingu, chingu.*'

'Absolutely right, old son.' Campbell turned to Alistair. 'Chin – his mother or mother-in-law, I'm not sure which – knows some old wives' remedies that are pretty potent. She'll probably be able to see to any scrapes you may have got on the way out. Let's go and collect them before anybody else comes along.'

Thankful beyond words for their sudden turn of good luck, Alistair led Campbell back the way he had come.

Hooper was awake now, bathing his ankle again. It looked dreadfully swollen. Pemberton jumped to his feet when he saw Alistair wasn't returning alone, then his eyes narrowed as he saw the face beneath the peasant hat was European. Alistair introduced Frank.

'Sir, this is Sig Frank Campbell; a friend of mine since we were both called up. He's been hiding from the Chinese with the farmer here.'

'Attached to the Royal Northumberland Fusiliers, sir,' Campbell said, snapping off a salute to his *satgat*.

'Northumberland Fusiliers?' Pemberton seemed to be suspicious. 'And how did you escape capture, then?'

'Long story, sir.' Campbell quickly glanced at Hooper's

ankle. 'I can give you a hand to get back to the farm. You can rest up there, and Shin can have a look at it.'

'Shin?' Pemberton asked.

Campbell grinned. 'Local healing woman,' he explained. 'Half doctor, half witch doctor, I think. Don't quite know which half we need the most. If you'll follow me, sir?' He helped Hooper to his feet, and hauled his arm across his shoulders. 'Just lean on me, mate. I'll make sure you stay upright.'

'Sorry, sir,' Alistair said softly to Pemberton, as Campbell moved off with Hooper. 'A couple of the locals spotted me, and called Frank in. But like I said, we were together in basic training. We can trust him.'

Pemberton looked sceptical. 'It's just a bit of a coincidence, finding him here. Don't forget Stan.'

Alistair knew Pemberton had a point, yet he couldn't bring himself to doubt Campbell's loyalty. And he hoped, in time, neither would Pemberton.

They made it to the small hut Campbell had originally appeared from. It turned out to be a sort of storeroom for foodstuffs. The sight of this almost made Alistair faint from hunger. Campbell laid Hooper down gently on the floor, and the Shin entered. She brushed them all aside and bent to examine Hooper's ankle. She poked and prodded and looked at it from various angles, in spite of the sapper's yelps of pain. Then she stood up and glared at them. She started growling and snapping foreign words at them and stormed out of the house.

'Well,' Pemberton said, 'I take it that she doesn't exactly approve of our treatment of Hooper's ankle.' He was clearly fighting to keep his face straight.

'Sorry, sir,' Campbell said. 'She gets a bit, well, direct at times. She didn't half give me a fair mouthful when she patched me up.'

'Patched you up?'

'Shot in the wing,' Campbell explained. He tapped his left shoulder. 'I was in quite a state when she got to me. I've mostly got the use of it back now. I don't know what she does, but it worked.' He grinned down at Hooper. 'Don't worry, I'm sure she'll get you fixed up in next to no time.'

Sure enough, the old woman came bustling back in with a bag slung over her shoulder, and a large leaf in her hand. She let loose a string of what were presumably instructions, which none of them could understand, and then set to work. She pulled various oddments of powders and pastes from the bag, and spread them on the leaf. Then she took a handful of some plant-stuff, crammed it into her mouth, chewed it up well, and then spat it onto the mixture of the leaf. Then she started to wrap it around Hooper's ankle.

'Hey!' he protested, struggling. 'I don't want her spit on my injuries!'

Shin issued some complaints and obscenities, and pushed his hands away as she finished wrapping the leaf in place using a strip of cloth.

'I think you'd better let her finish, Hooper,' Pemberton said tactfully. 'Whatever you think of that stuff, it can hardly make your ankle any worse, can it?'

'I suppose not, sir,' he replied, hardly mollified.

The old woman straightened up and pointed emphatically at the dressing. She let loose a string of instructions not to touch it until she came back, gave them all the withering look of an elderly spinster teacher to unruly pupils and then stormed out.

'Well,' Pemberton finally said. 'I suppose that's telling us.'

The door opened again, and this time it was Yung-Sun. He carried a steaming pot and four bowls, which he set down carefully. '*Sigpum.*'

'Food,' Campbell translated. 'Looks like you could all do with this.'

Alistair had to work hard to avoid drooling. Hooper and Pemberton looked almost as starved. It was simple enough – rice, with chopped up vegetables – but pleasantly seasoned, clean and filling. Yung-Sun left them to it. This was a farm, after all, and he undoubtedly had chores to do.

If he could be trusted. He might just have popped out to alert the authorities… It felt horrible to have to suspect everyone of evil intentions all of the time.

With a supreme effort, Alistair put down his bowl and crept to the door and glanced out. Shin and Yung-Sun were

114

both in the fields, weeding away. Alistair felt guilty for suspecting them, but knew he would have been foolish not to. Was this the sort of person war turned you into? He didn't like the way it made him feel.

'Don't worry,' Campbell assured them. 'They're really good people. They hate the Communists, but they can't get away from their family farm. Sheltering us is their way of fighting back.'

'I thought they were all Reds up here,' Alistair said.

'Yes, well, supposedly. Practically, though, quite a few of them don't like the regime. They'd move south if they could, but the Communists won't let them. They execute the odd family sometimes as a warning to stop the others fleeing. Despite that, there are still some good folks left in these parts, as you can see.'

'We'll hole up here for a few days, if we can,' Pemberton decided. 'Hooper badly needs rest, and could do with recovering our strength a bit.' He glanced at Alistair. 'You especially, Grimnod.'

Campbell raised his eyebrows at Alistair. 'Grimnod?'

Alistair pulled a face. 'Shut up, Oxtail.'

Pemberton threw a questioning glance at Campbell, and the other signalman sighed. 'As in Campbell's Soup, sir,' he said, a little wearily.

Pemberton gave a snort of amusement. 'Well, after we've recouped then we can try to make it back to our own lines.' He glanced sharply at Campbell. 'That's all of us, Campbell.'

Campbell grinned widely, obviously missing Pemberton's implication. 'Absolutely, sir! I was only waiting for my wound to heal enough, then I was going to try my luck.' He went suddenly serious. 'Yung-Sun and his family have hidden me out for a couple of weeks now. There are enemy patrols every few days, so I take to the woods until they're gone. Yung-Sun is fairly safe, but if the Communists even suspect we're here, they'd execute the entire family.'

'I can imagine,' Pemberton said soberly. 'And I have absolutely no intention of getting them into any trouble. The first sign of a patrol, and we'll follow your example and take to the hills.'

'Thank you, sir.' Campbell's relief was palpable; he was

clearly – and understandably – fond of this family. 'In the meantime, I'll keep watch if you want to grab some rest. You all look like you've been through hell.'

'Perhaps,' Pemberton said. He levelled his gaze at Campbell. 'But first, Oxtail, why don't you tell us a bedtime story?'

Campbell exchanged a baffled glance with Alistair, who shrugged. 'Uh, if you like, sir. What would you like to hear?'

'Tell us how you got here.'

'Oh, that!' Campbell breathed a sigh of relief. 'Well, it's kind of funny, in an odd way, how I ended up here...'

OXTAIL

CAMPBELL RUBBED his chin as they settled down. 'As I said, I was attached to the Royal Northumberland Fusiliers. Well, we were advancing, heading up to Haaju, and the KPA counter-attacked. They had some support from a handful of Tupolev bombers, who attacked our lines, doing a fair bit of damage. One of the bombs didn't go off, but it had fallen pretty much smack on my company, and with a fairly hefty wallop at that!

'I don't rightly recall what hit me or what happened to the rest of my company, but I woke up in the bottom of the crater, half-covered in soil and lying next to a dirty great bomb. Then I looked up and saw I was surrounded by a bunch of Korean soldiers, not my mates. Needless to say, I was more worried about them than about the bomb, since they were pointing their guns at me. I figured that it was all up for me.

'Then one of their officers yelled at them, pointing at the bomb. I realised that he understood that if they shot at me, they risked the bomb going off, killing the lot of them. He ordered two of his boys into the crater, bayonets fixed, to come and fetch me out. They weren't keen though, dead scared, I can tell you!

'Don't know how the idea came to me, but I'm glad it did. If they thought the bomb was about to go off, they'd probably scarper and leave me for dead. So I started to shout, scrambled to my feet and starting running, waving my arms about, pointing at the bomb and yelling at them to keep away. Well, they almost pissed themselves, diving out of the way. I jumped the closest one and grabbed his rifle, managed to crack the butt on his head and get a shot off at another, then legged it for cover. Fortunately, everyone else seemed too pre-occupied to chase me. Then I saw that the enemy advance had passed over the area my company had been in, and they were about half a mile behind me now, between me and our lines. Obviously, I couldn't go that way, and the only thing for me to do was to try and circle around make it back a different way.

'So, I set off north-east, praying I wouldn't run into any trouble. Clearly the Lord was busy elsewhere that day, and I promptly ran into a handful of PVAs. They were more surprised than I was, but I still had my borrowed rifle, so I opened fire. They went down, but the last man managed to get a few shots in, and one caught me right in the shoulder.

'I was desperately afraid that there would be more of them nearby, so I bolted for it. Trouble was, I'd become turned around in the dark, and I was in pretty bad pain from being winged, so I wasn't thinking too straight. I had absolutely no idea which direction I was going, and even less idea which direction I *should* be going. I just had the idea that I'd be a lot better off if I didn't hang about.

'Well, I stumbled over this Korean lorry parked by the side of the road. The driver had stopped for a smoke and a piss. I had sort of half an idea that this truck was going to the front, and maybe I could hitch a ride in the right direction, so I hopped in the back. I must have passed out, though, because I didn't wake for a few hours – didn't even know that the lorry had started up again. Well, I soon found out that the driver hadn't been heading for the front, but back to resupply, and instead of going south, we'd gone north. I was in a worse position than ever, and I couldn't stay in the lorry any longer – I could just imagine what would happen if I passed out again and woke up in some enemy supply dump. I waited for the driver to slow down a bit, and took a chance and jumped for it.'

Here Campbell paused, breathed a deep sigh and shook his head.

'Well, with my run of luck being so bad, I should have known that was a stupid idea, because I landed on my injured shoulder. The pain made me pass out again, but I'd rolled off the road, and it was dark, so I suppose my luck hadn't been entirely bad. All I had with me was the rifle, and I was completely lost. And thirsty. And hungry. So, when I saw this farm, I thought I'd sneak in and steal some grub. And the first person I ran into was old Shin.' Campbell shook his head, ruefully. 'She wasn't at all scared of me, gave me a mouthful. Then she saw the blood on my shoulder, and the fact I was about falling-down sick. She called Yung-Sun in, and they brought me here and looked after me.

'So, I laid low here, and they fed me, and Shin treated my wound. It was just healed enough that I was thinking it was about time for me to try and make my way back to our lines, when you three showed up. I'm wondering if I dare start believing my luck has changed at last.'

With the tale finished, Alistair stole a bleary glance over at Pemberton, but it seemed at some point the lieutenant had been overcome by fatigue and fallen asleep. Alistair couldn't blame him. He too felt exhausted, and he had a full stomach for the first time in weeks.

'Oxtail,' he said.

'What, Al?'

'Shut up and let us sleep.'

When Alistair awoke, it was in darkness. He rolled over and opened his eyes, and saw Campbell grinning at him.

'Just in time for reveille,' the man said. 'You've slept away almost an entire day. It'll be dawn soon.' Then his face turned serious. 'It must have been hell in that camp. They abused you terribly.'

'It was, Oxtail,' Alistair admitted. 'I'd rather not talk about it.'

'I can imagine. And Stan...?'

'Keep the noise down, you two,' Hooper complained from the gloom. 'Some of us are trying to sleep.'

'In your case, it's more like *hibernate*,' Campbell shot back.

Privately Alistair was glad for the interruption. Although they hadn't been close, Frank had still been friendly with Stan.

There was movement, and then Pemberton spoke. 'Well, lads, it looks like we're all awake now. That's a good thing, because we've got some planning to do. We may be safe here for the moment, but that won't last – and we're putting Yung-Sun and his family at risk by staying here. Sig Campbell, do you know where *here* is, exactly?'

'Not entirely, sir,' Campbell admitted. 'The family and I have a bit of a problem with the lingo. All I really know for certain is that we're in the north-west, too close to the Chinese border for comfort. Yung-Sun did manage to tell me that the small river out there flows vaguely south and exists in the Yellow Sea. I had been thinking of trying to steal a small boat and head down-river. But my boating skills are limited to the row boats at Yarmouth.'

'I've done a bit of sailing, sir,' Alistair admitted. 'I'm not exactly skilled, but I could help out.'

Hooper snorted. 'I'm with Oxtail on this, sir,' he said. 'Not done any water stuff since I was in the bucket and sandcastle brigade as a kid.'

'Well, I've experience, though not with the kind of boats they have here,' Pemberton mused. 'Still, I think it's probably the best bet we have. Trekking out through the jungle behind enemy lines is asking to be found again. If we can make the coast, we should be able to follow it down to Seoul.'

'Assuming we still control Seoul, sir,' Alistair observed.

'It's still a possibility, Grimnod,' Pemberton said archly. He rubbed his hands together. 'Well, that's the start of a plan, at any rate. It's going to need some thought, but at least we can all put our minds to it. Now, what's next?'

'If you don't think I'm being personal, sir,' Campbell said, 'I think it's time you all had a change of clothing. Not meaning any disrespect, but you stink.'

'Yes, I imagine we do,' Pemberton agreed. 'Not too many opportunities to spruce up in that prison camp.'

'Yung-Sun hooked out some clothing. It's a bit ancient, but serviceable. It'll make you all blend in to a casual glance – if it's *very* casual.'

Alistair frowned. 'If we're captured wearing that, we'll be in danger of being shot as spies,' he pointed out.

'Better than getting dragged back to that camp, if you ask me,' Hooper said.

'It's a risk,' Pemberton agreed. 'But it's one I'll gladly take. We can't wear these rags any longer.'

The sun was rising now, and Alistair could see the other three clearly at last. Campbell jerked his thumb over his shoulder. 'River's out there,' he said. 'Have a good wash and change clothing.'

'Bring the old rags back here,' Pemberton said. 'We'd better burn them; can't risk them being found here, for the family's sake.'

Alistair picked up one of the piles of clothing. 'I'll go first,' he said, and slipped out of the door into the soft morning light.

He headed towards the river, and then saw a small figure hurrying up from it. It was a petite, dark-haired young woman, obviously Yung-Sun's wife. She ducked her head to avoid catching his gaze, and hurried up to the farmhouse. He had only caught a glimpse of her, but she seemed like a pretty young thing, with a distinct resemblance to old Shin. Obviously, she was Shin's daughter, or even granddaughter.

She was also the first young woman he'd seen in months.

She had probably been doing her own morning ablutions. Well, at least she wasn't likely to surprise him at his own. Mercifully. At the river, he stripped off his filthy shreds. He was immune to the smell, but Campbell was probably right about them stinking. Cold water. Good. He washed himself off as well he could. Then he left the water to drip off his body before dressing in the soft, old clothes he'd been given. If you squinted and he stood with his back to the sun, a casual observer might just take him for a local. Might. He picked up the remnants of his uniform and his battered boots and headed back to the storehouse.

Shin was there now, examining Hooper's ankle. The swelling appeared to have gone down a lot, which was an improvement. Shin clucked to herself, and then fastened the poultice back in place.

'I'm much better,' Hooper protested. 'I don't need that stuff any longer.'

The old woman might not understand English, but she clearly understood his attitude. She let loose another of her long harangues, and held one finger under his nose, repeatedly striking the air with it.

'It looks like you're keeping it on for one more day,' Pemberton said, grinning. 'I think it might be wiser to do as she instructs.'

'I wouldn't argue with her,' Campbell added, laughing.

Hooper subsided, grumbling wordlessly. He and Pemberton then took their turn to wash and change. None of them could shave, unless they felt like passing around Yung-Sun's razor among them. Alistair didn't like his beard, but there was nothing he could currently do about it.

Yung-Sun came by with a breakfast bowl of rice, this time with some cooked white fish in it. He nodded in approval at their change of clothing, and then went off to his work. The food was delicious – well, after the prison camp, *any* food was delicious – but Alistair felt troubled.

'I feel like we're just sponging off this poor family,' he finally said. 'Can't we help them in the fields, or something, to repay them for their kindness?'

'It's not very practical, Grimnod,' Pemberton said. 'We're a good foot taller than the locals, and, despite the clothing, we don't blend in at all well. If one of his neighbours happened to pass by...'

'What I've been doing, sir,' Campbell piped up, 'is to repair the houses. I'm not the world's best carpenter, but I've been able to fix a few things for him. And we can do that inside, so nobody sees us.'

'That's actually not a bad idea, Campbell,' Pemberton acknowledged. 'Let's see what we can find to keep us busy, then. Not you, Hooper – you rest that ankle of yours. That's an order. From me, as well as from Shin.'

'Sir,' Hooper agreed miserably.

As Campbell had suggested, there were plenty of small repair jobs to do for the family. No doubt Yung-Sun would have done them in the winter, when there were no tasks in the fields for him, but this would give him a bit of free time. He probably didn't get much of that. Alistair was fairly good with his hands, so he was able to fix windows and so on.

He would see members of the family from time to time. Shin seemed to be out in the fields constantly, weeding. If old age had affected her limbs or back, she showed no evidence of it. She probably treated herself, as well as the family – and visiting soldiers on the run. Yung-Sun worked the fields also, mostly in the vegetable patches. His shy wife – Frank said that her name was Hee Won – stayed inside for the most part, avoiding interaction with the strangers. The child was a small boy, Jintao, and he was – like most children – into everything. The family didn't rein him in much, but one of them constantly kept an eye on him to ensure that he didn't get into *too* much trouble.

Alistair was starting to feel much stronger now. A few days' rest, some decent food and hope had made all of the difference. His mind was a lot clearer, and he could concentrate once again. A lot of his thinking, though, was about Stan Hodgeon.

He knew that there would be people who would call him a coward and a traitor for having been broken, but Alistair knew far better. He'd been quite close to doing the same thing. And if it hadn't been for the voice in his head, he may well have done so.

The voice, he noticed, had more or less gone quiet since he'd met up with Campbell again. Perhaps, surrounded by allies, Alistair didn't need it to keep him focused.

Alistair took the chance to talk with Pemberton and Hooper about the matter of Stan's actions.

'I know we have to make a report about Stan's death,' he said. 'But… What are you planning to say, sir?'

'The absolute truth,' Pemberton answered. 'Hodgeon was one of the bravest men I've ever met, and he willingly gave his life to ensure that we could escape.'

'Dead on,' Hooper agreed. 'Don't worry about it, Grimnod.'

Alistair smiled at the nickname. Still, it was a huge weight off Alistair's mind. He wasn't too surprised by this. The other two men had suffered the same hell he and Stan had, and they knew how close they had come to the breaking point themselves.

Poor old Stan – all he had ever really wanted out of life was quite simple: to follow the family tradition of being a butcher, and to marry Gladys. And now he wouldn't even get to be buried in England…

What about the rest of them? Did they actually have a chance of escape, and making it back to British lines? True, they were no longer prisoners, but that could change at any time. One bit of bad luck, one small slip-up, or even betrayal – any of those would mean that they would take them again.

They had a plan, true, but it was horribly shaky – steal a boat, make for the sea and then run south, hoping that the Allies still held Seoul. The enemy had been strongly on the offensive when he had been captured – who knew how far they'd got? They had broken the Gloucestershires, and pushed back the Yanks. Had they broken through completely? Had they reached Seoul? Had the city fallen? Pemberton didn't seem to think so, but if it had, then even if the four of them somehow managed to make it that far – against all of the odds – then it wouldn't be their salvation, but their damnation.

TERROR

THE FOLLOWING morning, Alistair passed Hee Won again as he went to wash up before breakfast. Once again, she cast her eyes down as he passed, though perhaps a shade less than she had the day before. She hurried back to the house, while he went down to the river. Maybe it was a cultural thing? Were married women here not supposed to look at other men? Well, either way, it didn't really matter; they wouldn't be seeing very much more of one another anyway.

Shin came by to check on Hooper, and this time she almost smiled, and allowed him to remove the poultice. She nodded as he stood up and moved around.

'Hey! It feels great,' he enthused. 'Well, maybe not great, exactly, but certainly a hell of a lot better.' He took Shin's hand and kissed the back of it gently. She giggled like a schoolgirl, clearly amused and pleased by this and hurried out.

'Then there's no reason we can't move now,' Pemberton decided. 'We've put this family at risk for long enough.' He sighed. 'If only we could talk to them; they'd probably know enough to be able to direct us. Well, we'll just have to do the best we can. Campbell, do you have any idea at all what lies ahead of us?'

'Very little, I'm afraid, sir,' Campbell replied. 'I chanced a bit of a recce, and there's more farms along the riverbank, but that's all I can tell you. Yung-Sun made it perfectly clear to me not to let myself be seen, so he clearly feels that they can't be trusted.'

Pemberton considered this. 'Then we'll have to swing around through the woods. We're going to have to travel when it gets dark, to reduce the chance we'll be seen.'

'One of us should go ahead and check out the lay of the land,' Alistair suggested. 'If I stick to the woods, I could have a shufti without being spotted.'

Pemberton looked thoughtful. 'It might be worth taking a risk,' he mused. 'All right, Stewart, but be very careful you're not seen. Come back if it looks too risky, and we'll wait for tonight.'

'I'll be careful, sir,' Alistair promised.

He waited until they'd all eaten, and then set off, keeping low, to the edge of the woods. He glanced back, and saw Shin and Yung-Sun at work in the fields as usual. Cautiously, he moved off into the trees, and then turned to roughly parallel the river. He went about half a mile, then slipped through the trees back towards the water. There was another farm, as Campbell had reported. He kept on, and saw a further three farms, and then, finally, a cluster of buildings. There was a distinct odour of fish now, suggesting a catch had been made recently. It was possible that this had been done simply with nets from the riverbank, but it meant that there was a chance that there were fishing vessels around, and that could be very helpful indeed. He toyed with getting a little closer to the small village to check, but decided that it simply wasn't worth the risk. That exploration could wait until tonight.

Alistair faded back into the trees and started back towards the family farm. It was late morning now, and time to report back to Lieutenant Pemberton. Pemberton wasn't a bad sort for a Para officer. He seemed to actually use his brain, and didn't flaunt his God-given right to issue orders. He had an air of calm assurance about him that inspired the others, and that was a good thing. He seemed to be convinced that they had a chance of getting back alive. Alistair didn't know whether the man actually believed it, or was just trying to keep their morale alive. Either way, it gave them all some hope.

And, he reflected, the voice in his head did rather suggest he and Pemberton would get to know each other well.

Alistair chuckled. Voice in his head. Look at him, taking the strange voice seriously as if somehow it really had come from the future. It was a way to cope, nothing more. And now he didn't need it, it was gone.

The war – sorry, *military intervention* – seemed a million miles away from this quiet place. Everything seemed to be so calm and normal here. It was hard to think of these farmers and fishermen as the enemy; they were just normal human beings, trying to do their best for their families. If it weren't for politicians, they would just get on with things, and not bother with political theories or boundaries on maps. Why did the people in power always have to muck up people's lives? Did it really matter whether these people were Communists or Young Conservatives? Why couldn't they just be left alone, to live their lives as they saw fit?

He came to the edge of the trees again, not far from Yung-Sun's farm. He could see the inevitable Shin and her son-in-law working quietly and efficiently in their fields. Then he saw Hee Won exit the main house, carrying a bin of some kind. She moved from the house towards the edge of the woods, not far from where Alistair was standing. Glancing around, he saw that there was a small area nearby that was used as a refuse dump, and it was obviously her destination. It was a large bin she was struggling with, and she was such a small woman, Alistair started to move to help her.

And then he saw motion over to the north, at the far end of the fields. Three Korean soldiers came out of the woods, each of them armed with rifles.

Dear God – if they decided to search the houses... Or if one of his companions should unthinkingly step outside... Alistair had the pistol with him. If there was need, he could fire a shot. At this distance, he'd probably miss the soldiers, but it would serve as a warning to the others.

Hee Won hadn't seen anything, of course, she had her back to the house and fields. And it didn't look like the soldiers had spotted her, either, as there was a bit of a dip where she struggled with the bin. But she wasn't in any danger from the men, was she?

Unless they were here looking for hidden enemy soldiers...

He pulled out his pistol, and peered out from behind a tree. One of the soldiers had called something out, and Yung-Sun looked up and waved.

The soldier raised his sub-machine gun and opened fire, raking bullets across the farmer. A second man did the same with Shin.

Alistair barely stopped to think. He threw himself down at Hee Won, and shoved her to the ground. She had started to turn and look back to see what the gunfire had been about. So far, the Koreans hadn't seen her – or Alistair – and he had to keep it that way.

Hee Won struggled to free herself, but he glared at her and put his finger to his lips.

'For God's sake, keep quiet,' he muttered.

But she was frantic, terrified – of him? She managed to scramble to the edge of the rise, and saw her husband and mother, their mangled bodies lying in spreading pools of blood. She started to open her mouth to scream, and he was forced to grab her and cover her mouth. A cracked sob was all that escaped from her.

What was going on? Did the soldiers know he and the others were here? Is that why they shot Yung-Sun and Shin? But the soldiers didn't look like they were searching for anyone. They ambled carelessly across the field toward the house, shouting and jeering.

They were looking unenthusiastically to see if there were any more family members around. But he had Hee Won here, and they probably wouldn't come this way to search – unless they knew she was somewhere around. He considered trying to shoot the soldiers, but that would draw their attention and accomplish nothing useful.

Then the door of the house opened, and Jintao stepped aside. He had obviously heard the shooting, and didn't know what it meant.

Surely these soldiers wouldn't...

The third soldier took aim with his pistol and fired just once.

Hee Won struggled furiously, tears streaming down her face. She fought Alistair, wanting to go down to her murdered family. It would do her no good. Clearly these men would simply kill her as well. Well, no, actually they would probably rape her first and *then* kill her. But the poor woman wasn't thinking logically – she only knew that everyone she loved was dead, and she wanted to go to them, to be with them.

Carefully, regretfully, he chopped down on her neck, and

she collapsed, struggling no more.

Alistair barely breathed as he watched the soldiers search the house very casually. They didn't know if there was anyone else there. With luck, they might think they had killed everyone who lived here, and leave again.

No. He saw flames in the windows of the farmhouse. They were setting fires....

They crossed to the two storehouses, and lit fires there also. They didn't even bother searching them. Clearly, then, they didn't have a clue that there were enemy combatants hiding here. Whatever their reasons for what they had done, it had nothing to do with Alistair or his companions.

That made him feel a tiny amount better, the idea that he might somehow have brought this upon the gentle family would have been too much to bear.

But where were the others? Were they inside the burning supply house still? He had to be ready in case they made a break for it. He lay flat on his stomach, his pistol steady in both hands. Only three bullets, so he couldn't afford to waste any.

But there was no movement, no breakout. The three soldiers, chattering and laughing together, walked back the way they had come, paying no heed to the bodies they left behind, and ignoring the fires that they had started and were now consuming their farm. Alistair stared at the scene in shock. He thought he'd seen sickening enough things already, but he had been completely caught off guard by this callous brutality. He couldn't help pitying poor Hee Won. She had seen her mother, her husband and her child all appallingly shot down, unable to do anything.

As soon as the soldiers were out of sight, Alistair jumped up and over the ridge, running down to where the storehouse was blazing intensely by now. If his companions were trapped inside, he'd have to do something...

'Stewart!' It was a soft call from the trees to his left. He cut across towards them, and saw his three companions crouched down. He joined them quietly. Pemberton nodded grimly. 'We didn't know if you'd seen them – or they you.'

'We should have killed the bastards,' Hooper growled. 'I wanted to, but...' He glared at Pemberton.

'Much as I would have liked to do that, Hooper,' Pemberton said coldly, 'it would have been the worst thing we could have done.'

'Letting them murder the family and not killing them for it was the worst thing we could have done,' Campbell said. 'It's *our* fault that they were killed.'

'No, it wasn't, Oxtail,' Pemberton said firmly. 'They didn't know we were here. If they had, they'd have searched the place before shooting anyone and letting us know they were here. And they certainly wouldn't have left without checking.'

'Then *why*?' Campbell cried. 'Why did they kill a harmless family?'

'I suspect it was what you said earlier, Oxtail,' Alistair murmured, still in shock. 'They kill random people to keep the others in line. Today they picked on Yung-Sun and his family. And if we'd killed them, then their superiors would no doubt have sent more troops in to annihilate the whole village in retaliation.'

'So we do *nothing*,' Campbell said, bitterly. 'After all they did for us. Is that how we repay them?'

'No,' Pemberton said. 'We repay them by getting back to our lines and keep on fighting the enemy from there.'

Hard as it seemed, Alistair realised that this made sense. He wished it didn't, but he understood and respected Pemberton's decision.

'We do have another problem,' he admitted. 'Those killers didn't get everyone. Hee Won's safe, for the moment. But what are we to do with her?'

'Safe?' Campbell looked hopeful, at last. 'Where is she?'

Alistair took them over to the dump site, where the young woman was still unconscious. 'Ah... I had to knock her out to prevent her from going to her family,' he admitted. 'She might not appreciate that when she wakes up again.'

'But you saved her life,' Campbell said, approvingly.

'Maybe,' Alistair agreed. 'But, what do we do with her, sir?' He gestured at the still burning houses. 'There's nothing left for her here. And her entire family is dead.'

'Perhaps somebody in the village will take her in?' Hooper suggested.

'I doubt that,' Pemberton said bitterly. 'Take a look around

130

– that fire has got to be visible for a fair distance – and yet not one person has shown up to help out. They *know* what this means – it's obviously happened before. And they will know that the soldiers intended to kill Hee Won also. If any of them take her in, they'll be in danger of being the next ones killed. The most likely thing that they'll do is turn her over to the KPA – and they'll kill her. If she's lucky.'

Alistair saw the cold logic in that. 'If she stays here, they'll murder her, one way or another.'

Pemberton looked unhappy. 'We can't take her with us. We're enemy combatants on the run.'

'She could hardly be in any better state if we leave her here,' Campbell insisted. 'We weren't in a position to help her family – but we *can* try and save her.'

'She may not appreciate it,' Hooper suggested. 'Her entire family has been wiped out. She may try and kill herself. You know, honour or something.'

'That's the Japanese you're thinking of,' Pemberton said. 'I don't think it's the Korean way.' He didn't sound too certain, though. For once.

'Maybe we should let her decide, sir?' Alistair suggested.

'How, Grimnod? None of us can talk to her properly.' Pemberton sighed. 'But it's probably the only thing we can do.' He glanced down at the three buildings, which were burning intensely now. 'I don't think we can salvage anything from that.'

'What about the bodies?' Campbell asked. 'Shouldn't we bury them? Out of respect?'

Pemberton chewed his lip again. 'I'm not sure that would be a good idea,' he said. 'It would show the villagers that there was somebody left alive after the killing – and it's likely that they'd be compelled to tell the soldiers.'

'They're going to realise that Hee Won isn't down there anyway,' Hooper pointed out.

'With a little luck, though, they'll assume that the soldiers took her away with them,' Alistair suggested. 'She's a pretty young thing, after all. And it *is* a logical thing for the bastards to do.'

'Quite likely,' Pemberton agreed. 'Well, we'll just have to pray that's what happens, at any rate.'

There was a moan from the fallen woman, and she sat slowly up. For a moment, she stared at them in bewilderment, and then the memories came flooding back to her. With a scream, she jumped to her feet and dashed down the hillside to the house.

'We'd better stick with her,' Pemberton said, and they hurried after her.

She had reached the house, now a mass of raging fire. Braving the heat, she dashed closer to snatch up her dead son's body and drag it clear. She collapsed over it, crying soundlessly, and hugging at him.

Alistair felt terrible for her – the pain that she must be experiencing was appalling. He wished that there was some way to comfort her, even a little bit, but he simply didn't know what he could do in this situation. He was ashamed that he couldn't help, and realised that his companions all felt the same way. They stood around, embarrassed and hurting for her.

After a few moments, she let her son down gently, and wiped away her tears with the back of her hand. She stood up and stumbled into the field, over to where her mother lay, half-submerged in the bloody rice water. She touched the old woman's body, her shoulders shaking, and then walked over to where her husband lay in his own drying blood. She knelt beside him, and bowed over his body. Her lips moved, but – thankfully! – they couldn't hear what she was saying, and wouldn't have understood it if they heard. She needed this time with her slaughtered family.

She took something from his body and slipped it inside her tunic. Then, wiping her eyes and nose again, she stood up and turned away. She marched determinedly over to where the four of them waited and watched, and stopped in front of Alistair.

For a moment, he was afraid she would scream or strike at him for saving her, but her tear-stained face seemed almost composed. She pointed to herself, and then to Alistair and finally nodded her head toward the woods.

'Ah – I think she wants to come with us, sir,' he said.

'So it would seem,' Pemberton agreed. He sighed. 'I suppose it's the best thing for her, for now. Let's go.'

Keeping an eye out in case the killers came back,

Pemberton led the way into the trees. Hee Won walked beside Alistair, her face stony, and she didn't look back once. Clearly, she felt that she had said goodbye to her family. She was obviously a lot tougher than she had seemed.

Smoke from the fire hung over the area, and there was a stench of burning. They moved softly through the forest. Alistair moved to look at the next farmhouse. It was quiet, with two men working in the fields as though nothing had happened. He could see the fire and smoke, though, rising in the background, and knew that they knew what had happened.

There was movement beside him, and Hee Won was there. She stared down at her neighbours, and the contempt she felt for them was clear. She spat on the ground and turned her back. Words were not needed to make her meaning any clearer. Alistair couldn't blame her for her attitude – and, at the same time, he could understand and empathise with that of the terrified neighbours. They could do nothing against armed foes – who were supposed to be their protectors. It was an awful situation to be caught in.

The military should *protect* the civilians, not prey on them.

He knew that he was starting to see some point in being a soldier, but put the thought aside. Now what mattered was survival. He glanced down at Hee Won, who was waiting stoically beside him. Her face was unreadable again, but, for the first time, she didn't look away from his gaze.

What was she thinking and feeling? There was no way for him to know.

They moved along to catch up with the others, and he reported what he'd seen to Pemberton.

'The cowards,' Campbell growled.

'They're just trying to survive as best they can,' Pemberton said. 'Don't judge them too harshly.'

Alistair didn't mention the widow's reaction. She had, undoubtedly, known these people well, probably played and laughed with them. She clearly felt that they had failed her and her family in their time of need. Her reaction was understandable, if unfortunate. He had been vaguely hoping that she would have wanted to stay with them. Wasn't there some sort of notion foreigners had that if you saved their life then you became responsible for them? Was this how she felt about him? If so, there could very well be a problem.

Well – what was one more problem at the moment?

Alistair pointed out the path he had taken earlier to the village, and they huddled there, on the edge of the woods, but well hidden, and looked out at the gathering of small houses.

'Yes, the fishy smell is quite… ripe,' Pemberton agreed. 'I think you're right, Stewart, there's probably some fishing boats here. Once it's dark, we'll nip down and have a look.'

Hee Won couldn't understand what they were saying, of course, but she clearly was no idiot. She caught Alistair's sleeve and looked up at him. She cupped her hands together and made an up-and-down motion with them, moving them forward. Then she pointed towards the houses and nodded firmly.

'I think she's caught on, sir,' he reported. 'And that's her way of saying there are boats down there.'

'Smart girl,' Pemberton agreed. 'Right then, as soon as it's dark, we'll go down and see if we can… acquire transport.'

Hooper looked a bit worried. 'Is that really right, though, sir?' he asked dubiously. 'I mean, we'll be stealing somebody's livelihood, won't we?'

'Indeed we will,' Pemberton admitted. 'But what other choice do we have, Hooper? I'm all in favour of *thou shalt not steal*, but this is war, and we have to get back to our lines. Aside from the fact that we're talking about our lives. And, technically, these people are our enemies.'

'Sir,' Hooper agreed, but he didn't look any happier.

Alistair could see his point, and he felt a bit bad about the matter himself. On the other hand, it didn't seem to be bothering Hee Won at all. If anything, she was probably glad to get a little revenge on the people who had ignored her family's need.

Pemberton looked up at the sky. 'It must be about noon, so we've got several hours yet. Better get what rest you can, lads. We're going to be pretty busy once it gets dark.'

Alistair picked out a spot that looked shady and relatively comfortable, and settled down to sleep. A moment later, he felt another person lie down at his back. He glanced over his shoulder and saw that it was the widow.

It was looking as if she had decided that he was her

protector – or, perhaps, the other way around. Was this because he had saved her life? Had she adopted him? Or was it because she thought he was attracted to her? Having lost one husband, was she looking to land a replacement? That was a disturbing thought. She was a pretty young thing, certainly, but they couldn't even communicate save through sign language. He was embarrassed by the thought, and at least a tiny bit flattered, too. Of course, there was no telling that this was what she was thinking. But if she *was* thinking that, he'd have to find out some way to let her down gently.

How had he managed to get into this mess?

Luckily, the soldier's knack of sleeping anywhere and at any time kicked in, and he fell asleep while he was contemplating this problem.

Pemberton shook him gently awake some time later. As Alistair stirred, so did Hee Won. She whipped to her feet, and there was a wicked-looking knife in her hand, pointed at Pemberton. When she realised who it was, she slipped the knife back into her tunic.

So *that* was what she'd taken from her dead husband. And she *was* protecting Alistair. That was… good to know.

'I'm going to get a couple of hours' rest,' Pemberton said, softly. 'Keep an eye on things, Stewart.'

'Sir.' He moved to the edge of the trees and studied the quite village. There were a handful of people about, but nobody seemed to be interested in the forest. If they looked anywhere, it was down the pathway beside the river. The way that the soldiers had come earlier.

Hee Won crouched beside him, her face impassive. There was no need for her to do that. Alistair put his hands together and then alongside his cheek in the universal (he hoped) symbol for sleep. She obviously understood, because she shook her head. She showed him her knife, and then hid it again. She was going to protect him…

Well, he was going to try and make her see some sense. He pointed to her, and then firmly at the ground. He repeated this to be sure she understood. She got the message all right. Shaking her head firmly, she pointed at herself, then at him, then at the others, and then down at the village. She clearly intended to go with them.

He thought for a moment, and then pointed to several of the people visible, and then at her, and then at the people again. She shook her head just as firmly. She didn't want to be with them. She thought for a moment, and then pointed at herself again, and then made a horizontal chopping gesture with her hand. This one had him stumped for a minute, and then he thought he understood. Was she afraid they'd kill her to appease the soldiers? How to ask that...

He pointed at her, then at the people, and then bowed his head, and made a downward chopping motion. Then he looked at her. She was puzzling through what he meant, and then got the point. She shook her head, drew out her knife and gestured savagely with it in the direction of the villagers. Well, she was obviously not afraid of them! But he suspected that they should be afraid of her if she remained...

She looked at him again and thought. Then she took his hand and placed it on her stomach. She made the horizontal motion with her hand and held it in place. Then she pointed to where his hand was on her stomach.

'Oh, good grief!' he muttered, and snatched his hand back as if burned. *Now* he understood what she was trying to say...

She was pregnant.

RIVER

'CRIKEY,' HOOPER said. 'That don't half complicate matters.'

Alistair had explained the problem to the others when he'd woken them just as the sun was setting. All three of his companions looked at Hee Won. She gazed calmly back at them.

'Well, she certainly can't come with us now,' Pemberton decided. 'We can't deal with a pregnant woman. She'll have to stay here.'

'Ah, I think she's made it perfectly clear that she has no intentions of remaining behind, sir,' Alistair said. 'And if we just abandon her, I think she's quite capable of slitting the throats of the entire village for not helping her family.'

Pemberton chewed at his lip again. 'Any idea how far along she is?'

'It's not really one of my fields of expertise, sir. I've never had to deal with this sort of thing before.'

'Our predicament seems to be getting worse by the minute. Well, she'll have to come with us for now, I suppose. Maybe we can drop her off at some other settlement further down the river.'

With that much, at least, decided, they waited for the sun to set completely and night to settle in. There were lights in a couple of the houses, but nobody moving outside. Hee Won tugged on Alistair's sleeve and gestured at the buildings.

'She seems to think it's safe to go now,' he said.

'Well, she knows this area better than we do, so I'm inclined to accept her word,' Pemberton said. 'Come along, lads.'

Hee Won led the way, her knife in her hand. Alistair felt

sorry for anyone who emerged from any of the houses. He glanced back at where Yung-Sun's farm had been, but the fire had burned itself out hours ago. He felt sorry that the bodies would still be left in the fields. The young widow seemed to have put them out of her mind, at least for the time being. She was being strong for the sake of her unborn child. Now he understood why she wanted to accompany them – she didn't want to bring up another child in this chaotic and violent place. He couldn't blame her for that.

They slipped quietly down through the houses. There were no streets as such, just pathways worn down by use. The fishy smell got stronger as they approached the river, and then they came across the water itself. There were gulls and other birds around, feeding on scattered fish guts and noisily fighting for what scraps they could forage. If they were disturbed by the five fugitives, there was no way to tell. They didn't move out of the way more than a slight shift if any feet got too close.

In the faint moonlight, Alistair could see that there were several small boats. Some were pulled onto the land, others were tied to a small jetty. Hee Won ignored the first few and gestured to one of the larger boats. It was big enough to hold all of them; some sort of a sampan. It was flat-bottomed, with a shortish mast, and a covered area towards the rear of the vessel.

There was a young man curled up there, sleeping on a mat. Hee Won pulled out her knife and started to move forward.

'No!' Pemberton whispered, furiously.

Instead, he moved quietly, and stepped lightly into the boat. He paused briefly as the lad muttered in his sleep and shifted. Pemberton moved softly forward and brought the butt of his rifle firmly and swiftly downwards. The youth grunted, and lay still. Pemberton beckoned for help, and Frank grabbed the youth's legs and together they hauled him onto the jetty. Using a length of rope they found in one of the other boats, they tied him up, gagged him, and placed him in a different boat.

Pemberton glared at Hee Won. 'No need to kill him,' he muttered. Hee Won clearly did not agree, but she made no protest.

They loosed the boat, and gently pushed it away from the jetty. There had been neither sound nor movement from the village. They drifted into the centre of the river. Hee Won stood beside the rudder, which was some sort of long oar. She gripped it, and started to twitch it gently from side to side. This was obviously how the boat was steered when the sail wasn't raised. The flow of the water bore them along, silently. Alistair sat beside the girl, and the others flopped onto the mat the young man had been sleeping on.

They drifted with the flow of the river, virtually the only thing moving in the darkness. There were signs of animal life in the trees, and the odd bat or night bird moving, but no people. They were soon out of sight of the small village, and alone on the river. The water rippled melodiously about them, and moonlight glinted off the surface, providing them with just enough light to make them comfortable that they'd see any obstructions.

If their situation hadn't been so desperate, it might almost have been relaxing.

'Hey,' Hooper said. 'Look at this.' He'd been looking around at what was in the boat, and had turned up a pot of cold rice and fish. 'Supper.'

Hee Won tapped Alistair's arm, and indicated that he take the rudder-oar. He wasn't entirely certain he knew what he was doing, but he accepted it and kept up the left-right rowing motion. She went to Hooper, and picked up a leaf that was beside the pot. Using her fingers, she scooped out some of the food, and dropped it onto the leaf. She then mimicked eating from this, and they got the message. The leaves – about six inches long – were the local equivalent of plates. Fingers were the local equivalents of forks.

She brought a leaf-full back to Alistair, along with one for herself. They alternated eating and rowing. The rice was cold, naturally, but it still tasted wonderful. Well, that was one thing he could say about the prison camp – it had certainly made him appreciate even semi-decent food! When they had finished eating, she tossed the leaves overboard, and leaned out to wash her fingers. The men did the same.

The moon was low in the sky, and setting. Just before it vanished completely, Hee Won steered the boat towards the edge of the river, and they moored it to a tree. It was clear that she intended them to wait for the morning light before going further.

'We've probably gone about five miles,' Pemberton guessed. 'I don't think the villagers back there will have spotted the missing boat yet, so they aren't likely to come looking for it before morning. If they look for it at all. They don't strike me as the sort who'll venture far from home.'

'Maybe they'll think the soldiers took it?' Hooper suggested.

'No, I'm sure that they'd know soldiers would take what they wanted by daylight and not sneak off in the night. If they work up the nerve to go to the farm tomorrow, they're bound to see that Hee Won isn't there, so she's the one they'd most likely suspect. They might even be glad enough that she's no longer a problem for them that they'll do nothing.' Pemberton thought for a moment. 'In any event, we'd better move on at first light. Until then, let's get some rest. Hooper, take first watch. We've no timepieces, of course, so try and estimate two hours before you wake Campbell. The same with you, Oxtail, then wake Grimnod here.'

Campbell grinned at the name, and Alistair winced. Looked like the name was going to stick after all.

'If it's not light by then, Stewart,' Pemberton continued, 'wake me for the last watch.'

They all settled down. Hooper sat in the stern, his rifle across his lap. Alistair lay down, and a moment later, Hee Won was against his back. She seemed to have adopted that as her customary post. Maybe she felt a little better having a man close.

A short while later, he could feel her body moving as she sobbed quietly to herself. Poor thing. She was putting a very brave – if sometimes savage – face on things, but she had to be emotionally raw inside. Alistair wished he could comfort her, but he didn't know how she'd interpret it if he hugged her; she might think he was making advances on her, and she *did* have that knife… Besides that, he felt terribly uncomfortable with attempting to console her. It was a role he'd never played before, and he wasn't at all certain how to go about it.

He'd never been that comfortable with girls. He vaguely recalled one from Bledoe. Jemima something or other. He seemed to remember she had a thing for him, even shared a first kiss with him, but he had never really known how to react.

Women, not really your field, right, Alistair?

He almost flinched at the unexpected voice.

I thought you'd gone.

The voice laughed. Definitely not *his* laugh. *No, just let you be. Didn't want you to think you're going mad.*

I see. So, why now?

Well, it's been fascinating seeing you with Old Spence. And your thoughts about Hee Won... Well, sorry, Alistair, but I couldn't resist.

Old Spence. That nickname again. Well, it was better than Grimnod. Of course, Pemberton wasn't that much older than Alistair. Ten years at the most. Maybe he should try the nickname out, see how Pemberton liked it.

What was he thinking? Playing with the idea of giving an officer a nickname – and to *his* face? Alistair's grandfather would go spare at the idea.

Well, thank you, future voice, but I'd rather my thoughts remain my own again.

The other voice was silent a moment. *Okay, I can see why.*

And with that the voice ceased talking.

Alistair returned his attention to Hee Won. Thankfully, the sobbing had stopped and all he could hear now was her breathing regularly. She'd fallen asleep. It was difficult to believe, but it had only been this morning that her family had been alive and happy.

Alistair slept, and then took his turn on stag. Again, when he awoke, so did Hee Won. It was as if she'd somehow become an extension of him. He might have enjoyed it if they had been able to communicate beyond hand gestures. Instead, they simply sat in dark silence until the sun started to nudge at the horizon. He woke the others, and they prepared to sail again. Hee Won gestured for him to take the rudder again, so he did. She moved to the side of the boat, where there was a bundle stowed. She unwrapped it, and it turned out to be a net. Hooper caught on, and took it from her, casting it over the side.

When he pulled it back in again five minutes later, it held half a dozen silvery fish. Hee Won nodded in satisfaction and, using her knife, expertly gutted them and threw the intestines overboard. Squawking gulls promptly dived for the discards. Working swiftly, she sliced open the fish and deboned them skillfully. Using leaves once more, she offered the fish around. Alistair stared at his, hungry, but unsure about eating. Hee Won rolled her eyes in a universal female gesture, and promptly ate a piece of her own fish. She then glared expectantly at Alistair. He had no choice now but to try it.

A bit rubbery, he decided, but definitely edible. And it did make a change from rice. The other three followed suit, and there was silence for a while as they ate. After cleaning up (throwing the leaves overboard and washing their stinky fingers), Hee Won took the tiller again, and the four soldiers tried to plan.

They were travelling mid-stream. The banks were lined with shrubs and trees, with no sign of people at all. That was a relief, but it wouldn't last.

Pemberton grimaced. 'I wish we knew how far we have to travel to reach the sea,' he muttered. 'I shouldn't think Hee Won knows, but even if she did, she couldn't tell us. We're at the mercy of chance – and I doubt chance has a great deal of mercy.'

'Maybe one of us should scout ahead, sir?' Hooper suggested.

'That would slow us down too much,' Pemberton decided. 'For all we know, there's an alert out to look for us. They know we escaped their prison camp, and even if nobody has seen us yet, they must know we'll be trying to get back south. They may not know our route, but they're bound to realise that a river is very likely. The faster we travel, the better our chances. Providing we're not spotted, of course. If we are, then the gig's up.'

As there really wasn't any further they could plan, they simply took it in turns piloting the boat.

Alistair examined the rest of the supplies. There wasn't much – a few blankets (or perhaps mats), the pot of rice, of which just under half remained, another fishing net and the sleeping mat. That was all. Not a great deal, it would seem, for them to use.

It was bound to happen, of course, but they caught a glimpse of another boat ahead of them about half an hour later. Hee Won hurried into action. She tapped Hooper and Pemberton, and pointed to the nets. She pushed Alistair to relieve Frank at the helm, and indicated that Frank should help Hooper fish. They set about doing this.

She settled down at Alistair's feet, and indicated that he keep his face down so that his wide hat would cover most of his face.

The other boat was tied up at the side of the river, with two men lazing in it. They sat up as the other boat approached, and called out. Hee Won conspicuously stuck her nose into the air, a clear sign of contempt. They called out again, roughly, and she stood up and let forth a stream of what was clearly insults. She'd probably learned them from Shin. The two men looked at one another, and then started laughing. Hee Won yelled again, and slapped Alistair – quite hard – on the backside. Then she stuck her nose in the air as their boat slid past the other, and sat down with her back turned in their direction. The two men called out something, laughed again and settled back down to serious lazing again.

'You know,' Pemberton mused, 'I'm starting to think that it may well be a good thing that none of us speak Korean... Whatever she said to them, I suspect it would have made some of us blush.'

'She's definitely related to Shin,' Campbell said. 'I was starting to get a bit jealous of the way she's been hanging around you all the time, Al, but now – not so much. She's got quite a mouth on her.'

Alistair said nothing to this good-natured teasing. He looked down at Hee Won, who looked back at him, fierce and proud.

'If you ask me, sir,' he said to Pemberton, 'we're very lucky to have her along. She can very obviously speak the lingo, and knows how to use it. And I thought she was the shy sort.'

'How's your arse?' Hooper asked, grinning. 'That was quite a wallop she landed you.'

'I hope she doesn't feel the need to do that with every boat we pass,' Alistair mumbled.

'Haul in those nets, lads,' Pemberton said. 'We're out of sight now.'

When they did so, they discovered another dozen fish. When these finished flopping about, Campbell stored them in the bows.

'Maybe we could make a living at this,' he joked.

Hee Won gestured at the nets and pointed overboard. She clearly wanted them to continue fishing for some reason.

'There's nobody watching us now,' Pemberton objected, shaking his head.

She nodded her own head and repeated the gesture. Then, to Alistair, she pointed at the fish in the bow. She made a sign of giving something away from her left hand, paused, and then one of taking something back into it. Alistair was starting to get the hang of understanding her.

'She wants to use the fish as trade,' he said. 'There will be villages up ahead, and she can probably exchange fresh fish for other supplies.'

'Good idea,' Pemberton agreed. 'I don't think I'll like a continuing diet of raw fish. Over the side with the nets, lads.'

'Ah, this is the life,' Hooper said, grinning. 'Floating down the river, catching the odd fish or three, a pretty girl in the stern... Much better than being shot at.'

'Except the pretty girl is a pregnant widow who saw her family massacred,' Campbell pointed out. 'And we could be shot at again at any moment.'

'Trust you to wreck my dream by letting reality rear its ugly head...'

The boat moved on.

Each time they hauled in the nets, they had between six and twenty fish. By late afternoon, there were signs of cultivation on the banks of the river. They floated into another small gathering of houses and outlying farms. Using one of the mats, Hee Won gathered up a batch of the fish. As they docked beside the houses, she gestured at them and then made a sleeping motion with her hands.

'Makes sense,' Pemberton muttered. 'We won't be disturbed by locals if we look like we're sleeping.'

They followed her instructions, and she came and went

several times as they dozed. Finally, she kicked Alistair quite roughly in the side and started yelling at him furiously. There was slightly embarrassed laughter from the riverside as Alistair shuffled to his feet and helped her cast off. Keeping his head low, he could see there were a couple of other women there. One called out to Hee Won, who laughed and replied, and then patted her stomach. The other women giggled in reply.

She had quite obviously been asked why she kept such lazy men around, and she had just as obviously said that Alistair was the father of her baby-to-be. It was a logical story, but he wished it didn't embarrass him quite so much. He was glad when the village was out of sight behind them.

He looked at Hee Won, who didn't seem to be bothered at all with the story that she'd invented. Instead, she was putting the supplies she'd traded for the fish into order. She'd managed to get fresh vegetables, some seasonings and a few more items in bags. One of those proved to be fresh rice, which would be handy.

He woke the others, and showed them what Hee Won had procured. He neglected to mention her story, knowing full well he'd get teased about it if he did. For some reason, the thought of that bothered him a lot more than it should have.

By early evening, Hee Won gestured for them to moor up. She leaped nimbly to the riverbank and picked up a few sticks, which she waved at Alistair and then pointed to the trees. She was very clear about getting her meaning across.

Frank went with him. They soon had kindling and wood, and started a small fire. Using the rice pot and fresh water from the river, Hee Won soon had supper cooking. She added fresh rice, chopped-up veggies and some of the remaining fish to the pot. Then she gutted the remaining fish (bringing in more of the omnipresent gulls for a feast), and salted them down to help them keep.

'What I wouldn't give for some good old roast beef and potatoes,' Campbell muttered. But he tucked into the resulting rice dish with great gusto.

They settled in on the boat for the night, and Hee Won curled up at Alistair's back as usual. She wriggled about a bit, but there were no silent sobs this evening. Satisfied that she was all right, Alistair fell asleep.

He didn't rest well, though. In his dreams, he saw himself killing Peng, over and over. Panic filled him, and he shot bolt-upright in the boat. Hee Won was already awake, concerned. She touched his shaking hand and spoke soft, completely unintelligible words.

Pemberton was on watch and he looked at Alistair sympathetically.

'We never forget out first kill, Stewart,' he said. 'I certainly can't forget mine. But that's a good thing – if we didn't remember it, then there would be a danger that we'd actually start *liking* killing, and that's something we should never do.'

'But... we're soldiers, sir,' Alistair protested. 'Isn't that our job?'

'No,' Pemberton said, very firmly. 'Oh, it's something we must do, certainly, but only when there's no other option. And it's something we should always regret, even when we know it's justified. Them or us. Them or some other poor bloody victims, like her family. That sort of thing. Your memories and nightmares about Peng will keep you anchored on the right side of things, lad, so that you'll kill with regret, whenever it becomes necessary.'

'Is that how it is with you, sir?'

'Very much so,' Pemberton admitted. 'And you'll learn that the way to being a good officer is to try to preserve as much life as possible – starting with the men under you, and the civilians around you.'

'I've no intentions of becoming an officer,' Alistair reminded him.

'So you say. But I have an idea or two about that.'

Alistair grunted, and settled down to sleep again. He glanced at Hee Won. 'Sorry I woke you.'

She somehow seemed to understand his meaning, if not the words. She snuggled in behind him again – but this time it was her front and not her back against his back. He wondered if there was any significance to this, or whether he was simply over-thinking the issue.

His dreams this time were a lot more pleasant.

SEA

AND SO it went for the next two days: fishing and floating gently downstream.

The river was widening out now, and there was about thirty feet between the banks. The currents were stronger, and they moved faster. The fishing remained quite good, though. The villages were slightly larger and less far apart now. Some of the houses that they saw were no longer simply wood, but had stone foundations. The roads were wider, though still not paved, and there were more people about. The latter was making things slightly more dangerous for them. They could hunch and feign sleep all they wanted, but it would take only one wide-eyed or suspicious person and they'd be exposed.

Hee Won continued to be a marvel. Her behaviour as a shrewish fisherman's wife was a clever act, ensuring that the people they met paid attention to her and not to the men. The villagers clearly found the thought of her large and rather clumsy 'husband' being constantly kicked and berated by his scold of a wife very amusing, and the fact that he didn't ever strike her back as quite pathetic. It was rather humiliating, but it diverted any suspicions beautifully.

When they were out of sight of other people, her behaviour changed completely, of course. She was always polite and considerate, and cooked cheerfully enough for the men. But Alistair could see that she was still haunted by the death of her family. There was an air of gloom over her, and the only reason she was still alive was the baby growing within her. He wished he knew how to comfort her, how to tell her the obvious – that without her the four of them would have been exposed by now. She was one amazing little woman.

He was growing awfully fond of her. He knew that this was a very foolish thing – they had almost nothing in common. Especially not language. She wasn't thinking about him, at least not in *that* way; all of her affections were for her murdered family. She was only *playing* at being his wife.

And she was a farm girl, used to living in primitive conditions in almost total seclusion. He couldn't picture her seriously as the wife of a maths teacher in built-up England. But, damn it all, she was a pretty little creature, and it was pleasant being with her, even innocently.

It was better, he knew, not to think along those lines. It was also almost impossible to control his thoughts.

He caught Pemberton looking speculatively at him from time to time. No doubt he'd seen Alistair's attraction to Hee Won and was wondering how to curb it without alienating either of them.

Campbell, it seemed, found the situation rather amusing. 'I'm glad she didn't pick me as her make-believe hubby,' he commented once. 'I don't envy you your bruises. But… I do envy you those nightly cuddles.'

'It's all for show,' Alistair said, rather stiffly.

'I'm sure it is,' Campbell agreed, cheerfully. 'It's not as if you two have any privacy, is it?' Chuckling to himself, he went back to his fishing.

Damn him! Alistair tried to scrub the thought of being alone with Hee Won out of his mind. And failed, miserably. Thankfully for his peace of mind, there was a village ahead, and she went into her shrew act.

And then he caught a slight tinge in the air, a smell he hadn't noticed in a long time, but one he was hardly likely to forget: salt.

Hee Won tapped his arm and pointed to the river. She held her hands together, slowly widened them and then gestured ahead.

'Yes,' he agreed. 'The sea.'

Pemberton perked up. 'By George, you're right,' he agreed, and smiled happily. 'We've reached the coast. Now all we have to do is to sail south from here and we'll be back with our lads again.'

'If only it's that simple, sir,' Hooper added. 'This could get quite dangerous. There may be soldiers here. And if they spot us…'

'We'll deal with that as we come to it,' Pemberton replied.

'We've made it this far; let's see if we can continue to rely on our luck.' He thought for a moment. 'We've more than enough food, so there's no need to put into shore here. We'll just go right on out. Less chance of us being observed if we do it by night, and this boat is virtually silent. Let's pull over now and rest, so we'll be fresh to go when it gets dark.'

They did so. Alistair took the first watch, and Hee Won sat up with him, as always.

When he woke Pemberton two hours later, he broached a subject that had been on his mind. 'What are we going to do about Hee Won?'

'Yes, I've been wondering about that myself. We should probably drop her ashore here before we head out to sea.'

'But she won't know anybody here,' Alistair pointed out. 'She'll be all on her own.'

'Grimnod, if there's one thing I've come to discover about her, she's one resourceful young lady. I'm sure she'll manage to cope. And these are, after all, her own people.'

'Perhaps we should allow her to decide, sir?'

Pemberton frowned. 'I was hoping that I wouldn't have to bring this up, but...' He gave Alistair a frank look. 'You're not letting yourself get too attached to her, are you?'

Alistair felt his cheeks flush. 'My own feelings have nothing to do with this, sir,' he protested. 'I just think we owe it to the girl to do the best for her.'

'And the best is for her to stay with her own people. She can lose herself very easily in a larger town and make a fresh life for herself here.'

Alistair wished he felt as certain that this was the best idea. But Pemberton was right in one respect: there would be no possible life for her away from Korea.

He settled down to rest, and Hee Won was there again.

Alistair awoke as it was starting to get dark. Hee Won was already up, preparing their evening meal on the shore. He ate it silently, wondering if this would be the last time he would see her. He couldn't decide whether he wanted it to be or not. Perhaps that would be the best thing all around, really. The mood among them all was quite sober, nobody talking much. Everyone was tense with anticipation.

This was very much the moment of make or break. If they could get through the village ahead and out to sea, then there was a good chance they'd make it. But if they were discovered or challenged here, then the best that they could hope for would be to end up back in a prison camp.

And Hee Won would almost certainly be shot for aiding them this far – if she was lucky. The thought of her fate disturbed Alistair a great deal.

'Perhaps we should drop Hee Won off here, sir?' he suggested. 'We're not far from the town, and she could walk there in an hour or less. If we're caught, and she's with us...' He didn't have to finish that thought; Pemberton had clearly had it also.

'Yes,' he agreed. 'That might be best for her.' He turned to face her, and caught her attention.

Pemberton pointed to her, and then at the ground. She seemed confused, and cocked her head to one side. He thought again, and then pointed to himself, Alistair and the other two men, and then at the boat and indicated it going away. Hee Won nodded, and stood, as if to start packing the cooking pot onto the boat. He shook his head, pointed at her, and then at the ground again.

She certainly understood the message this time. She looked angry and shook her head firmly. She pointed at herself, then at the boat, and then folded her arms.

'I think that's a *no*, sir,' Alistair said.

Pemberton was worried. 'But it's the safest thing for her, to stay here.' He repeated the gesture, a little less certainly. Hee Won glared at him, then she repeated the gesture. He nodded, enthusiastically. She pulled the knife from her tunic and pretended to run it across her throat.

That needed no translation whatsoever.

'Bloody hell,' Hooper muttered. 'I think we had better let us accompany us, sir.'

'It would appear so,' Pemberton agreed, sighing.

He pointed to Hee Won, and then to the boat. She nodded, stone-faced and took the pot back aboard. Silently, they all followed her and cast off.

In the fading light, they moved into the middle of the river.

Alistair paddled hard, as the boat was feeling the effect of the tides now. Hee Won stood impassively beside him. The others crouched down, their rifles within easy reach, just in case. Alistair felt his palms sweating. What were they getting into?

There was a final bend in the river, and then they could see the waters ahead of them. It had to be the Yellow Sea, and the route to freedom, if luck was with them. They could also see the port here. This was a substantial city, with stone and brick buildings, not the usual native shacks. It looked to be decades old, if not a century or more. There were freighters docked along the shore, and warehouses and other large buildings. Unlike the smaller villages, where people huddled indoors at night, there was activity there, on the quays and docks. Voices carried across the water.

Hee Won tapped Alistair's arm urgently, and pointed to the shore. He couldn't see anything that might have disturbed her, so he frowned. She repeated the gesture.

'She appears to want to go ashore, sir.'

Pemberton looked relieved. 'I suppose she didn't want to walk. Well, let's drop her off and we can be on our way.'

Alistair steered for the jetty she had indicated, and pulled in.

So, this was it, then – goodbye to Hee Won. He hadn't known her for very long, but he was going to miss her.

He held the boat steady and waited for her to climb off.

She glared at him, and gestured to the rope.

'Uh, she appears to want us to tie up here, sir.'

'Well, we're not doing that,' Pemberton said, flatly. 'Tell her to go ashore, and we'll be on our way.'

'Right-o.' Alistair pointed to Hee Won, and then at the shore. Then he gestured at himself, and gestured at the open sea.

She rolled her eyes and punched him on the arm, quite hard. Scowling at him, she made a cup of her hands and stamped her foot. Obviously she meant the boat. Then she pointed at the sea. He nodded. She made the cup again, and rocked it from side to side. He nodded again.

Then she twisted her hands upside down, and showed falling with her fingers.

'Good Lord,' Alistair muttered, catching on. 'Ah – she thinks that this boat isn't seaworthy.'

Pemberton glanced about. 'Yes,' he said, slowly. It clearly

hadn't occurred to him before. Well, they were soldiers, not sailors. 'She's probably right. It's got a flat bottom; any serious waves could swamp it.'

'*That's* why she wanted to pull in here,' Alistair said. 'She's telling us that we have to steal another boat. One that's seaworthy.'

'We're going to run up quite a criminal record, aren't we?' Campbell remarked. 'I wonder what the penalty is these days for stealing boats. Do they still make you walk the plank?' Hee Won tapped him and pointed at the rice pot and the bag of her vegetables and leftover fish. 'Heigh-ho, I guess I'm on donkey duty...' He started to gather things together.

'Well stick together,' Pemberton said. 'It'll be safer that way. Let's go see what the local selection of pre-owned boats might be.'

Alistair looked back at their small boat. Oh well, it had served them well until now. It was time to trade up.

They started to walk along the jetty. All that they could see, though, were boats that would need far bigger and more experienced crews. These weren't sampans, but ocean-going vessels. There was no way that they could handle them.

They passed a few knots of people, most of them laughing and drinking. There were young women among them, most of whom had overly painted faces and shrill laughs; obviously the local tarts out to give as many sailors as possible a good time. And syphilis, too, no doubt.

None of the people they passed even gave them a second glance.

And then they hit the jackpot.

Hooper whistled and grinned. 'Now, *that's* what I call a boat.'

It was battered and needed a fresh paint job, but it would be perfect for their needs: it was a World War II era Elco motor torpedo boat. The Yanks had used lots of them in the Far East, and this one had obviously been left behind after the war's end.

There was a North Korean soldier on guard duty at the gangplank. He looked bright and alert and would undoubtedly prevent them from getting anywhere close.

'Well, we're sunk now,' Hooper muttered. 'One good look at us, and he'll howl his head off and start shooting.'

He was undoubtedly correct. The only way to take him out

would appear to be to shoot the soldier, and that would certainly alert anyone else aboard the vessel.

Hee Won looked at them and shook her head. She grabbed Alistair, and then pointed to a throng of sailors and girls. The girls were laughing and allowing themselves to be pawed. Hee Won looked at him, and pointed to herself and then him.

'She's obviously had a bright idea,' Pemberton said. 'Stewart, follow her lead. We'll wait here and follow you when we can.'

'Right, sir.'

Alistair put an arm around her shoulder, and they started out down the dock toward the guard. He gave them a wary glance and shifted his rifle slightly. Whatever Hee Won had in mind had better be good, because he was very definitely on the alert. She laughed rather loudly, and then grabbed Alistair for a kiss. As she did so, she glanced downwards. He didn't understand what she meant, even when she growled softly and repeated the eye-dropping routine. With her back to the guard, she laughed again and pointed to her breast. She spun around again, so that the guard would have a good view. Alistair took the plunge and grabbed her breast.

She yelled, loudly, pulled back and started screaming what was obviously invective. She glanced down at her breast again, and Alistair make a pretend drunken lunge to grab it. She slapped him hard across the face, and ran the few paces left to where the guard was standing, an amused expression on his face. She pointed at Alistair and called out. The guard's grin spread, and he started to gesture with his rifle for Alistair to move on. He probably thought it was his lucky night.

He was right – only his luck was all bad. Hee Won made as if to hide behind him. Then her hand slashed swiftly upwards, and she buried her knife into the astonished man's rib cage. As he started to fall, she jerked the rifle from his hand, and threw it towards Alistair, who fumbled before he caught it. The guard was down, bleeding profusely. She spat on him with contempt and then used her foot to push him over the edge of the quay into the water.

The others came running now. As he passed, Campbell muttered, 'You'd better make sure you never, *ever* make her mad, mate.'

'Shut up, Oxtail!'

There was a fierce look of satisfaction on her face as Hee Won ran with them up the gangplank. She had obviously repaid the Korean Army in part for her murdered family, and was clearly eagerly anticipating adding to her score.

Pemberton gestured, and they went softly onto the boat. There would hopefully only be a couple of sailors aboard. 'Knives only,' he whispered. 'Don't need to alarm anyone ashore.'

He went forward with Campbell and Hooper. Alistair followed Hee Won inside, his own knife at the ready. Hers still dripped blood.

There were two sailors sleeping in a bunk. She had slit the first one's throat even before Alistair could kill the second man. The man she had knifed took a moment to die, choking in his own blood. She watched him die, her face impassive, her eyes gleaming. It made her seem almost terrifying.

Campbell came in. 'Got two upstairs. That's the lot.' He saw Hee Won's face, and heard the death rattle from the man she had killed. 'Grief; she looks like she enjoyed that.'

'I'm sure she did,' Alistair replied. 'Revenge for her family.'

She wasn't as civilized or meek as she had seemed on their first meeting.

'We'd better dispose of the bodies,' Campbell said. 'Unless she's planning on eating their hearts or something. I wouldn't put it past her.'

He took the arms of the man that Alistair had knifed, and Alistair took the feet. They carried him onto the deck and then pushed him over the side. When they returned for the other man, Hee Won had cleaned her knife off on his uniform and put it away. She calmly watched them dispose of the other corpse.

Pemberton came up from below. 'Hooper's almost in love,' he said. 'With the engines, that is. He says they're in good shape, and he'll have them up and running inside ten minutes. We'll have to keep a sharp eye out for the moment – just in case.'

'Sir,' Alistair agreed. He nodded to Campbell, and they both grabbed rifles and watched the docks. 'Probably safer for everybody if we leave Hee Won below decks for now.'

Campbell looked at him curiously. 'Is she starting to worry you?'

'Well, she's a tad too quick with that knife of hers to make me easy in my mind,' Alistair confessed. 'She's enjoying taking her revenge a bit too much for my liking.'

Campbell grinned. 'You going to let her curl up with you tonight?'

'I don't think I should try to stop her.'

'What do they say about the female of the species?'

'I never really believed that. Until now.'

There was still a fair amount of activity on the docks, but none of it was at all close to the old PT boat. The sailors were far too interested in the girls, and the girls far too interested in the money; nobody cared about the boat at all.

A few minutes later, the engines roared into life. It was too late to try hiding now, so Pemberton called out, 'Cast off the lines, chaps!'

Alistair and Campbell did so. Pemberton engaged the engines. Slowly at first, then with increasing speed, the torpedo boat moved away from the dock. The gang plank fell into the water, but nobody on land seemed to find that of interest. Pemberton guided the boat out of the harbour and out to sea before turning the wheel to follow the coast southwards.

Their luck was holding – so far.

'Anything we can do, sir?' Alistair asked Pemberton.

'You could check our inventory, see if there's anything useful on board – weapons, food, that sort of thing. Enlist Hee Won's help for the latter. Oxtail, take a look through the drawers there and see if you can find me any charts. Can't be any harder to decipher than Ministry of Defence maps.'

Alistair left them to it, and went below to take inventory.

Hee Won was still in the cabin. She'd stripped the bloody bedding from the bunks and was using it to mop up the spillage on the floor. She gave him a shy smile and continued with her chores. He checked the room, which held four beds, a table and a few chairs. The cupboards held cans of food, all neatly labelled – in Chinese. Not a helpful picture on any of them. They had plenty to eat now, even if it would be potluck on opening the cans. They could include the rice pot and the food Hee Won had insisted they bring with them. There was a small galley tucked behind that cabin with a burner so they could cook. The pans looked as if they were surplus from World War I, but they would be serviceable.

Next to the galley was the WC – complete with an abundance of shiny-white toilet paper. And, almost better, there were a couple of straight-edged razors.

'The lap of luxury,' Alistair commented, happily.

There was a small supply room, and then the engine room, where Hooper was clearly in his element. He looked as happy as a dog with a bone. A large, meaty bone. He laughed when he saw Alistair.

'This is more like it, eh? We'll be back behind our lines in no time.' He tapped one of the gauges, then frowned. 'Hard to tell how much of this equipment is still working properly. Take a look up on deck, will you? See if there's any extra fuel; this beast gets mighty thirsty.'

'Right-o.'

Alistair popped up top. There were a number of cans of diesel strapped into the back of the boat. They looked to be about hundred-gallon drums, and he counted a dozen of them. They were all full. He also spotted the Korean flag the ship flew, so he went forward to talk to Pemberton.

'We're flying the Korean flag,' he pointed out. 'Should I take it down? We don't want our own chaps to open fire on us.'

Pemberton thought about it, and then shook his head. 'Let's get a bit further south first, Grimnod. At the moment, we're more likely to run into enemy shipping than our own.'

'Right, sir.'

Alistair told Pemberton what he'd found so far, and then went downstairs again. Downstairs? He was certain that the Navy boys would have a different word for it – they had their own separate parlance for these things – but he didn't know what it might be. He went back to Hooper.

'There's what looks like a dozen hundred-gallon drums.'

'Hmmm… They were planning just a shortish trip, then.' Hooper slapped the closest engine cowling. 'These babies drink about two hundred gallons an hour, and we're making about twenty-three knots – about twenty-five miles an hour. Only enough fuel for six or seven hours. Something like a hundred and forty miles or so. If we're not at Seoul by then, we'll be in trouble. Better tell the lieutenant.'

'Right.'

*

Pemberton was worried a little by the news.

'Well, we've got some charts. The problem is that there's no way of knowing where we started from, and the ruddy things are presumably written in Korean or Chinese, so there's not much to go on. If it was daylight, we might make out some landmarks, but, frankly, even if we saw city lights, there's no telling *what* city it is.'

'Is there anything else we can do, sir?'

'Actually, yes. Well, something *you* can do.' Pemberton gestured towards the stern. 'There's a small radio back there – see if you can get it working, and have a shufti to see if you can pick up anything from our side. If you can, we might get some advice.'

Alistair hesitated. 'I can do that, sir – but as soon as I try transmitting, the Koreans will almost certainly pick us up. They've probably realised the boat is missing by now. At the very least, somebody's bound to spot the dead bodies floating in the harbour. If they're not already looking for us, they will be any time. And if I give a yell, they're bound to come running.'

'Hmmm… Good point. Perhaps we'd better put off a call until we're closer to home waters, then. Just check out the radio, make sure it's working. We'll wait a while before calling for help.'

Alistair set to work. The unit was in good shape; whoever the operator had been, he'd clearly known his stuff and maintained the set. He scanned and found a couple of incidents of chatter, presumably in Korean. While he was working, Hee Won turned up with plates of rice and fish – on actual, battered tin plates, and with genuine spoons.

'Half-way back to civilization,' Pemberton said approvingly. He thanked her with a smile. She bowed her head and went to sit beside Alistair.

She seemed fascinated by the headset. Well, that made sense; she'd never have seen anything like it in her life. He found one of the transmitting stations and held the earphone to her head. Her eyes widened in astonishment, and then she frowned. When Alistair tried to remove the earpiece, she shook her head firmly, and pressed it into place.

When she finally let go, she looked worried. After thinking for a moment, she pointed at herself and him, and then at the floor. She flattened her palm and made a motion forward with it. Alistair thought he got the point. He pointed at her hand, then at themselves, and she nodded. Then she held her other hand out, flat, and waved it around, getting close to her other hand, and then farther away.

'Sir,' he said, urgently. 'Hee Won says that the enemy are searching for us.'

'Well, we knew it would happen,' Pemberton said. 'I wish she could translate this chatter for us.'

'She could listen, and warn us if they're getting close,' Alistair suggested. 'I'm sure she's quite intelligent enough to do that.'

'So am I.' Pemberton looked at her and nodded. 'All right, my girl, you're in the Army now. Or should it be Navy?'

Alistair sat her down in the chair, and placed the headset over her ears. She nodded, firmly, and scowled as she concentrated on listening.

'Meanwhile, Stewart, you'd better check what armaments we have aboard. I don't think our rifles would be of much use if they find us.'

'Right, sir.' Alistair gave Hee Won an encouraging smile, and then went out on deck to check the vessel's weaponry.

It was obvious right away that they had no torpedoes – the tubes clearly hadn't been used in quite some time. In some ways, though, that was a good thing, since he wasn't sure they'd know how to arm, aim and fire one anyway. There were two mounted deck guns in blisters, one on either side of the boat. They weren't the originals, but some sort of Chinese or Russian equivalent. Each gun had an armaments locker containing boxes of spare ammo. It looked to be about fifty-millimetre. Depending on what was after them, and how their luck held out, they might be able to do some damage with those.

There was evidence that a larger cannon had been mounted in the stern at one point, but it had been removed. The Koreans probably couldn't have had access to the appropriate shells, and removing the gun had lightened the load the boat had to carry. There was still the depth charge holder and mechanism, but no depth charges. A shame, but, again, he didn't have a clue how those things would have been fired anyway.

He reported back on his findings, and Pemberton nodded.

'Better than I expected, but not as good as I'd hoped. Ah, well, we'll have to hope they don't find us.' He nodded at where Hee Won hunched, grimly listening to the radio. 'She's not said a word, so I'm hopeful that's a good sign.'

'It's going to be a long night, sir,' Alistair commented.

'Yes. I'm afraid we daren't allow anyone to get any rest. Hooper's going to have to nurse the engines for us, and I'm stuck here, steering. Better go find Campbell and then both of you prep those two guns. I'm hoping we don't need to use them, but we'd better be ready.'

Alistair found Campbell eating his second plate of rice.

'Making up for lost time,' he said, unapologetically. 'My stomach's finally remembered what real food tastes like.'

Alistair filled him in, and Campbell reluctantly pushed his plate aside.

'Just as I was starting to enjoy myself again, too.'

He accompanied Alistair onto the deck and started to check out the starboard gun.

Hooper suddenly stuck his head up from below. 'Need some more fuel,' he called. 'Fill her up, boys!'

'Always fancied myself as a petrol station attendant,' Campbell said. 'Let's hop to it, Grimnod; wouldn't want our shop to get a bad rep, would we?'

It was obviously going to be a long and weary night…

FIRE

IT WAS still dark, but Alistair knew that sunrise had to be close. They'd been going steadily south for hours. He'd seen absolutely no signs of land, but the surface of the sea was only a smidge darker than the star-strewn skies. It was clouding over, though, probably close to the start of the monsoon season. Not only did they not know the time, but they didn't even know the date. He couldn't be at all sure how long they had been captives. The last date he knew for certainty had been April 25th. It could well be early June by now, but he could be off by as much as a month. There was a certain freedom to just living day by day. It would feel a bit strange to put on a wristwatch again, and have access to a calendar.

The enemy were out there, somewhere. Hee Won had stuck firmly with the radio, but she'd issued no further warnings, for whatever that was worth. And, hopefully, there were friends out there also, somewhere. It was just a matter of trying to find the latter before being found by the former.

And now he and Campbell had to refill the fuel tanks yet again. They had been doing this at regular intervals and this was the last of the spare drums. Once they had burned through this – in about an hour – that would be it. It was still too dark to tell if there was any land nearby. But the moment of decision had arrived.

He reported to Pemberton. 'Last of the fuel now, sir. An hour's supply, give or take.'

Pemberton nodded. 'Time of reckoning,' he said. He glanced back at Hee Won. 'We're going to have to risk the radio now,' he decided. 'It'll alert the enemy to our position, but with a bit of luck they'll be too far away to stop us.'

'Right, sir.'

It was taking quite a chance, but there really was no other option. With luck, they'd be close enough to the UN forces that the Koreans wouldn't dare attack them. Without luck...

Alistair tapped Hee Won on the shoulder, and then slipped the headphones off. 'Thank you, but you'd better go below now. Things might get rough.' She couldn't understand him, of course, so he pointed to her, and indicated she should go below. She shook her head firmly and indicated that she wanted to stay with him. Ah, well, why not? They weren't in danger – yet.

He started to scan, but could detect nothing in English. Well, that wasn't surprising, really, especially if they were still in Korean waters. There was only one thing to do. He set the frequency to the old one he used with the Glosters, and hesitated just a second before transmitting the out-dated codes he'd used then.

The problem was that if the British or Yanks picked the signal up, they might think it was an enemy trick. His call signs were well over a month out of date, and HQ would have marked his codes as possibly compromised by the enemy. They might just ignore it.

What other choice did he have? He repeated the signal, and listened. Still no response. A third time, and then there was a crackle.

'Identify yourself.'

Alistair did so.

There was another pause, and then: 'Use current codes.'

'I can't,' he explained. 'Don't have a blessed clue what they are. We've been prisoners of the Chinese for at least a month.'

'Kindly confirm.'

Alistair sighed. 'I wish I could.'

'What is your position?'

'Desperate,' he replied. 'We have no idea where we are and we're low on fuel. Can you guide us to land?'

That one went unanswered for several minutes. Well, he couldn't blame them. There was no doubt a frantic discussion over whether to believe the call or not. No doubt officers were being called in to make the decision, and that would certainly create a delay. How far up the chain of command would it have to go before a decision would be made? He was sweating again. He had to stay on the air, waiting, and all the time. The tension was terrible.

Finally, the air crackled with a reply. 'Make for land.'

'Yes, but which way? And which land?'

'Head east. You can't miss it.'

As long as we don't hit it... 'Roger. Over and out.'

He reported all of this to Pemberton.

'Can't blame them for being cautious, Stewart,' he observed. 'If I were on their end, I'd be highly suspicious, too.' He swung the wheel over, and started heading due east. 'Come on, sun, wake up...'

About fifteen minutes later, there was a faint glow on the horizon, indicating it was dawn at last. With agonising slowness, the light crept upwards, and then the first rays of the sun flashed. Hee Won gave a sharp intake of breath and pointed.

Towards the north, there was a small, dark shape on the horizon.

And to the east – nothing. Just sea. Not a sign of land at all.

Their situation was bad, and getting more dire as the minutes passed. The Korean ship had altered course to intercept them. They still couldn't make much out, and there were no binoculars aboard, so they couldn't yet say what was chasing them, except that it was clearly larger and faster than they were. And there was still no sign of land.

'Better prepare for a fight, lads,' Pemberton said. He glanced at Hee Won. 'Go below.' He gestured. She shook her head and pointed at Alistair, as he ran for the port gun. 'Do as you're damned well told, woman!' Pemberton shouted. This somehow cowed her, and she meekly obeyed his order.

The sun was firmly above the horizon now. The day was broody and overcast. It seemed to be rather appropriate. Alistair sat at the gun mount and readied his weapon. He glanced over at Campbell, who gave him a thumbs-up. Alistair felt a stab of fear. This could well be the end of their escape.

Their pursuer was clearer now, a gunboat of some kind. It was at least twice their size and certainly packed a lot more firepower. Oddly, the thing that bothered Alistair the most was that poor Hee Won had come all of this way in an attempt to protect her baby. He felt as though he had let her down by not protecting her properly.

The gunboat crept closer. The radio crackled to life again, spouting unintelligible words. It had to be a call from the gunboat for them to surrender. But why wasn't it in English?

And then he realised why; the Koreans thought that they were simply defectors who had stolen the boat and run for it. They hadn't yet worked out that the boat was occupied by enemy soldiers! They probably didn't have anybody aboard that spoke English, and they didn't understand what Alistair had been saying. And he and the others were still dressed like Korean farmers...

He rushed to Pemberton and told him this.

'I'm certain you're right, Stewart,' he agreed. 'That gives us one advantage – they won't expect us to seriously fight back. We may be outgunned, but we'll show them what a fight the British can put up. I think now is the time to strike the Korean flag, don't you?'

'Yes, sir!'

Alistair did so. There weren't any other flags to raise in its place, though. Then he dashed back to the gun. For some inexplicable reason, he felt almost buoyant. He thumbed off the safety and waited.

The gunboat was closing in now. They had a deck gun, something like a Bofors, and there were men moving to man it. The ship was still out of range of his gun, but it was drawing closer. If the enemy waited long enough before opening fire, then he and Frank should be able to get some shots in. The Koreans probably wanted to capture the 'traitors', so they could be taken home and executed publicly to dissuade others from attempting to defect. The cannon was therefore probably more intimidation than real threat, at least at this moment.

Closer, closer...

The radio was still yelling orders and threats in Korean, still not aware of who they were actually facing.

Alistair glanced about. Pemberton still had their boat heading due east, and there was still no land visible. They weren't going to make it. Even if they could somehow survive this encounter with the Koreans, they had to be just about running on fumes at the moment. There weren't even signs of a possible Allied ship steaming to their rescue. It was just them against the nearing Koreans.

Alistair rubbed his palms on his tunic and gripped the gun again. He no longer had the time to feel scared. They were just moments away from action...

They wouldn't be able to hear the lieutenant give the order to fire over the roaring of the engines, but Alistair could see him raise his arm then lower it in a surge.

He aimed at the deck of the gunboat and started firing. It took him a moment to get the range right and to adjust to the feel of the gun, but he and Campbell shortly had bullets ripping savagely across the deck. Two of the sailors at the gun went down.

The gun belched flame, but the shot passed clear over them. The enemy hadn't got their range right! With grim exultation, Alistair fired across the deck again. More of the sailors went down, and the others dived for cover. The gunboat sheered away, and he stopped firing. Campbell's gun fell silent a moment later.

'That showed them!' Campbell yelled triumphantly.

But Alistair knew there was no cause for rejoicing. The Koreans now knew what they were facing – not frightened, desperate farmers, but proper soldiers. They wouldn't make the mistake of approaching too closely now. They could simply sit out of range and lob shells at the boat without fear of reprisal. He was sure that this was what the Korean captain would do.

His prediction was shortly to be proven accurate. Unfortunately.

The gunboat paralleled their course, and a few minutes later, the deck gun fired again. Again, the shot fell short. But they would get the range in the next shot or two. Campbell let loose a burst from his gun, but it was completely pointless. The gunboat was out of their range.

Pemberton tried to weave. The next shot missed them, but only barely.

The engines started to misfire. The fuel was almost gone now. They couldn't fight back, and, without fuel, they couldn't even dodge. The situation was utterly dire.

The next shot hit the sea close to the stern. The PT boat rocked under the impact, and a huge chunk was ripped from the rear of the vessel. The engines died completely. It didn't make any difference whether it was because they'd been hit or simply run out of fuel.

They were dead in the water.

Amazingly, despite the horrendous damage to the stern of the vessel, the ship remained afloat. Alistair had heard that these boats were tough, but he hadn't understood just how tough. Many other boats would have sunk with that sort of damage.

What about Hee Won and Hooper? They'd been below decks, and Hooper had been close to where the hull had been hit. There wasn't much point in sticking with his gun while the enemy were out of range, so he hurried below.

Hee Won wasn't in the cabin, and he felt a stab of fear that she'd somehow been killed. Then he saw that she was at the entrance to the engine room, dragging at something. He rushed to join her, and saw that the *something* was Hooper. He was unconscious and bleeding from a gash to his forehead, but he was still breathing, albeit in a laboured fashion. Hee Won smiled at him as he bent to help her drag the injured man to safety.

He couldn't understand why the Koreans hadn't fired again, unless they were satisfied with their victims being dead in the water. He hurried back on deck to see what was happening.

Their boat was tossing up and down in the choppy waves produced by the gunboat, which was circling them slowly. Someone had a megaphone and was yelling unintelligibly. No doubt calling on them to give themselves up; the Koreans clearly wanted to take them prisoner.

'There's only one thing they can be thinking,' Pemberton said, 'that we're spies making an escape from the north. They'll want to take us alive if possible, for interrogation.'

'Logical, sir,' Alistair agreed. 'Frankly I'd rather go down fighting than be taken back there.'

'I quite agree, Stewart. I don't see any other way out of

this. We'll have to lure them in somehow and then try and take them out.'

'Luring them in should be easy enough,' Alistair said. 'We can pretend to surrender. They'd close in on us then. But they won't come near us if we try to man the guns.'

Campbell had joined them. 'Could we blow up the boat somehow?'

'We don't have any explosives aboard,' Pemberton pointed out. 'And we used up the last of the fuel making a run for it.'

'We've still got oil,' Alistair said, thoughtfully. 'Hooper's an engineer – I'm sure he could rig something up. If only he were conscious.'

'I might be able to cobble something together,' Pemberton mused. 'There's oil and the dregs of fuel left in the engines, so it would just be a matter of starting a fire of some kind.'

'There's the stove in the galley,' Alistair pointed out.

'Splendid idea.' Pemberton looked almost eager. 'Right, Campbell, you come with me and we'll work something out. We won't be able to sink that gunboat, but we'll do them some damage.'

'What about me, sir?' Alistair asked.

'You'd better try and get across to Hee Won what we're up to, Stewart. She deserves a chance to live through this. If we get her off, then the Koreans will pick her up, I'm sure.'

'And then what would they do to her?' Alistair demanded.

'God knows,' Pemberton admitted. 'But she deserves the chance to decide if she wants to live or die, doesn't she?'

Alistair glanced at where the gunboat was still circling them, out of firing range, and then he went below to Hee Won.

She was sitting beside Hooper's unconscious form and looked at him, stony faced. He hesitated, wondering how he was going to explain her choice to her. Finally, he gestured all around, and then threw his hands up wildly in the air. She grasped it immediately and nodded. She grabbed his hand, pulling him towards her, and then down beside her. Then she nodded.

'You don't have to do it,' Alistair said, but she couldn't understand his words. He pointed to her, and then made a diving motion, over the side. She frowned, not understanding. He repeated it, pulling her to her feet and gesturing over the side of the boat. That she understood. She shook her head firmly, and sat down again.

Worried, he bent over her, and she looked up at him almost angrily. He touched her stomach, and made a rocking motion – baby. Then he pointed over the side. Again, she caught on. She pulled out her knife, and made a slashing motion across her stomach.

Well, that was absolutely clear: she would rather kill her baby herself than go back. Well, he couldn't blame her. In her position, he'd probably make the exact same decision. She was a brave and determined woman.

Pemberton and Oxtail came through.

'Just need a fuse now,' Pemberton said.

Alistair pulled the bed linen out, and together they tore it into strips. Hee Won didn't know what they were doing or why, but she helped with her knife. They started tying the strips together, and laid them out towards the primed engines.

In ten minutes, they had a fuse ready to be lit. Then they went above decks again.

The gunboat was still circling.

'I hope they make themselves ruddy dizzy,' Campbell muttered.

'Guns overboard,' Pemberton ordered. 'We have to make it look like we've decided to surrender.'

He held his up, and threw it over the side. Campbell and Alistair followed suit. Hee Won stood close to Alistair, gripping him fiercely. He glanced down at her, and she looked back at him and smiled ferociously. Clearly, she was at peace with this idea.

The gunship changed direction slightly, and started to close in. Several sailors moved to the side, aiming their rifles toward the smaller boat. But they didn't fire – it was clearly only a precaution.

'Let them get closer,' Pemberton said.

He'd found a cigarette lighter somewhere, and he held it ready to light the makeshift fuse.

Just minutes left to live…

Alistair held Hee Won closely; she was extremely calm, resigned to her fate. He wished he was quite as firm. He wondered if it would be over quickly. Dying was one thing, but suffering was something else entirely. But he wouldn't let her be braver than he was.

Closer… closer… Pemberton's hand inched towards the fuse…

There was a faint roaring sound in the distance. Campbell and Alistair exchanged glances, wondering what the Koreans were up to now. It hardly mattered, really. And then Alistair saw a shadow in the sky.

'What's that?'

Pemberton followed his gaze. 'Aircraft,' he announced. 'Why the blazes would they call in an aircraft?'

'They didn't, sir,' Alistair said, excitedly. 'That's an F-84!'

'Thunderjet?' Pemberton looked upwards, shielding his eyes. 'By George, you're right. It is!' He pulled his hand back from the fuse.

The Koreans had seen the plane also, and were gesturing and yelling. The Thunderjet swooped in and raked the deck of the gunboat with cannon fire. The sailors screamed, scrambling for cover, and the F-84 was over and gone.

'Let's give it some help,' Pemberton yelled, cheerfully, running for the port gun.

He swung it into position and fired at the Koreans as well. The captain clearly made a decision that this was getting too much to handle, and the gunboat started to veer away from them. But he wasn't leaving it at that. There were sailors running to man all of the guns. It was clear that he was going to try and sink the escapees before fleeing. They were still in range at the moment, though, and Pemberton's firing was making them all keep low.

Then the Thunderjet screamed past again. It must have dropped one of its bombs because there was a huge explosion at the side of the gunboat, and it rocked like crazy. Huge waves pummelled the side of their boat, and Hee Won hung grimly on to Alistair to stay on her feet.

The gunboat was damaged now. Part of the ship above water had been torn apart, and it was listing rather badly. Someone was still yelling orders, however, and several of the sailors tried to man the deck gun. But the way the ship was leaning in the water meant that they couldn't lower the barrel to aim at the small boat. They gave up the attempt. Then the captain obviously had a fresh idea. He had the gunboat change course to head directly for his enemy.

He was planning on ramming them. The PT boat was tough, but it wouldn't be able to survive such a collision. Alistair shook Hee Won free, and went down to drag Hooper up to the deck. It was possible that they'd get thrown free of the collision, and he'd stand more of a chance on deck than trapped below.

Once again, the Thunderjet was back and firing at the gunboat. There was an anti-aircraft gun on the Korean ship, but Pemberton's hail of fire from the PT boat meant nobody could get near it. The F-84 let fly another bomb, and this one caught the gunboat squarely in the bows.

A huge spout of fire and water hurled into the air, and Alistair went temporarily deaf. The boat shook and almost swamped, but he could see as everything started to settle that the gunboat was little more than a burning hulk that slowly slipped beneath the waves. There was a burning debris field, but no sign of survivors.

Gradually, he started hearing things again. The boat had steadied in the water. Hee Won was still holding onto him, completely confused by the carnage they had witnessed. He spotted the untouched makeshift fuse and laughed in relief.

They had come incredibly close to killing themselves, but now they were okay...

It felt absolutely bloody marvellous to be still alive.

He could hear the radio crackling, so he hurried to answer it.

'Your man showed up just in time,' he reported. 'Got the vessel trying to capture us. Give him our thanks. Ah – we're out of fuel, though. Any chance you could spare us a couple of gallons?'

WRAP-UP

THEY SENT a pocket battleship instead. The Yank captain was cheerful when he brought them aboard his craft to head back to land.

'Inchon,' he explained. 'You almost made it without our help. Mind you, the intelligence fellas are still not certain you're who you say you are – you were all listed missing in action a couple of months back. You've no proof of identity on you, I gather?'

'Nothing. Even our tags were taken,' Pemberton said.

'Except mine,' Campbell added.

'And a young woman, I see.' Captain Langdon shook his head. 'And you can't really vouch for her. The spooks think she might be a plant.'

'Silliest thing I've ever heard,' Alistair growled.

'She seems attached to you,' the American observed. 'Are you and she…?'

'Not at all,' Alistair replied stiffly. 'We've just been through a lot together.'

'Quite. Well, is there anyone who might be in Inchon that might be able to vouch for any of you?'

'No British troops?' Pemberton asked.

''Fraid not.' Langdon looked around. 'Ah, here's coffee all around. No tea, I'm afraid.'

A sailor brought in a steaming pot, several mugs and a jar of milk on an old tin tray. Alistair shuddered at a sudden memory of the old man in the prison camp with the silver server and bows of filthy water.

Pemberton grinned. 'We're so desperate, we'll even cheerfully drink coffee.'

'I do know a couple of Americans,' Alistair said, and accepted his mug gratefully.

Hee Won stared at hers in deep suspicion. Alistair sipped the piping hot brew and sighed with pleasure. She essayed a sip and then spat it out, letting loose a string of complaints.

'Some mouth on that gal,' Langdon commented.

Alistair looked at him, amazed. 'You can understand her, sir?'

'Sure. Well, not *every* word, but I studied the lingo. You were saying about knowing some Americans?'

'Right, yes. Privates Izzy Rivkin and Stu Weiss.'

Captain Langdon burst out laughing. 'Well, that sure as hell proves you're not spies,' he chuckled. 'No spy would be dumb enough to admit knowing that pair of goldbricks.' He looked at them all. 'We'll be back in Inchon in a couple of hours, and you'll be formally debriefed there. You might want to clean up a little, and I'll see about getting you some fatigues and throwing those clothes out you have on. You stink like Fulton Fish Market.'

'What about Hee Won, sir?' Alistair asked.

'I'm not sure she'd look good in fatigues, soldier,' Langdon answered. 'But she's welcome to clean up.' He spoke to her, and her eyes widened. She launched into quite a long speech, talking quickly, and gesturing like crazy, often in Alistair's direction. 'Slow down,' the captain begged often, sometimes in English. Finally, he sighed when she shut up. 'Boy, she's had to bottle all of that up for days, it seems.'

'Is there any of that you'd care to repeat, sir?' asked Pemberton.

The American grinned. 'Not a lot of it.' He looked at Alistair. 'She doesn't seem to think she should be separated from you, soldier. I had to be quite firm that she couldn't take a shower with you.'

Alistair felt himself go bright red. The thought of sharing a shower with Hee Won was a little too attractive…

'Ah, no, sir. I'm afraid she's rather attached to me, sir.'

'Attached?' Langdon laughed. 'Ah, not in *that* sense, fella. She seems to think you're some kind of an idiot, and that it's her job to look after you so you won't get hurt.'

'Too late,' Campbell muttered, stifling a laugh.

Alistair was too embarrassed to try and shut him up.

All this time he had thought he was protecting her – and she thought she was protecting him! Ah, well, he'd rather suspected all along that this was what she'd had in mind.

He was rather glad that they were separated to clean up and get showers. He was less happy about it later, when he learned that it had been done to keep them all apart, just in case they were Korean agents.

He didn't see any of his companions for weeks – and Hee Won not at all.

It was an amazing relief to have an almost proper shower, and – heavens! – he found that they had provided him with a razor. He doubted he'd ever get used to facial hair. It may have suited his father – probably suit an officer like Pemberton, too – but it would never be him. Alistair didn't think he'd even ever be one to carry off the clipped moustache look successfully. Although, he supposed, it might make him look a bit older.

A familiar laugh sounded in his head.

Oh, you're still there, he thought.

Looks like it, Grimnod, the future voice said. *Clearly whatever I was sent back to witness hasn't quite happened yet.*

Alistair frowned as the water caressed his tired muscles.

And I still have no idea why I'd create such a silly notion. From the future indeed! Listen, it makes sense that I'd create you to help me survive the prison camp, even everything that has happened since, and I appreciate your support, but I really don't need it anymore. I'm free, and soon be reunited with the Royal Signals.

Yes, the voice agreed. *But you haven't chosen your path yet.*

Alistair decided he'd had enough. He knew his path; he'd known it for years. Nothing in his National Service had changed that.

There's still time, the voice said.

With a harrumph, Alistair turned off the water and climbed out of the shower. There were fatigues and underwear waiting for him, courtesy of the US Navy. He noticed that his peasant clothes had disappeared. Their absence didn't break his heart in the least.

The captain had been correct. The ship docked in Inchon in less than two hours. He was escorted onto the docks, where there was a British jeep waiting for him, with a driver and two soldiers, both conspicuously carrying rifles. Alistair wasn't offended – the Army would have to have been stupid not to consider the possibility that he'd been turned by the Koreans during his captivity.

He was taken to a British base – they didn't tell him where – and given a decent meal. Good old bangers and mash! Then he was ordered to wait. An hour later, a soldier escorted him to a small hut and left him in a room with two chairs and a desk. After a few minutes, an officer came in.

'I'm Captain Anderson,' he said. Alistair noticed that he didn't identify his unit. This meant he was probably Army Intelligence. 'Glad to have you back with us, Sig Lethbridge-Stewart.'

'Believe me, sir, I'm very glad to be back.'

Anderson took the seat behind the desk and gestured for Alistair to take the other chair. He had a slender file in his left hand, which he opened and glanced over. Alistair was sure he probably knew every detail in it already.

'Right, Lethbridge-Stewart, why don't you tell me your story? In detail.'

They went through it three times in all, strengthened by cups of tea part-way through. Anderson didn't ask many questions, merely about small details. After the third time he closed the file, clearly signifying the end of the interrogation. He had made no notes, which suggested to Alistair that somebody else had been listening in for that purpose.

'Well,' Anderson said, standing up. 'I think that's about it for now. I'm sure you'd like to get some rest; I'll have a man escort you to your quarters.'

'Am I permitted to ask a few questions, sir?'

That brought a slight smile to the captain's face. 'You don't seem to understand how debriefing works, Signalman.' Then he relented. 'Ask – I'll answer if I can.'

'Thank you, sir. The Glosters; what happened to them?'

Captain Anderson considered that. 'Mostly wiped out or captured, I'm afraid. Brave lads, all.'

'Yes, sir,' Alistair agreed. 'So, it was a disaster, then? Hill 235?'

'Depends on your definition of the word, Signalman. The

Glosters paid heavily, but they held up the Chinese long enough for our men to fall back and establish a line the Chinese couldn't cross. It's only thanks to their actions that we still hold Seoul and Inchon.'

So, not a *total* disaster. They hadn't suffered for nothing.

'That's good, sir. And, can I ask about my companions?'

'You can *ask*, but I'm sure you must realise that all I can tell you is that they're being debriefed also.'

'Of course, sir. But – Hee Won? The Korean girl?'

'Oh, the Yanks kept her. We didn't object, naturally.'

Oh. 'Do you know what will happen to her, sir?'

'Well, from what you say, I'm sure she'll apply to stay in the south. That means the Yanks will be vetting her. She'll probably end up on Geoje Island. That's where they have their internment camp.'

Alistair scowled. 'She's a *prisoner?*'

'Don't be naïve, soldier,' Anderson growled. 'She's North Korean – she's hardly likely to be greeted with open arms. But the Americans treat their… internees… very well. They'll process her application to remain and – if she's cleared – she'll be freed.'

That was not the best of news, but Alistair knew that it was the way things were done. Poor Hee Won; and he'd not even had a chance to say goodbye to her.

He was taken to a barracks, given a room alone and told to wait. He was under no illusions: at the moment, he was just as much a prisoner as Hee Won. It would last until the Army felt that they could trust him, and there was no telling how long that would be.

It turned out to be almost a week. He was taken back to see Captain Anderson again, who actually shook his hand and told him that he was being reassigned – and promoted.

It seemed that Pemberton had kept his promise to mention his name.

THE OBSERVER V

BILL FELT Alistair's unhappiness at the promotion. It wasn't something he had wanted. And, although, Alistair may not have consciously worked it out, National Service had already changed him. Sure, he hadn't made the decision to remain in the military yet, but he wasn't the same man who had been conscripted months earlier.

Bill wondered what would change his mind. He'd been sent back to find out. Just like Sir Alistair had known.

As the black swirled around him, Bill felt himself leave Alistair's consciousness once more. And something occurred to him...

When he and Sir Alistair had talked about his National Service, the conversation and sound of Bill's voice must have made something click in the old officer's mind. That was why he'd told Bill that one day he'd find out, and why Sir Alistair had left the Gnome to him. Sir Alistair had recognised Bill's voice as that same voice he'd heard so often during his National Service, the voice he'd no doubt convinced himself he'd made up.

Which meant this wasn't the end. Bill wasn't returning to 2012, he was simply moving forward a few months in time...

GEOJE ISLAND

LANCE CORPORAL Lethbridge-Stewart was enjoying some well-earned R & R in Tokyo in October when he ran into now-Lieutenant Pemberton again.

The lieutenant laughed, clapped him heartily on the back, and bought him a pint. 'American, I'm afraid. Tastes like chilled dishwater, but better than we drank up north, eh?'

'Indeed, sir.' The bar they were in was overcrowded and busy, but they found a couple of seats and waved away the inevitable women. 'You haven't heard about the others, have you?'

'Hooper and Campbell are back at the front.' Pemberton smiled and shook his head. 'You're doing well for yourself, Lance Corporal.'

'Thanks, sir. Didn't really ask for it.'

'I'm glad you didn't turn it down this time, Grimnod.' Pemberton sipped his beer, pulled a face, then grinned. 'I know you have this idea that you'll quietly work out your time and then go back to civilian life – but permit me to say that would be a damned shame. You're as natural an officer as I've ever seen. It would be a pity if you left us.'

'It's not the life I want, sir,' Alistair pointed out.

'It's not the life you *wanted*,' Pemberton corrected him. 'But the Army has a way of changing people, you know. Some for the worse, some for the better. You, I think, for the better. It could provide you with the motivation you need, you know. And frankly, Stewart, the change in you is obvious. Never mind the rank, it's clear you're not the siggie I met at that prison camp.'

'My father and grandfather were both career officer,'

Alistair replied. 'We hardly ever saw either of them. And my father was shot down in the last war.' He hesitated. 'If I had a family, I wouldn't want them to have my experiences.'

'That's understandable, I suppose,' Pemberton agreed. 'But, just maybe, they were career officers because it was in their blood – and *you* have their blood too, you know. Have you ever thought you're simply pushing back against fate?'

'It's a possibility. But I don't think so.'

'Well – can I ask you to promise me one thing, though? Don't simply dismiss the idea of staying in the Army out of hand. Give it some serious, honest thought.'

Alistair nodded. 'I can promise you that I will, sir.' He relaxed slightly.'

'Glad to hear it.' Pemberton smiled. 'I have some contacts, you know. Could pull some strings, get you another shot at the selection board. Reckon I could make a good case for you.'

Alistair nodded grimly. 'Sir, I understand that, and I appreciate your effort on my behalf, but…'

Pemberton finished his pint. 'Your round, I think.' He stared at his glass. 'Sometimes the Yanks do things semi-right.'

'Speaking of whom,' Alistair said, giving up arguing for the moment. 'have you heard anything about Hee Won, sir?'

'Not a sausage, I'm afraid. You neither, it would seem. I think she's been in Geoje-do, but I don't know if they passed her through yet or not.'

Alistair ordered a couple more pints. Pemberton gave him a sombre look.

'You'd better hope she's out of there by now. I hear conditions there are not good.'

'What do you mean, sir?'

'It's a big mess,' Pemberton explained. 'The Yanks have taken too many prisoners, but they are still trying to treat them well. The Koreans have been taking advantage of them, and there are what amounts to gangs in the compounds. It's hard to say, sometimes, just who's in charge there. But the Communists are pressuring the ones who want to stay in the south – beating them up, sometimes even knifing them. And you know how Hee Won could be…' He shook his head. 'Still, there's nothing we can do about it. The ball's not in our field of play.'

The conversation ruined Alistair's enjoyment of the rest of his leave. He couldn't help feeling somehow that he was responsible for Hee Won, and he was determined to find a way to check up on her. There was only one thing he could think of doing, and so he sent a message to Izzy Rivkin, asking if he knew anything.

Alistair heard nothing for more than two weeks. There was plenty to keep him busy, but he had enough free time to worry, and not a word back from Izzy. He asked around about Geoje, and what he heard was far from encouraging. Pemberton's assessment of the situation sounded accurate – and, if anything, on the optimistic side. The situation was a mess working its way up to a disaster.

He was disturbed by the screech of brakes and a loud horn outside his hut. He stormed out.

'Hey, lookit that!'

Alistair's mood lifted almost immediately. 'Izzy! Stu!'

Izzy jumped out of the jeep, grinning widely. 'Glad to see you can still recognise us lowly privates. A lance corporal! Who'd have believed it?'

Stu glanced around. 'Can a man dying of thirst get a drink around here?'

'I think there's some tea, yes.'

'I'd sooner die of thirst.' Stu pulled out a hip flask and took a slug, then smacked his lips. 'You want some, Al?'

'Not at the moment, no. Are you two reprobates here for any specific reason, or are you just disrupting the entire front and it's our turn?'

Izzy scowled. 'Come on, Al, you invited us.'

'I don't recall that,' Alistair said. 'I asked you to check up on Hee Won for me, that was all.'

'And that's what we did, and that's why we're here, chum,' Izzy said. 'Reporting in person. Say, that's some good-looking gal you got there, friend.'

'She's *not* my girl,' Alistair replied. 'I just feel somewhat responsible for her, that's all. And I heard some disturbing news.'

'Yeah, there's lots of disturbances,' Stu agreed. 'But we met with Hee Won and had a chat with her.'

178

Alistair looked at them in amazement. 'You *talked* with her? I didn't know your Korean was that good.'

'It ain't,' Izzy admitted. 'She's been learnin' herself English. Manages quite well. Anyhow, we told her that you was worried, and she seemed kinda pleased to hear you'd been askin' after her. But she said she wants to talk to you real urgent-like.'

'The poor woman,' Alistair said. 'She's been in Geoje prison all this time?'

'Whadda ya talking about?' Izzy asked. 'We don't keep gals in prison. She's free as a bird. Well, maybe shackled a bit, but she ain't *in* jail – she's workin' there.'

That was quite a surprise.

'Working?' He wished he had better information. 'Then she's fine?'

'If she was fine, she'd hardly want to talk to you so urgent, now would she?' Izzy shook his head. 'Ya know, Stu, I'm startin' to think that gal got it right when she said Al here ain't too bright.'

'Of course he ain't too bright,' Stu replied. 'He got himself promoted, didn't he? And after we warned him time and again what a dumb idea that was.'

Trying to ignore their banter, Alistair considered the matter. If Hee Won wanted to see him, then it would have to be something very serious. There was only one thing for it, he'd have to wangle some way to get out there.

'You two wait here; I'll be back as soon as I can.'

'Maybe he's natural-born Brass,' Izzy said. 'See how easy he slips into givin' us orders?' They were still discussing it animatedly as he hurried off to see the captain.

In a short while, he was back with a pass.

'Will you two jokers be able to take me to Geoje?' he asked.

'Why else do ya think we're waiting around here?' Stu asked him. 'Haul your ass into the jeep, and we can be on our way.'

Alistair complied, and Stu sent the vehicle roaring out of the British compound and heading south towards Geoje Island.

Alistair had brought with him a short briefing on the camp they were heading for. Geoje was Korea's second-largest island, and was off the south coast. Ostensibly under UN command, it was mostly occupied by US troops. A camp had been established to contain the North Korean prisoners captured in fighting. It was meant to be a humane and decently run camp, but good intentions had gone out of the window when far more prisoners were taken than could be handled.

The camp had been a logistical nightmare from the outset. The island had no natural water resources, and over a hundred thousand inhabitants. Engineers had been forced to build dams and reservoirs as well as the enclosures to contain the prisoners. There were two sections to the camp, each in an adjacent valley, and each camp was split into eight separate compounds. Each compound was supposed to hold around a thousand men, a total of sixteen thousand men or less.

There were more like 170,000 there, over ten times the planned capacity. Prisoners were crammed in wherever they could be placed, and supplies had to be increased. There were only about nine thousand guards, who were outnumbered around twenty to one.

As if that wasn't bad enough, the prisoners didn't get along well with each other. Most were from the Korean People's Army, but a lot of those were not actually Communists. Many had been impressed into the Army and hated the Communists. Confining the two groups together resulted in a lot of bad blood – literally. There were internal squabbles and struggles for power, often resulting in bloodshed or murder. A lot of the prisoners managed to make crude clubs or even makeshift knives. And the knives made bodies.

The guards were in a dangerous situation – if they went into the compounds, they were liable to be attacked and even knifed. While they were certainly a lot better armed, they were also hampered by the orders they were given. They were forbidden to open fire under almost any circumstances. Peace talks were going on, and the United Nations made it quite clear that any shootings of unarmed prisoners would harm the peace process, hence the moratorium on shooting. The prisoners had no such worries, and were easily provoked into stone-throwing and other demonstrations. From time to time, despite their orders, troops would fire on rebelling prisoners. Each such occurrence was a black eye for the negotiators.

As a result, the guards were ordered to stay out of the compounds, which resulted in something of a stalemate. The guards couldn't go *in*, and the prisoners couldn't come *out*. It was not the best of solutions, but there didn't seem to be any way around it.

Alistair shook his head in despair.

But it got even worse. Many of the prisoners didn't want to be freed just to be sent back to North Korea. They wanted asylum in the south, which was understandable. But all such requests had to be screened, to make sure that there weren't Korean agents among them. And there *were* Communist agents in the camps. A lot of the prisoners believed firmly in the Communist cause, but they were augmented when the Korean – and Chinese – command realised that they had a perfect opportunity to put pressure on the UN. They would deliberately allow undercover agents to be captured, knowing they'd be sent to Geoje. Once there, they organised the prisoners. Because the guards couldn't (and daren't) enter the compounds, the prisoners were given their rations and left to fend for themselves. The agents communicated back and forth almost at will and tested their power by staging acts of rebellion and defiance. They also refused to allow the Americans to carry out their screening of prisoners to see who would be allowed to remain in South Korea.

Prisoners who were considered viable for asylum were transferred out of Geoje and into another camp on the mainland in Busan. Thankfully, that was well-ordered and peaceful. But certainly not Geoje.

They were living on a knife-edge, and any slight spark could instigate a huge problem.

And poor Hee Won had somehow been caught up in all of this.

Alistair didn't know what her problem was, but it was almost certain to be complicated – and difficult to resolve.

There were only two bridges leading from the mainland onto Geoje – good for defence, at least, but all traffic had to pass over one or the other of them. Even with Stu's manic driving, that meant that they were delayed. There were a large number of supply trucks heading in either direction.

'Transport is all ballsed-up,' Izzy explained cheerfully. 'The South Koreans were supposed to provide the grain for the camp, but their economy isn't up to it, and they handed it over to our guys. Like overnight. We're shipping in the grain, but those Commie bastards in the camp are complaining that the mix isn't to their liking, and that we American oppressors are trying to starve them to death. Or poison them, or somethin'. Doesn't stop them eatin' it, though.'

'Add in all the refugees fleeing the war zone and ending up here, and there's a lot of need for food,' Stu added.

Wonderful. Alistair didn't envy the Americans the headaches all of that had to be causing.

'I wouldn't want to be in charge here,' he commented.

'Neither would any of the guys actually in charge here,' Izzy replied, grinning. 'The brass turns over so fast that they're gone before we can even memorise their names.' He laughed. 'No idea who's even currently in charge. I don't *think* it's a Commie – yet.'

'Though the Commies probably do,' Stu added.

It was late afternoon as they approached the camp. They had to show their papers several times before being allowed in. Stu braked the jeep to a sudden halt outside one of the admin huts.

'You'd better go see the Duty Officer, Corporal. We mere privates ain't invited. Good luck! Give us a howl when ya need a lift back, okay?' And they wandered off to look for the nearest beer.

Alistair reported in, and was allowed in to see a Captain Austin, who listened to his story, after examining his papers once again.

'Hee Won?' he mused, and then checked through a file on his desk. 'Oh, yes, one of the civilian washer-women, I see.' He looked confused. 'You sure you want to see her?'

'Yes, sir. We went through a good deal together, and she's asked for my help.'

'With what?'

'I don't know yet, sir.'

The captain sighed. 'Okay, Stewart – I'll give you a pass. The guard outside will point you in the right direction.' He paused. 'She's not…?'

'No, sir. We're just friends.'

Austin seemed relieved. 'Fine. Just report back to me when you're done, okay?'

Alistair assured him that it was indeed okay.

He followed the guard's directions to the laundry area, where he asked for Hee Won. There was an American female officer in charge, and she sent an underling off to find the Korean girl. She frowned at Alistair. 'We don't approve of fraternizing with our females.' She was a young woman, pretty enough, with her blonde hair pulled tightly under her cap and a frown that seemed etched into her face.

'I'm not here to fraternise,' Alistair complained. 'I'm here merely as a friend, to talk with her.'

'Well, mind that's all you do.' She gestured to an empty office. 'You can talk with her in there. Leave the door open.'

Good grief...

A few minutes later, Hee Won was there. Her face lit up, and she rushed to give him a huge hug. '

'Al-ee-stur!' she cried, sounding his name as three separate words. 'Good to see!'

He hoped the officer in charge hadn't seen that. He managed to disentangle himself from the enthusiastic embrace. 'It's wonderful to see you again, Hee Won,' he said, smiling. 'Are you well?'

'Yes, well,' she said. Then, proudly, 'Speak English good, no?'

'Speak English good, yes,' he replied. She looked very different, and then he realised that there was a bundle tied about her back. 'Did you have your baby?'

She grinned and swung the baby around to show it to him. 'Good baby,' she announced. 'Name for you.'

'For me?' He was astonished and a little embarrassed at the thought. No wonder the officer had been so suspicious...

'No,' she answered, snorting. 'Joke. Fool you, yes?'

'Yes,' he admitted, feeling rather relieved.

'Is girl,' she explained. 'Shin.'

He smiled and touched the child. 'It's a very fine name. Shin.' Named for Hee Won's mother. It was highly appropriate, and a little emotional. He hadn't thought about the dead family in several months. 'She looks very healthy and content.'

Hee Won nodded. 'People good here. Good to Shin. Good to Hee Won.'

'I'm very happy to hear that,' he said, somewhat relieved. 'But I was told you needed to see me very urgently.'

'Need help,' she answered. 'Bad, bad help.'

'What's the problem, Hee Won? Anything I can do, of course I'll help. But what is it you need?'

'Father for Shin.'

Alistair stared at her, aghast. 'I can't do that!'

She rolled her eyes and shook her head. 'Not *you* father,' she said. 'Idiot.' She pointed at the POW camp. 'Father there.'

The conversation was filled with far too many ups and downs, tearing at his emotions. He was having trouble understanding her, even though she was now speaking English. There were times it might as well be double Dutch.

'He's a prisoner?'

'Idiot idiot,' she growled. 'Guard.'

Oh. 'The man you aim to marry is a guard in the camp?' It was slowly starting to make some sort of sense – except he still couldn't see the problem.

'Guard,' she confirmed.

'Right. So, what's wrong with that?'

'In camp.'

'Yes, he's a guard in the camp. I understand that.'

'No – prisoner guard *in camp*.' She glared at him as if he was an imbecile.

They were getting nowhere like this. He walked to the door, motioning for her to stay still. As he had expected, the American female officer was in the next room.

'Could you help me here?' he asked her. 'I seem to be having some sort of a communications difficulty. Do you know anything about Hee Won?'

'Yes,' the officer replied. 'She's a hard worker and a dedicated mother. She's engaged to one of the guards here, I believe.'

'So I gather. But there is some kind of problem that I can't make head nor tail out of, and I'm hoping you can get to the bottom of.' He turned to Hee Won. 'Can you explain to this young lady?'

'Idiot,' Hee Won said, gesturing at Alistair.

'Yes, dear. Many men are. Now, what seems to be the problem?'

'Husband guard. In camp.'

'So I understand.'

'No!' Hee Won shook her head violently. '*In camp*! Prisoner guard.'

'Oh…' The American turned to Alistair, looking worried. 'I'm afraid I think I *do* understand. A few days ago, some of the prisoners lured three of the guards close to the wire. The gates are never locked, because we're always going in and out to question the prisoners to see who wants to apply for asylum. A bunch of the KPA grabbed the guards and spirited them inside the compound. We don't know whether they're alive or dead.'

And *now* it all made sense. He turned to Hee Won.

'So your husband-to-be is one of them?'

'Yes! Prisoner guard.'

Alistair looked at the officer again. 'Can't something be done to determine if he's alive or dead?'

'The guards can't go into the compounds,' she answered. 'It's more than their lives are worth.'

'Then he's probably dead?'

'Maybe, maybe not. You see, the KPA sometimes hold the guards as hostages, to leverage for concessions. So they could just be holding him. If he was an American, they certainly would. They know if they don't ask for too much, then we'll trade. But with the Korean guards, it mostly depends on whether anybody has a grudge against the man. If he's unpopular, then they'll simply kill him.'

'Aren't they afraid of reprisals?' Alistair asked. It sounded like a crazy way to run a prison.

'No, because the Brass have issued orders not to shoot under any provocation. There are peace talks on, you see, and we don't need any negative press. There are Commie agents in the compound, and they can get messages out of here. If they say we're mistreating them, then it would hurt the peace talks. And the red press would spread the news that we're shooting unarmed men. Technically, of course, they're unarmed – but they can throw a hunk of rock a good distance. I could raise a mean baseball team from among them. They throw rocks, we have to retreat.'

'So, there's no way to find out if her man is still alive or not?'

'Oh, there's one way,' the officer answered. 'Somebody would have to go in and take a look-see.'

Alistair was definitely getting the picture now. 'And whoever went in…' he said, slowly.

'Would be very unlikely to come out again,' she finished for him. 'At best, they would just become another hostage. At worst…' She shrugged.

Alistair turned to Hee Won. 'And you want *me* to go in there and find out for you?'

'Trust you,' Hee Won replied. 'Good man. Idiot, but good man. No killed.'

'Well, she's right about that,' the American said. 'I mean, the *no killed* part – I'm not sure about the *idiot*. You'd be far too valuable to them for them to hurt you. But you can't seriously be thinking of going in there?'

Alistair didn't know what to say. It was a crazy idea, he knew, but he *was* likely to be safe. Well, *mostly* safe…

'My friends and I were captured by the enemy,' he explained. 'Hee Won helped us get to safety. We all owe her a great debt. And this might be one way to help repay it.'

'She was right,' the officer said. 'You *are* an idiot.' Then she smiled. 'Though I wish I knew a few more men like you.'

'I'll tell you what,' he said. 'If I come out of this in one piece, allow me to buy you a drink. As long as it's not another of those horrible chilled beers.'

'You've got yourself a date. I always was a sucker for an English accent.' Then she was serious again. 'But this is still a crazy idea. I don't think the brass will go for it.'

'Surely they want to know the fate of the missing men, too?'

'Yeah, but they may consider the cost to be too high' She looked from him to Hee Won, who was looking hopeful. 'She seems to have a lot of faith in you. Let's hope it's not misplaced. You do know that if the brass let you go in, you won't be allowed to carry any weapons – they'd fall into the hands of the Reds.'

Alistair raised an eyebrow. 'Walking unarmed into a prison full of Commies,' he said. 'What could possibly go wrong?'

WHAT WENT WRONG

THE OFFICER turned out to be named Captain Maggie Hickenlooper (which might explain why she hadn't volunteered the information earlier), and she became suddenly quite helpful. She went off to talk to her superiors about allowing Alistair to attempt to talk to the prisoners. While she was gone, Hee Won gave him another big hug, and then fished around inside her clothing until she produced a rather battered photograph. It showed a young man in an ROK uniform, smiling nervously.

'Jae-ho,' she explained, looking suddenly shy.

'He looks like a kind man,' Alistair told her. 'Is he good?'

'Good,' she confirmed. 'Get?'

'I'll do my very best, I promise you.'

Captain Hickenlooper returned a short while later, accompanied by a major she didn't introduce. The middle-aged man examined Alistair thoughtfully. 'You need your head examined,' he said, finally.

'Hee Won would agree with you, sir.'

'But we're going to agree to this anyway,' the major added. 'Against my better judgement. You're nuts to think this will do any good.'

'In that case, sir, why are you agreeing to it?'

The major pulled out the butt of a cigar and rammed it in his mouth. He made no attempt to light it; he seemed to enjoy simply chewing on it. 'You're aware of the state we're in? The problems we face?'

'Only a few of them. But enough to be glad I'm not stationed here.'

'Yeah, you get the picture, then. Well, the Commies have

been taking out their anger on any guards they can grab, and, naturally, this makes the South Koreans kinda nervous. There's talk among 'em that we're abandoning them, and that doesn't do a lot for camp morale.'

'So, you need to look as though you're doing something about it, sir?' Alistair guessed.

'That's about the size of it, yeah.' The major pulled out the cigar, glared at it, and tossed it into a garbage bin. 'You do understand that once you're in there, we won't be coming to drag you out?'

'Yes, sir.'

'Well, you're either a brave man or an incredible fool. I don't know which.'

'Perhaps you'd be so kind as to enlighten me when you decide, sir?' Alistair suggested. 'I'm not entirely certain myself, either.'

The major grunted – it might have been an attempt at a laugh. 'Okay, Limey, come with me.'

Hee Won clutched Alistair tightly, then let him go. Captain Hickenlooper gave her a reassuring smile (which she didn't seem to believe herself) and then touched his arm.

'Don't forget our date,' she said. 'I hate to be stood up.'

He nodded curtly to her and left the two women together as he followed the major out to the inevitable jeep. The major gave a barked command, and the jeep shot off towards the compounds.

They were taller, strong enclosures, but internal divisions were no more than a few strands of barbed wire. The compounds were jammed with prisoners. Some watched sullenly, others called out insults in pidgin English. Many simply turned their backs. They all looked fairly healthy and they certainly hadn't been abused. It was the polar opposite of the Chinese camp he'd been in a half a year – a lifetime – ago. But his briefing had obviously been correct; there were far too many prisoners and far too few guards.

The officer on duty led them to a gateway, where two of the guards were on duty. The entrance to the compound was merely a double gate, separated by about eight feet. On the outside were about a dozen US soldiers and several Korean guards. On the inside was a host of sullen, angry or impassive Korean males.

Alistair steeled himself. This was no time to have regrets, or an attack of nerves. Like pack animals, the Korean prisoners would be able to sense if he showed any fear of them. He was relieved that his hands were calm and steady as he unfastened his gun belt and handed it to the duty officer. The officer saluted him, and he saluted back. He then saluted the major, turned and marched to the gate.

There was an eerie silence about it as he reached the gate. One of the guards opened it and held it as he passed inside. Alistair fought down the fear he felt as he walked the few steps to the inner gate. Then he stood there, waiting. It was important that he seemed unhurried and unconcerned. And that he didn't open the gate for himself. Eventually, a couple of the prisoners dragged the gate open and he stepped inside. He didn't make eye contact, but didn't flinch away, either. Again, he waited.

Slowly, reluctantly, a pathway began to form among the prisoners. Breathing evenly, and resisting the urge to wipe his moist palms on his uniform, he marched steadily through the assembled ranks. It led to a small cleared area in front of one of the barracks buildings. A chair had been placed in the open, and a Korean in a colonel's uniform sat, bolt-upright, in it. He was equally calm and impassive. Behind him, to his left, was a thin Chinese officer with a pinched face. He had a very decided scowl.

Acting as though there was nothing at all extraordinary about this, Alistair marched up to the colonel and saluted him. After a moment, the colonel saluted back.

The pathway he had walked closed in behind him, as the prisoners moved forward in anticipation of what was to happen.

The colonel inclined his head slightly towards the Chinese officer, who then looked directly at Alistair.

'The colonel asks why you have given yourself into his power. You will reply.'

'I have every intention of replying,' Alistair answered. 'The prisoners have seized three of the Korean guards; I am here to ask for their safe return.'

The Chinese man bent to whisper in the colonel's ear. The

colonel considered and whispered something back.

'*Ask?*'

'Ask,' Alistair repeated firmly.

'Do you not mean *negotiate?*'

'No.'

The two conferred in whispers again. Then the Chinese man snapped a short order. There was a flurry of movement near the hut, and then three prisoners dragged out a guard. His arms were tied across a thick stick, and he'd obviously been beaten and starved. There was blood on his face and pain in his eyes, but it was quite clearly Jae-ho. That was some measure of relief in Alistair's mind, and a dark cloud in his memory of suffering like that.

'You may have two of them for nothing,' the interpreter said. '*This* man, however, you will have to *negotiate* for.'

Alistair glanced around. 'Where are the two I may have for nothing?'

There was a low-level laugh, and several of the prisoners moved aside, exposing a pit.

'They are in there. We have no further use for them. Neither will you.'

Beaten and tortured to death... And Jae-ho was to be the next if Alistair couldn't talk them out of it.

'What do you offer for this man?' the Chinese asked.

'Myself.' Alistair tried not to think what might be in store for him as he said this. He had once promised himself that he would never be taken alive again.

The Chinese man barked a sharp laugh. 'We already have you. We need something... more substantial.'

'What would you suggest?'

The two enemy officers conferred again. Alistair stared straight ahead. He would not look at the prisoners, and certainly would not give them the pleasure of seeing him afraid. He was starting to become more certain that Hee Won had been right about him all along. He *was* an idiot.

The interpreter straightened up, opened his mouth to speak, and then paused. He scowled, and then moved closer to Alistair.

'There is something familiar about you,' he said. 'I have seen you somewhere before.'

'I've been somewhere before,' Alistair admitted. 'But I can't say I remember you.' But that wasn't entirely true. Closer in, there was something definitely familiar about the man's face. But he was right – he couldn't recollect ever seeing it before.

The colonel said something in a low, commanding tone, and the interpreter snapped back from Alistair.

'The colonel says that as you are our prisoner…' His voice trailed away, and then there was a look of exultation on his face. 'Now I recall! You were a prisoner. You were my brother's prisoner.'

'Your brother's…' And just like that it all came rushing back. Everything that had happened to him at the prison camp, every humiliation, every torture tactic, and the voice.

Be careful, Alistair.

Well, of course the voice would return now. If it ever went away. Maybe he'd just succeeded in silencing it? Thoughts of the prison camp had brought it back.

'Your brother was *Peng*?'

'Yes.'

Now he had something to offer.

The colonel seemed to be annoyed at this diversion from his discussion. He snapped a command at Peng's brother. Instead of backing down, though, the Chinese man argued, which clearly didn't sit well with the colonel. His face clouded over, and he spoke very softly, and Peng's brother appeared ready to back down.

Alistair couldn't allow this; these two men were obviously in charge of the prisoners here. If he could get them at odds with one another, and keep them there, then he would become the one in command of the situation and not them.

'I remember Peng well,' he said. 'I can still see the expression on his face when I killed him.'

With a howl of fury, the brother jumped at him. Alistair side-stepped and brought his hand down in a heavy blow across the man's neck. He went down, rolled, and started to get to his feet. The colonel snapped out a command, and two of the prisoners jumped to grasp the brother's arms and hold him still.

'That was well played,' the colonel said in perfect English. The whole 'translating' business had been a subterfuge to let

192

him be in command of the situation.

'And so was your pretending not to understand English,' Alistair replied.

'So.' The colonel smiled. 'Then let us speak, face to face, eh?'

'That would be a good thing.'

'Did you really kill Chen's brother? Or is it another ploy?'

Alistair could still see the expression on Peng's face. 'No ploy, I really did kill him.' He ignored the snarl and Chinese curses aimed at him. 'I was his captive and he tortured me. But he was an idiot, and gave me the opening I needed. It showed great weakness and foolishness on his part.'

'And yet you now provoke his brother into fury… Why would you do that?'

'May I ask first why you killed the two guards, and why you torture this one?' Alistair nodded at the fallen Jae-ho.

'Look around you, Englishman. There are a great number of us, and there is little for us to do here. A little… entertainment is appreciated by my men.'

'But it would be of greater entertainment to punish me, would it not?' Alistair smiled slightly. He knew that this thought had undoubtedly occurred to everyone here. 'But if you did, you would pay dearly for such sport, would you not?'

'Indeed.' The colonel nodded toward Jae-ho. 'Such wretches as these the Americans do not care about. If we kill them, their loss is not felt. They are of no real consequence. But if we were to slay you – *then* the Americans would grow angry. This they could not allow. They would lose face. So, we must keep you alive – fortunately for you. We lose great sport – but we are not killed.'

'And what if I could offer you a chance for sport when you would *not* be killed?' Alistair's mouth had gone dry now, knowing what he was offering and what he would face.

'You intrigue me.' The colonel licked his lips. 'What is it that you propose?'

'A fight. One on one. Here and now, to the death.' Alistair jerked his head towards Chen. 'He and I.'

'I will kill you!' Chen shouted, struggling to free himself.

'You see the hatred he has for me,' Alistair argued. 'It would be a good fight. Your men would enjoy it greatly. They would be grateful to you for providing it.'

The colonel glanced around at his assembled men. 'You are quite correct – they would. And, yet – if I were to agree to it, and you were slain, then the Americans would come in and punish us all.'

'And if I can guarantee that they won't?'

There was true interest in the colonel's eyes now. Alistair could imagine the prestige he would accumulate with his followers if he could share such entertainment with them…

'In exchange for what?' the colonel asked.

'In exchange for your word that if I win the fight, then I should be allowed to go free, unmolested.'

The colonel considered and then nodded. 'That would seem a reasonable request,' he agreed. 'I would agree to that condition. Whichever of you survives, my men will be… entertained.'

The question was, of course, whether the colonel would keep his word. There was no guarantee about that. Alistair couldn't dwell on minor problems, though. 'Then what I suggest is that I write a note to the American commander, which that man…' He indicated Jae-ho. '…will take to him.'

'Why him?'

'Because he is the only man here that the guards will allow to leave.'

The colonel inclined his head. 'That is true. Very well, I agree. And what will this clever note of yours say?'

'That I have a personal grudge to settle with Chen here, because his brother once held me captive and tortured me, and that we wish to settle the matter man-to-man. And that, regardless of the outcome, you are to be held blameless.'

'You appear to have considered everything,' the colonel said approvingly. 'Very well, I accept your offer.'

He barked a command, and one of the men rushed off, returning moments later with paper and a fountain pen. The man offered his back for Alistair to lean on as he wrote. The colonel chuckled.

'I am quite aware, of course, that you believe that you are… playing me, I believe the expression is? At the same time, of course, I believe that I am playing you. But I suspect that we shall both be satisfied with the outcome. Well, *if* you

194

manage to survive, of course.'

'Yes,' Alistair said, drily. 'There is always that, of course.' He finished writing and signed the letter. He offered it to the colonel. 'If you speak English this well, I am sure you can read it just as easily.'

The colonel waved his hand airily. 'I do not think I need distrust you,' he said. 'You English are widely known for your sense of fair play.' He chuckled. 'Besides, the fact that you would allow me to read it tells me there is nothing amiss about it.' He gave a quiet command to the guards standing over Jae-ho.

They sliced the ropes holding him to the pole through his arms and jerked him to his feet. Uneasily, he stood up, then stumbled across to Alistair. Alistair handed him the note.

'Go,' he ordered.

The soldier nodded, and then started towards the gateway. The colonel waved his hand, and the prisoners parted. Slowly, painfully, Jae-ho made his way to the first gate and through it. He reached the outer gate and the guards there helped him out. The prisoners closed in again, gathering silently around Alistair and the colonel.

'You have seen that I have kept my word,' the colonel said. 'The man you came to rescue is now free. It is time that you paid the price.'

Alistair took his jacket off and handed it to the closest man. 'Very well, I am ready.'

Well, as ready as I will ever be.

My money's on you, Alistair, the future voice said.

It would be, as you're my inner voice.

The colonel shook his head slightly. 'There is one more tiny condition,' he said. 'For my men to properly enjoy this fight, there must be blood. The more blood, the greater their enjoyment.' He gave another order, and one of the men handed something across to Alistair.

It was a very crude knife, made from a door hinge. One end was wrapped in cloth, the other had been sharpened to a knife point. A second, identical, weapon was snatched quickly by Chen.

'Now,' the colonel said, 'the fight can begin.'

The men holding Chen released him, and the man snarled

viciously and threw himself at Alistair.

THE OUTCOME

ALISTAIR DROPPED into a crouch, ready to meet the attack. At the last second, Chen gave a quick stab with his knife, and moved aside. The blow didn't even reach Alistair, but it was clearly only meant to test. Alistair turned as his opponent slowly started to circle. Again and again, Chen slashed out cautiously, but couldn't get close enough to strike a real blow. The tension was oppressive, but Alistair knew that this would start to bore his audience shortly, and that might prove more fatal than the fight. They wanted to see action and blood, not dancing with knives.

He waited a further moment. Chen made another feint. This time Alistair moved towards the blow instead of away from it, hacking out and down with his knife. Chen barely avoided the blow, snarling. There was real hatred in his eyes, but he wasn't allowing it to control him. Chen was no fool – he knew that too great anger could make him lose proper caution. He was feeding *on* his anger, not feeding it.

They circled again. Once more Chen lunged and spun and lunged again. Alistair avoided the jabs and countered. They backed off, moving slowly. He abruptly danced forwards, thrusting upwards with his knife. Chen back-peddled quickly – too quickly. He stumbled and fell to one knee. Alistair crowded him, stopping him from rising. He feinted with his empty hand, then slashed down.

Chen rolled, then struck back. Then he was on his feet again. It was clear that he was no mean athlete – far better than Alistair. Perhaps this fight hadn't been such a good idea after all.

Chen started circling again, and then thrust. Alistair twisted, but this time the knife caught him and scored across his shirt. There was a sharp stab of pain in his left chest as he broke away.

He could see blood on Chen's knife, and felt a slow trickle of his left pectoral and chanced a quick glimpse down. It was a shallow cut, nothing more, but it stung. First blood to Chen.

Alistair willed himself to ignore the pain – it was more annoying than damaging. And it wouldn't slow his responses. He could hear favourable murmurings – or were they bets being placed? If it were the latter, it was unlikely many people would be betting on him right now.

More circling, more feinting. He was starting to breathe heavily now. He still had problems with the heat and humidity in Korea, and being so close to the sea, the humidity was worse than normal. He could feel sweat trickling down his back. Chen probably had the advantage there, also. Not good.

He struck and then jumped back out of range of Chen's counter. There was a sudden, sharp blow on the back of his leg – someone had kicked him from behind! – and he fell abruptly, completely off-balance. The fall took the wind out of him, and Chen seized his chance, leaping at him, knife raised high.

There was an abrupt command. Chen hesitated for a second, glanced around, but then moved forward to strike. Alistair didn't have a chance to move, and he'd fallen on his right shoulder, the knife trapped under his thigh. He was wide open to Chen's murderous attack.

Then two of the Koreans grabbed Chen and pinned him in place. The colonel strode angrily across, ignoring Alistair and Chen. He stood in front of the man who had sent Alistair tumbling. The man was being held firmly by two more Koreans. The colonel said something soft and angrily, and held out his hand. A club was placed in it. He spoke to the man again, and then brought the club down viciously on the man's shoulder.

The man screamed in pain. The colonel struck again and again. Blood splattered everyone in the vicinity. The man finally stopped screaming, but the colonel continued to strike furiously, blow after bloody blow. Then he handed the club back and turned his back on the shattered victim. The men holding the body up let it drop to the ground. He glanced down at Alistair.

'I gave my word,' he growled. 'This fight was to be one-on-one. I keep my word.'

He did indeed. Well, that, at least, was one thing less for Alistair to worry about – if he won this fight, then the colonel would allow him to leave.

If…

The colonel waited for him to regain his feet, and then he nodded at the two men restraining Chen. They immediately released him and stepped hastily back.

Chen was enraged now. He'd been made to look a fool by the colonel, for taking an unfair advantage. He had to regain favour in his eyes. He swung quickly, slashing out almost wildly. Wary that this might be a ruse, Alistair held back his counter-attack, staying just out of reach until he felt confident enough to strike.

He caught Chen across his forearm, but the left, not the one holding the knife. Chen grimaced, but struck with his own blade, scoring a gash along Alistair's back. Unlike the first strike, this one penetrated beneath the skin and he had to bite back a cry of agony. He twisted around; Chen slashed again, and he managed to duck under it. Chen was off-balance, stumbling slightly. Alistair's blade flickered out, cutting deeply across Chen's thigh.

This time Chen did cry out. Blood was pouring down his leg – not leaking, but pouring. Alistair must have severed the artery there. The interpreter looked down in shock. Alistair couldn't be generous and take any chances now. He kicked out, savagely, sweeping Chen's leg from under him. As Chen went down, Alistair buried his blade into Chen's chest. He heard it grate across one of the man's ribs, and then penetrate deeper in an instant.

For the second time in his life, he stared into the eyes of a man as he died. The brother of the first…

Alistair wished there had been some other way he could have dealt with this business, but there hadn't been. He'd taken the only course he could, and he now had the blood of another human being on his hands.

He stood up, and threw the blade aside. If the colonel reneged on his word the knife wouldn't do him much good against hundreds of Koreans. Breathing heavily, he turned to face his enemy.

The colonel's face was impassive. It was impossible to read anything in his eyes. He then gave a short command to the men closest to him. Two of them walked forward, grabbed the still bleeding corpse and dragged it to the pit. One of them kicked it in, contemptuously.

He'd lost to an enemy; clearly they thought he deserved no better.

Alistair stood still, waiting on his own fate. He was too exhausted to even be afraid for his life right at that minute.

The colonel looked at him, stood up and approached him. 'It is a shame we should be on opposing sides,' he remarked. 'You appear to be a very brave and efficient soldier. In other circumstances, perhaps we might be friends. At the moment, however, that is impossible.' He turned his back on Alistair and started to walk back to the barracks. 'They will allow you to pass,' he said over his shoulder. 'I keep my word.'

'Yes,' Alistair answered. 'Yes, Colonel, you do.'

He turned and limped towards the exit. The crowd was silent, but they parted for him and allowed him to pass, unmolested. He was weary and hurting, but he also felt good about himself.

He'd feel a hell of a lot better after he was cleaned and patched up, though.

It was impossible to know what they were thinking, or whether they had enjoyed seeing a man die. But, frankly, Alistair didn't give a damn about any of that. He was tired; he was injured; he was hurting.

But he was alive.

Lance Corporal Lethbridge-Stewart walked through the inner gate, and the soldiers on duty hastily opened the outer one, big smiles on their faces. Maggie and the major were both there, grins on their faces also. It made Maggie look a lot more attractive, but it didn't work for the major, thankfully.

Maggie moved towards him. 'You're covered in blood!'

He looked down, and saw that his trousers were soaked in it. 'It's not mine,' he said. 'Well, most of it isn't.' He gave a wry chuckle. 'It looks like I'm going to have to borrow some US fatigues again, though. Then I believe I owe you a drink.'

The major slapped him on the arm. 'Congratulations, son. I wish I could have seen that fight. Still…' He fished in the inside pocket of his jacket. 'Have a cigar.'

'Don't mind if I do,' Lethbridge-Stewart said, accepting the offer. 'Can you point me to the infirmary?'

'I'll take you,' Maggie offered. 'Only – try not to bleed too much in the jeep, okay? The motor pool guys hate having to mop it up.'

*

At the infirmary, there was another commotion as Maggie helped him in. Then Hee Won was there, laughing happily. He didn't think he'd ever before seen her truly happy. She threw her arms around him, completely ignoring the mess he was covered in.

'Idiot,' she said, with great affection. 'My idiot. Thank you.'

As he was being patched up, Lethbridge-Stewart saw that she'd returned to the bed in which Jae-ho lay, and she clutched his hand tightly.

He'd made her happy. After all of the horrors and pains in her life, *this* would probably be the one great memory she would have of him, and that pleased him a great deal more than he had expected. Then he winced as the medical orderly started to patch up his wounds.

Later, after everyone had gone, he relaxed slightly. He'd been forced to postpone the date with Maggie – the medics had insisted on giving him painkillers. Maggie had insisted she could kiss everything better, and he was sorely tempted to let her try. But the doctors had thrown her and Hee Won out, leaving the men to recover in peace.

His clothing had been removed, and probably burned. It was certainly beyond salvaging. But he had rescued the cigar he'd been given, and, ignoring doctor's orders, lit it up. If he was the hero of the day, then he was damned well going to enjoy *something*. He sat back, contentedly, savouring the taste of the cigar. It was much better than cigarettes, he decided. He'd lost all pleasure in those after Peng had blown smoke into his face so often.

He wasn't sleepy, but he was feeling introspective. It had been one hell of a day. He just hoped that the Yanks didn't do anything embarrassing, like give him a medal. He was sure he didn't deserve one. He was concerned that he might have nightmares again once he drifted to sleep – he'd killed his second man today, after all – up close and very, very personal. But the one thought he couldn't get out of his head was the Korean colonel.

He had been a cultured, eloquent man – and a savage killer – but he had admired his foe.

And he had called Lethbridge-Stewart a 'brave and efficient soldier'.

Was he? Oh, yes, at this moment he was a soldier. And for a while to come. But then he would return to civilian life, and become what he had always intended – a teacher. He was still sure that this was what he wanted to make of his life.

Well… *mostly* sure.

Only mostly?

The voice was back.

Yes, mostly.

The voice seemed to smile. *Old Spence was right about you, you know. You have changed. The past half year has changed you, and I expect the next year…*

Lethbridge-Stewart wasn't sure he liked the idea of another year of this life. But then…

Perhaps he was right, he thought to the voice. *Perhaps I can be a decent officer.*

That's the spirit, Alistair. When you get back, make contact with Pemberton.

Alistair nodded. *I think I shall.*

The voice was quiet a moment. *Ah, here I go. Well, I can't say it's been fun, but it has been an education. You won't hear from me again, Alistair. At least, not like this.*

And then, just like that, the voice was gone. And for the first time in months Lethbridge-Stewart felt like himself. He closed his eyes.

Him. An officer. Yes, he supposed he might get used to it…

THE OBSERVER VI

'...**YOU NEVER** return? You know, Bill, I don't think I can—'

Bill blinked. He was back in the living room of his house. And Anne was speaking. He looked around.

'How long was I away?'

'Away?' Anne frowned. 'You mean you've travelled back in time already?'

'Yes. For months. I was there, with Alistair, from conscription right up until... What is it?'

Anne laughed. 'Bill, darling, it happened in less than a second.' She climbed to her feet. 'You must tell me everything. I will make a pot of tea.'

As she passed him, Bill reached out for her hand. For a moment she stood there beside his chair, her hand in his. He squeezed it gently, then let her continue on her way to the kitchen.

He placed the Gnome on the floor and stood. He walked over to the mantle and the picture of Alistair Lethbridge-Stewart. He was in his Blues uniform at Anne's and Bill's wedding. Although he wasn't wearing a cap, or even a uniform at all, Bill saluted the man in the picture.

'You always were a splendid chap, Alistair,' Bill said. 'And my hero.'

AUTHOR'S NOTE

AS WITH the best Hollywood movies, this book was based on real-world events, but told with a liberal sprinkling of dramatic licence. Or, to put it another way, the events of the Korean War in the *Doctor Who* universe were not quite the same events as history records.

National Service was quite real. It lasted until 1963, and my own father did his stint. Unlike Alistair Lethbridge-Stewart, however, my father *did* have flat feet, so he served his time doing office work. He was taught book-keeping, and he spent the rest of his working life using the skills he'd learned in the Army.

The attack on Hill 235 was, sadly, all too real as well. There was a huge loss of life, and the Gloucestershires suffered as badly as I described. But they were heroes, and did delay the Communist attack. Hill 235 was renamed Gloster Hill as a result. And the man who single-handedly took out the machine gun nest at the cost of his own life was Lt Philip Curtis. He was awarded a posthumous Victoria Cross for his actions.

And the POW camp on Geoje Island also existed. The problems I mentioned were unfortunately all too real as well.